DO
NI

Also available in the New Adventures series

TIMEWYRM: GENESYS John Peel
TIMEWYRM: EXODUS Terrance Dicks
TIMEWYRM: APOCALYPSE Nigel Robinson
TIMEWYRM: REVELATION Paul Cornell

CAT'S CRADLE: TIME'S CRUCIBLE Marc Platt
CAT'S CRADLE: WARHEAD Andrew Cartmel
CAT'S CRADLE: WITCH MARK Andrew Hunt

THE NEW

DOCTOR WHO

ADVENTURES

NIGHTSHADE

Mark Gatiss

First published in Great Britain in 1992 by
Doctor Who Books
an imprint of Virgin Publishing Ltd
338 Ladbroke Grove
London W10 5AH

Copyright © Mark Gatiss 1992

'Doctor Who' series copyright © British Broadcasting
Corporation 1992

Cover illustration by Peter Elson
Typeset by Type Out, London SW16
Printed and bound in Great Britain by
Cox & Wyman Ltd, Reading, Berks.

ISBN 0 426 20376 3

A catalogue record for this title is available from the British
Library

This book is sold subject to the condition that it shall not, by
way of trade or otherwise, be lent, resold, hired out or otherwise
circulated without the publisher's prior written consent in any
form of binding or cover other than that in which it is published
and without a similar condition including this condition being
imposed on the subsequent purchaser.

For my dear friend Paul Howard
Kindest and gentlest of men
So much missed

Grateful thanks to Peter and Ríona; to all my friends and family for their love and support and particularly to my father for his boundless help and enthusiasm.

'...*the true paradises are the paradises that we have lost*'.

Marcel Proust
'Time Regained'
Remembrance of Things Past (1927)

Prologue

All around the cluttered cloisters, musty rooms and high, vaulted halls there was a deep and tangible hush. The only light in the virtually impenetrable gloom was of a peculiarly pellucid green, spilling out feebly from every heavy wooden door and misaligned stone. Everywhere, there was a terrible sense of stagnancy, imbuing the whole place with a fetid, neglected atmosphere as though some great cathedral had been flooded by a brackish lagoon.

From out of the cobwebbed shadows emerged a little group of very old men, resplendent in their ornately decorated robes.

The least ancient of the group, a white-haired individual with piercing eyes and a down-turned, haughty mouth, lifted the hem of his robes as he detached himself from the others, sending little flurries of dust over the flagstones. He murmured a few words of apology to his comrades and melted away into the shadows.

After a time he came to a small door inset in the crumbling stonework. He looked about him, senses alert, and lifted his hands to grip the lapels of his robes. His twinkling eyes darted from side to side. It was time.

A man with a face like a deflating balloon, dressed in dark gold robes which were too big for him, crossed the corridor, mumbling happily to himself. The white-haired man pressed himself into a doorway until the fellow had passed. It wouldn't do to be discovered now.

When he was certain that he was alone, the old man opened the door with a spindly key and squeezed himself through into darkness.

Beyond the door was a flight of stone steps, which he descended nimbly, leading into a huge, ink-black, domed chamber.

Arranged in a row were eight featureless objects about the size of horse boxes, their dull grey surfaces tinged by the familiar underwater-green.

The white-haired man lifted the heliotrope robes from around his shoulders and let them slip to the floor. He steepled his bony fingers and looked up at the ceiling high above his head. What was the night like out there? It had been so long since he'd ventured outside, smelled fresh air, seen the first frosts, watched the pale silver and bronze leaves disappearing under melting snow . . .

But now all that would be different. It was time to go.

There was a noise from somewhere close by and the old man hastily unlocked one of the featureless grey boxes.

'I must be quick,' he muttered. 'Yes, I must be very, very quick.'

A look of profound sadness seemed to come over his wise old face as he gave the hall one more sweep of his searching gaze. Then, with a heavy sigh, he vanished inside the box and closed the door.

There was a raucous, grinding moan and, quite suddenly, the old man and his protesting grey box simply faded away.

For a long time the seven remaining boxes stood in silence with only the steady drip of the leaking roof to disturb the gloom. Then the man in the dark gold robes appeared in the doorway, tutting to himself. He regarded the seven boxes, and the space where the eighth had been, with some annoyance.

'Oh no, no,' he said. 'This really won't do at all.'

1

Perhaps the world was dreaming. Dreaming as it drifted like an exotic butterfly through those gossamer summers which seemed like they could never end, stretching pacific arms around its people under a billion-dollar blue sky. And there were those who said there'd never been a better time to be alive. Perhaps the world was dreaming . . .

Jack Prudhoe scratched his bristly chin and cleared his throat loudly. He was in no mood to argue. Standing in the draughty hall of his little house, he wearily ran a hand through his thinning hair and rattled the walking sticks which cluttered the umbrella stand.

'Are you listening to me?'

Win's voice stabbed at him like a needle. Jack kept his rheumy old eyes fixed on the umbrella stand. Had it always been like this? Dreary days. Arguments. Going to the pub. Coming back. Apologies. Another argument. Bed. Silence.

Jack looked at Win's angry, pinched face as she continued to berate him in a shrill monotone. Mouth like a horse's backside, he thought idly. Win's grey eyes flashed dangerously.

'Same old routine isn't it, Jack Prudhoe?'

Yes, he despaired, yes, yes. Same old bloody routine.

Jack selected his favourite walking stick. The one with the horse's head carved on it. The one Win had given him on their tenth anniversary. He buttoned up his heavy raincoat and eased his feet into a pair of wellingtons. With two pairs of socks on they almost fit.

'Off you go to the pub to get tanked up. And not a thought for me, oh no. Well, I've had enough. Either you start facing up to your responsibilities . . .'

Jack didn't hear the rest. He lifted the latch on the solid front door and stepped out into the rain.

There was a dismal, slate-grey quality to the light which did nothing to lift his spirits. A wintry dusk was creeping remorselessly over the village in defiance of the early hour.

A short walk across the square stood The Shepherd's Cross, a pub in which Jack had been drinking, man and boy, for nearly fifty years. He nearly chuckled as he remembered his dad smuggling him his first pint.

The pub's comforting atmosphere of red flock wallpaper, old wood and frosted glass rarely failed to cheer him up. Except, perhaps, on bleak days like this one.

'Afternoon, Jack.'

Jack nodded his hello to the landlord, Lawrence Yeadon, who stood drying glasses behind the long mahogany bar. Lawrence tossed the teatowel on to his shoulder and grinned. He was always grinning. Or whistling.

'Filthy weather,' he said cheerily. Jack grunted and looked Lawrence up and down, noting with disapproval the younger man's turtleneck sweater and fashionably exaggerated sideburns. Silly bugger was too old to be following trends.

Back in the days when the colliery was still open, Jack had been a good friend of young Lawrence, especially after he'd married such a pretty young lass as Mrs Cockayne's eldest and produced a son, Robin. But his wife's untimely death had left such a profound impression on Lawrence that he had virtually withdrawn from village life, becoming sullen and uncommunicative. However, after some years (much to everyone's relief), he pulled himself together, got the tenancy of the pub with little bother and married a lovely widow from York called Betty Harper.

These days, Lawrence was all sweetness and light. He and Betty had recently returned from a holiday in Jersey and were already planning their next excursion, rumoured to be a cruise on the new *Queen Elizabeth II*.

Lawrence grinned at Jack. The old man turned away thoughtfully. There was something about Lawrence which nagged at him. Perhaps he was just a bit too eager and cheerful to be true. And there had been a lot of gossip recently about how ill Betty was looking.

4

Jack shrugged off these thoughts, turned back to the bar, ordered a pint of mild and asked after Betty.

'Oh fine, fine,' said Lawrence, a little too quickly.

Jack sat down at a table and closed his eyes, listening to the gentle crackling of the fire. He was grateful that the recently installed jukebox (one of Lawrence's efforts to 'liven the place up a bit') had fallen silent. Honestly, the drivel people listened to nowadays. You couldn't tell the boys from the girls half the time.

Sipping his pint thoughtfully, Jack glanced into one of the shadowed corners where a hefty wooden and cast-iron table stood, its surface littered with sodden beer mats. It was in that corner sometime during the Great War (1916, wasn't it?) that he'd first seen Win. She and her mother had just arrived in Crook Marsham and moved into the old Shackleton house on Faraday Street. Win was such a beautiful woman in those days. Lovely thick auburn hair and soft, soft skin that seemed to shine . . .

'Can I get you girls a drink?' Jack had asked in a nervous voice. Win and her new friend Veronica Railton giggled into their hands. They were already feeling rather daring having gone into the pub unchaperoned. Jack looked down at the oversized uniform he'd been given and suddenly felt a fool. His army haircut was horribly severe and he felt self-conscious about his sticky-out ears. Veronica peered at him from behind her thick spectacles. Win's big eyes looked him up and down. She was wearing that red dress which her mother had made for her. It was always her favourite.

'Well?' said Jack. Veronica giggled again but Win held his gaze. 'There's something about a man in uniform,' she'd said quietly.

Always had spirit that one. So beautiful. So beautiful . . .

Jack Prudhoe shook himself out of his reverie and took another sip of his pint, leaving a creamy semicircle on his upper lip. His eyes strayed to the tatty Christmas decorations which Betty Yeadon had put across the bar only the other day.

His mind began to drift again. He and Win saying their farewells just before he was posted. Endless laughter and chatter. Going on trips over to Leeds and Ilkley Moor. Kissing

5

by the falls at Haworth. And then parting. Jack waving to Win as she stood in that lovely red dress at the station. Waving as the steam from the engine enveloped her.

After that had come the worst time of Jack's life: foul and wretched war. Up to his knees in freezing water as star-shells blossomed overhead. Half his comrades slaughtered in that filthy mud. And then came the day he saw his best mate's head blown off and Johnny Hun put a bullet through Jack's chest, sending him home within the week. Home to Crook Marsham and his mum and dad. And home to Win, who had waited for him, despite the best efforts of the local lads.

The year after those university men came to the moor looking for old relics, Jack and Win finally tied the knot.

'We'll have a dozen kids,' he told her. 'And a house as big as Castle Howard. A garden full of roses, and chrysanths... Aye, you like chrysanths, don't you?'

She'd turned her big eyes to him and smiled warmly. 'Oh, Jack. What am I going to do with you?'

Jack turned back to his pint and rubbed the ribs which the bullet had smashed all those years ago. They still ached a bit in damp weather.

He sighed heavily. Sometimes he just couldn't believe that the Win he'd loved and the woman who was now such a thorn in his side were one and the same. They'd had their ups and downs, of course, like anybody else. One kiddie still-born. The other, named after his father, run down by a bus. Jack could see himself there even now, standing helplessly as the great, lumbering vehicle lurched around the corner. Then young Jackie running into the road. Time slowing around them, moving like treacle. That awful noise as the bus's brakes howled, and then Win, turning to him with such a look in those grey eyes. Accusing him. Little Jackie breathing his last on that rain-washed street and, perhaps, something inside Win quietly dying. The passing years became like a physical weight, pressing her down, breaking that rare spirit, transforming her into the stooped and bitter woman she now was. They'd never even left the village. Despite all those plans, all those promises...

Something caught Jack's eye as it flashed by the smoked glass of the pub window. He turned full around and his old neck wrinkled in the none-too-clean collar of his shirt.

A flash of red. There was something darting past the window, the smudged red of their clothes bobbing into view like a lone poppy seen through a curtain of fine rain.

Jack moved closer and peered through the little area of clear glass which spelt out the pub's name in big Victorian letters. There was a girl out there, dressed in a light summer frock. A red frock. Jack sensed its familiarity and something turned in his stomach.

And then there was a face at the window. Pressed against the smoked glass. A pale, lovely face with a halo of thick hair. The girl giggled lightly and was gone.

Jack stood up sharply, sending both table and beer crashing to the floor. Lawrence looked at him oddly.

'Jack?'

The red blur began to diminish. Over towards the moor.

'Jack? Are you all right?'

Jack Prudhoe turned and his careworn face was full of wonder. He suddenly knew he didn't have much time.

'It's her, Lol,' he breathed. 'It's her!'

'Who?'

Jack let out a high, hysterical laugh and stumbled out of the door. Lawrence hastened after him.

'Jack! Your coat, man! You'll catch your death! Jack!'

The policeman and the old man are tired. Their faces, in tight close-up on the television screen, blurred by the crude film process. The policeman's nerves are close to breaking point.

'What do you mean, "not of this world"?'

The older man puts a comforting hand on the constable's arm. 'I know it's difficult to accept, my boy, but I've encountered these things before. They are the vanguard of an invading force from the planet M...'

The policeman screams as a huge, scaly claw bursts through the window.

'Professor! Professor Nightshade! For God's sake...!'

The older man's face zooms into view. Grim and determined. Fade to black. Thunderous chords bellow out the familiar theme tune as the word *Nightshade* is superimposed on a roll of rather

7

jerky credits.

Professor Nightshade — *Edmund Trevithick*
Constable Chorley — *James Reynolds*
Staff Sergeant Ripper — *William Jarrold*

The blue light from the television screen threw garish shadows across Edmund Trevithick's chuckling face as he watched his name flicker by. He smiled, a little indulgently, and leant forward in his chair to switch off the set. The room seemed suddenly very dark and quiet. Trevithick cleared his throat loudly and smiled his famous lopsided smile. It hadn't really dated much at all, even if he did say so himself! Even so, it had been a good few years since he'd last played old Professor Nightshade. Nice of Auntie Beeb, though, to give the series a dusting down and a slot on their new second channel.

Trevithick looked around the room at the circle of elderly people, all sound asleep; their gentle snores rising and falling in pitch like steam from old copper kettles. He harrumphed loudly, considering himself a sprightly seventy years old and nothing like the poor old dears with whom he shared a roof, now clustered around the television in a sea of tartan blankets.

He huffed again at his compatriots. They'd promised to stay awake for his programme, they'd *promised*.

'I don't know why I bother,' he said out loud.

'Bother about what?'

It was Jill Mason, the warden of the old people's home, sneaking up on him again.

'Don't do that!' snapped Trevithick. 'Gave me the shock of me life.'

Jill was lifting up cushions and looking under chairs.

'You haven't seen the *Radio Times* about, have you, Edmund?'

Trevithick smiled his lopsided smile. He'd hidden the period-ical during one of Mrs Holland's fits. That way no one would know there was anything else but *Nightshade* on the television that night.

'Perhaps Mrs Holland has eaten it.'

'You're wicked,' said Jill, smiling.

She peered out of the window into the darkness and closed the curtains in one decisive movement. It was getting late.

Trevithick had to admit that he was fond of the girl, even if she was a little patronizing at times and wore her hair too long. She'd even taken to sporting false eyelashes (of all things) which Trevithick thought resembled copulating insects. He objected less to the length of her skirts which barely reached her shapely knees. Girls had been far too prim in his youth. This bra-burning mularkey certainly had its advantages.

He kept his thoughts to himself, however, and steered the conversation back to his old series.

'We had a lot of trouble with young Jimmy Reynolds.'

'Mm?'

'Jimmy Reynolds. The lad who played a bobby in this week's episode. Not long out of drama school, I seem to remember. And a bit fazed by all the lights and excitement. Of course, it was all live in those days. He was sick in his helmet just before he went on!'

'Really?' Jill said distractedly.

'Queer as a dog's hind leg as well. We used to call him Debbie Reynolds!'

Trevithick guffawed into his handkerchief, then looked over at Jill. 'Oh, you're as bad as this lot. You don't care. That's a piece of history you missed tonight.' Trevithick adjusted his blanket and huffed again.

Jill brushed a lock of hair out of her eyes and crossed the room to check on Mrs Holland.

'Believe it or not, Edmund...'

'Mister Trevithick to you, girl.'

'Believe it or not, I have more important things to do than watch you on the TV.'

Trevithick grunted. 'Oh yes? Rather be with your bloody anarchist friends, would you?'

'What?'

'In Paris? Isn't that the "in thing" for young people today?'

Jill felt a rush of blood to her face. She was silent for a while and then said simply, 'No.'

Mrs Holland, who had slowly woken up, began to cackle wildly. Her toothless, sunken face reminded Trevithick of one of those laughing sailor dolls at the seaside.

'Ooh, Mr Trevithick,' she cried. 'When are you on the telly?

You keep telling us you're going to be on the telly...'

Trevithick raised his eyes heavenward. 'I've just been on the television, you stupid old woman. You were too busy snoring...'

'Eh?'

Mrs Holland had become deaf again as she often did in moments of stress.

'Oh, never mind,' grumbled Trevithick.

'When's he on the telly, Jill?' pleaded the old woman, gripping Jill's arm. 'I do so want to see him. Tell me when he's on.'

Jill nodded vigorously and reassuringly, soothing Mrs Holland back into her chair.

'And let me know when Wilfrid gets home,' she said finally, drifting back into sleep.

'Wilfrid?' said Trevithick with a raised eyebrow.

'Her husband.' Jill tucked the blanket around the old woman's knees. 'Killed in the First World War, I think.'

'Hmmph,' Trevithick grunted. 'Mad as a hatter. Well, if you'll excuse me, I think it's time I got this old body to bed.'

Jill nodded distractedly and then looked up.

'Oh, I almost forgot. I got a phone call today. Someone from the BBC. They want to come up and interview you.'

'Interview me? Whatever for?'

Jill pulled a face. 'Apparently they've been flooded with letters since they started repeating your series. Seems you're famous all over again.'

Trevithick grunted. 'Probably just amazed I haven't dropped dead yet.'

'Shall I tell them it's all right then?'

'Hmm?'

'Shall I tell them it's OK to send someone up to see you?'

Trevithick shrugged non-committally. 'If you like,' he said and left the room.

Jill sighed. That man was so exasperating!

Once in the corridor, however, Edmund Trevithick's sulky expression changed. He laughed delightedly and his face broke out into a beaming, lopsided smile.

10

Famous! All over again!

He shambled excitedly to bed.

In the TV room, Jill was trying to ease old Mr Peel into a sitting position. She knew from bitter experience that if she couldn't make him sit upright, his medicine would run like syrup down his leathery chin.

She stopped suddenly and stiffened. There was an odd rustling sound coming from outside, as if tree branches were scraping against the window. But there were no trees that close to the wall. The heavy velvet curtains seemed to stare at Jill, daring her to open them.

Don't be scared. You're a grown woman. What do you have to fear?

Jill swallowed nervously, feeling the back of her throat suddenly dry up. Then, grateful that there was no one awake to see her, she hurried from the room.

Jack Prudhoe staggered on. He splashed through puddles in the cobbled square, careered around the post office and finally found himself on the moor path.

The moor. It stretched in front of him in the teeming rain; a great, dismal expanse of purple. Billowing clouds, like strokes of charcoal, lowered over the desolation.

Jack felt his wellingtons sink into the sodden ground. Ahead of him, still discernible despite the darkness, the girl in the red dress was running. Almost skipping. Oblivious to the driving rain which soaked her auburn hair, she spun around, jumped into the air, shouted for Jack to follow her.

'Follow me, Jack! Follow... Follow... Follow me!'

Jack could hear her light, musical laugh resounding in the air. It was a sound he knew well. There was no mistaking it. The laughter of a delicate, carefree girl he'd once known and loved.

'Win!' he called.

She turned and he could see little beads of rain shining on her lovely young face. She laughed and Jack's head crowded with memories.

'Win!'

He pounded on, his old legs buckling under him. Once or twice his boots sank completely into the marshy ground and corpse-cold water stained the knees of his trousers.

'Win! You've come back!'

She beckoned to him and the old man ran on, his heart in his mouth and his face wreathed with smiles. It was impossible. Impossible!

Follow me, Jack. Follow me... Follow... Follow...

'Wait for me, Win. Wait for me!'

Win vanished into a little copse of scrubby, stunted trees. Jack plunged on until he reached the withered foliage which sheltered an enclave in the rocks too small to be called a cave but large enough for him to stand upright. He pushed aside the sharp branches and peered into the hollow beyond.

It was very dark now. Jack's mind was reeling. Somehow she was back. The years had been rolled away. Perhaps they had a chance to start all over again. Win was here. It didn't matter how. His beautiful young wife had come back to him. That was enough.

'Win?'

There was silence in the little hollow. Jack looked around, bemused. Then, to his right, he heard a soft, soft rustling sound. Something was emerging from the shadows. Something huge.

Jack tried to say Win's name but the sound died in his throat as the vast darkness closed around him. No time to turn and run. No time, even, to scream.

Out on the moor, in the darkness, there was only the steady hiss of the rain.

Trevithick shut the door of his room. He rubbed his hands together excitedly and looked at his face in the battered old shaving mirror he kept by the bed.

'Not bad,' he said happily. 'Not bad at all!'

Those roguish good looks had stood him in good stead in the old *Nightshade* days. Why not again? And after those charming make-up girls had worked their magic he'd look twenty years younger. Perhaps they wanted to make a new series?

He undressed carefully, laying his tweed trousers over the arm of the chair, and clambered into his soft blue pyjamas.

The Dalesview Residential Home had been converted from an eighteenth-century farmhouse and still retained its deeply inset windows, although the leaded panes had been replaced by thick modern glass. Trevithick was always reminded of prison-cell windows.

He paused to draw the curtains and glanced outside.

The lashing rain was only visible in the weak yellow light of a distant streetlamp. Trevithick started. Something moved through the pool of lamplight into the darkness. He saw it only for a moment but it felt oddly familiar. A big, crooked, hunched figure. Scuttling like a crab.

Trevithick dismissed it with a shake of his head, drew the curtains and clicked off the bedside lamp. It was good to be inside and warm when there was such foul weather out there. He looked at the ceiling, his eyelids making a gentle tick-tick as he blinked into the dark. It really *was* good to be inside. Inside the Dalesview Residential Home and away from all that uncertainty. Much as he railed and protested and argued, there was a degree of comfort to be derived from being an old man in such extraordinary times. Exciting times, to be sure, but frighteningly unstable. Surely it was all going too fast? The certainties of his own young days, the ethics, the institutions — all seemed to be flooding away like precious wine from an unstoppered bottle. And it scared him.

There were wonders, of course. Hadn't he cheered with the rest when Apollo 7 returned to Earth only a couple of months before? Now they were saying man would be on the moon by next summer! Trevithick huffed to himself. All well and good, but at what cost? Half the world starving to death. Brave lads pointlessly slaughtered in Southeast Asia. Bloody bolshy students tearing Paris to bits. Give 'em a taste of the birch. That'd teach 'em. No, it was all going too fast ... Much too ... fast ...

Trevithick felt himself sinking into sleep. Rain drummed against the window in relentless, sweeping waves. Then there was another sound. Rustling. As if branches were scraping at the thick panes ...

'Wake up, Vijay. Vij? Come on, love.'

Vijay smiled to himself as he heard Holly's voice but kept his eyes shut all the same. It would be nice to tease her for a while. The smell of hot coffee tempted him to stir but the chair with its fat cushion was so comfortable...

'Come on, Vij. If Hawthorne finds you asleep...'

Vijay opened one eye and winked at Holly. She smiled back at him and pushed a mug of steaming coffee into his hand. Vijay sat up and shuddered, rubbing his shoulders and back in an effort to wake himself up.

'Happy now?' he said, stifling a protracted yawn.

Around them, the great grey room twittered and buzzed with energy. Banks of monitors, scopes and readouts covered every available surface, rising high towards the domed ceiling where a forest of gantries also hummed with life.

Holly was checking one of the smaller screens, a green, luminous display speckled with figures and oscillating curves. She glanced idly over her shoulder as Vijay stood up and loosened his tie.

'If you're going to snooze, don't volunteer for night shift. You know how crucial this stage is.'

Vijay laughed bitterly. 'Volunteering didn't really come into it, Holly. When Cooper or Hawthorne say "jump" then we...'

'Drop off to sleep?'

'Very funny.'

Vijay sneaked up behind Holly and put his arms around her waist. Holly craned her neck and gave him a light kiss on the cheek. Vijay grinned.

They'd been colleagues at the Space Tracking Station for eight months and lovers for four. Vijay had unfashionable hopes that one day Holly would cease to be Miss Kidd and become Mrs Degun. But, like saying 'man' at the end of his sentences or admitting that he preferred Peter Noone to Jim Morrison, plucking up the courage to ask her was something Vijay hadn't quite pulled off.

'Missed me?' he asked.

Holly shrugged. 'Suppose so.'

Vijay smiled but couldn't quite suppress the little twinge of panic which rose up in him. What if she meant it? What if she really were indifferent to him?

Vijay looked at his reflection in the darkened windows and sighed. He'd tried to swing, he really had, growing his thick black hair to shoulder length and sporting a long, drooping Lennon moustache. But he felt uncomfortable with this image. It wasn't Vijay Degun expressing himself, it was Vijay pretending to be something he wasn't in order to impress Holly. Perhaps all those childhood stories about old Imperial England had made him yearn for security and normality. Certainly, he'd loved his adopted country with the zeal of a convert, ever since he and his father had stepped off the boat in 1951.

Now he'd fallen in love with a wonderful woman who might just regard him as a little diversion to help pass the time during the yearlong slog at the station. There was so much to discuss. So many hurdles to be scaled. How could he tell his father he wanted to marry a white girl?

Holly turned and gently stroked his cheek.

'Get some sleep, Vij. I'm not tired. Besides, I've got some stuff to work on.'

He almost refused for the sake of chivalry but then remembered that chivalry wasn't hip; he nodded, grinned and found himself yawning again.

'OK. What time am I on in the morning?'

He never checked the roster. Holly, who used to find that infuriating, now thought it rather endearing. She looked at the clipboard which hung on the wall by the main display screens and rubbed the sleep out of her large green eyes.

'Er... eleven... eleven to nine. Yeah. Same as last Thursday. Cooper's on too. Then Hawthorne at four.'

'Oh, Christ.'

Holly smiled sympathetically. 'Think yourself lucky. I've got Hawthorne right through Saturday while you're off enjoying yourself.'

Vijay pulled her towards him and kissed her. Around them, the instruments whirred and ticked soothingly. Holly wrinkled her freckled nose as Vijay's moustache brushed against it.

'Enjoy myself?' said Vijay, laughing. 'In this place?'

'Well, get yourself over to York or somewhere. How about the Brontës' house?'

'Vijay shrugged. 'Been there, seen it et cetera. Besides, how can I enjoy myself if you're not around?'

Holly pulled away, blushing a little in spite of herself. Again that reluctance, thought Vijay, that reticence...

'Go to bed,' said Holly. 'I'll see you tomorrow.'

Vijay picked up his lab coat and nodded. He turned as he reached the door to the interior. 'Keep smiling.'

He disappeared into the darkness.

Holly sat down in Vijay's chair and rubbed her face. She really did wish Vijay didn't have the day off on Saturday. Dr Hawthorne would be breathing down her neck all day. Another interminable shift of doubles entendres and sarcasm from that nasty, rat-faced man. Always patronizing. Always smiling that sickly smile.

'You must pay more attention, Miss Kidd, you really must,' said Holly to herself, imitating Hawthorne's funny, high-pitched voice. Then he'd probably get in a dig about Vijay, something about staying where nature intended or about parts of London resembling Calcutta.

Hawthorne's resentment was firm, clear and diamond hard. If Mr Wilson had any sense, he used to mutter, he'd deport the lot of them.

Holly sighed and looked at the clock. It was two in the morning. She drank a little more coffee and glanced at the ink tracers which measured the radio waves from the stars they monitored. The thin line of green ink was straight and unperturbed. They were on the lookout for pulsars, mainly — this year's great discovery — sweeping the heavens for likely sources.

The ink tracer continued on its placid path. Smooth as a knife through water.

Holly went to the window and gazed up at the brilliantly lit disc of the radio telescope which towered above the station. There were few stars visible in the murky black sky. She recognized Gemini and part of Taurus. Then a little of Orion, the constellation on which they were presently concentrating. But it rapidly vanished under a blanket of greasy cloud.

Yawning, Holly moved away from the window and, more through a desire to avoid starting work than any real need, walked into the corridor to make herself some more coffee.

Outside, the rain lashed the great parabola of the telescope, bouncing off into the guttering and cascading down the stained concrete walls of the station.

A mile away, in the village, Win Prudhoe spent her first night alone in forty years.

Trevithick awoke with a start. His gaze darted about the room as he took in the familiar shapes, still enveloped in thick darkness. The chair with his trousers laid across it and the old wardrobe with the wonky door were still there, but there was something wrong.

It was only when a sharp gust of freezing air wafted into his face that Trevithick noticed the window. His heart began to slam against his ribs and he felt a great tide of adrenaline pulse unpleasantly to his head.

Slowly, with great deliberation, Trevithick folded back the top blanket and tiptoed softly across the room. He clicked on the light.

A huge hole had been smashed in the thick pane of the window and the curtains hung in shreds, swinging from the broken rail like gibbet corpses. The shattered glass rattled as a stiff breeze from the moor ebbed and flowed against it.

Trevithick licked his suddenly dry lips and sat down heavily in his chair, crumpling the trousers he had so carefully laid out. His eyes moved quickly from the devastation around the window to his bed and then back again. He could see the pool of yellow light from the same streetlamp. Nothing there now. He glanced at his old brass alarm clock. Half past four.

And suddenly there was a voice. A shocking, twisted rattle of a voice, like dead air expelled from the lungs of a drowned man.

'Night... shade...' it hissed. Chuckling, chuckling.

A dreadful smell — a rancid stench like bad meat — blasted through the smashed window. Trevithick felt his head becoming insanely light, almost as if it were about to leave his shoulders and fly away. He felt sick and dizzy all at once. Then the chuckle came again and the fearful stink rose up in his nostrils till he felt the room shuddering and blackening around him.

* * *

17

Holly looked at the clock. It was still ten past five. She must've looked at the thing a dozen times and there seemed to be no difference. Clockwatching, she thought. Naughty, naughty.

Ten past five. December 23, 1968. God, it was nearly Christmas. A fact which had totally escaped her until she'd looked at the calendar instead of the clock. The exhausting routine at the station had numbed her to the passage of time. Once, she would've been all excited, preparing presents and puddings. But all that was back in Wales with Uncle Louis. The only festive spirit she could imagine inside Hawthorne and Cooper was a couple of glasses of sherry.

Holly could remember playing snowballs with her Uncle Louis, using a pair of his old pit socks instead of gloves. Little bobbles of snow clung to the wool. She'd pulled a face.

'They are clean, you know, flower,' Louis had said, laughing in his big, barrel-chested way.

Their breath hung in the air like smoke. After several snowball fights their hands were red raw and cold as marble. Warming them by the fire induced a delicious tingling pain, soon sorted out by a little ginger wine. Then there would be steamy stuffing smells and the King on the radio. The last bits of rationed chocolate left over from the morning's gluttony would be consumed as Uncle Louis' tuneless singing drifted in from the kitchen...

Holly sighed. That was all such a long time ago. It made her think of another Christmas. Her first without James. And how Louis had comforted her as she wept into his cardigan, orange firelight glowing around them.

'It's all right, Holly, love, it's all right. Shhh now...'

A klaxon wrenched Holly from her thoughts, its violent screech echoing through the station. Holly stood up too quickly and banged her knee against the console.

'Bugger!'

The klaxon wailed at her accusingly. She whirled around, trying to locate the source of the emergency. The banks of lights twinkled on in innocent placidity and the ink-tracer continued to draw its steady line.

Holly dashed to the window and strained to make out anything in the gloom. Still the klaxon blared on. Theoretically, it should only be triggered by a breach in the security fence. Holly swallowed. There was no way she was going out there on her own.

Without warning, the ink-tracer began to oscillate crazily. The line broke up, rose and fell, creating an astonishing pattern of curves and waves in a seizure so rapid that the pen could hardly keep up with it. New information flooded through the monitors. Screens flared with light and energy.

Dr Hawthorne tumbled into the room, a heavy jumper over his pyjamas and his steel-rimmed glasses hanging off the end of his nose. He struggled to get the wire arms hooked over his ears.

'Kidd! What the hell do you think...'

He swung his head towards the ink-tracer and then over to the screen which crackled with data.

'Grief!' he said, swallowing hard. 'Where's all this coming from?'

Holly looked at him dazedly. The klaxon was still blaring in her ears.

'What?'

'I said, where's it coming from? Which quadrant?'

Holly checked her files and joined Hawthorne.

'Erm... quadrant...'

'Come on, woman.'

'No change. It's Orion. Same as before, Dr Hawthorne.'

'You haven't changed the scan?'

Holly shook her head. Hawthorne whistled. 'I don't believe this. Get on to Cooper would you?'

'Righto.'

'Where's Sabu?'

Hawthorne shot a nasty look up at Holly. She took a sharp intake of breath, almost wincing at Hawthorne's transparent racism.

'Vijay's asleep. I relieved him.'

'Did you now?'

Holly ignored him. She turned her attention to a stream of print-out which was piling at her feet.

'Why's the klaxon going?' she said distractedly.

Hawthorne shook his head and tapped a series of figures into

19

the console. 'I don't know. Why don't you find out?'

Holly let out an exasperated sigh and stalked off towards the internal phone. Shaun, the new security man, should've reported in by now.

Holly called Dr Cooper, who was none too pleased to be woken up, and then Vijay shambled into the room, his face slack and drunk with sleep.

'Holly? What's going on?'

She hugged him, grateful for an ally, and led him back into the main room.

'We're getting massive emissions on the feed. Piles of data. I've never seen anything like it. Tons of the stuff.'

Vijay shook his head as if to clear it and opened his eyes wide. 'Why's the klaxon . . . ?'

Holly turned him towards the double-doored exit and patted his backside affectionately. 'I don't know. Why don't you find out?'

Vijay sniffed resignedly and pulled on one of the thick parkas which hung by the doors. The klaxon's screech was beginning to get on his nerves. Why hadn't Shaun done something about it? It was his job to see to the thing, after all. Privately, Vijay sympathized with the security man. It couldn't be much fun patrolling the perimeter fence every night. Things were so quiet he often wondered why they had security at all.

'It's just that nothing ever happens around here, Mr Degun,' Shaun's predecessor used to say. 'And what's the point of me walking around when we all know that no one would dream of breaking in?'

He'd finally left and gone off to work in an open prison somewhere down south. Very much the same line of work, Vijay thought, smiling.

Vijay opened the doors and stepped out into the hallway. Within a moment, he was outside. The icy wind blasted him full in the face. Darkness swallowed him whole.

Freezing rain was once again lashing across the moor in great, sweeping waves. There were still a few lights on in the village and Vijay recognized the bedroom light in The Shepherd's Cross. Distractedly, he wondered whether Betty Yeadon was having another of her sleepless nights. There was a lot of gossip about how ill she'd been looking. Lawrence, though, never said a word. Just grinned.

Vijay swung round his torch in an arc and the perimeter fence loomed into view, gobs of rain splashing off its barbed-wire top.

Out of the corner of his eye, Vijay saw something move; a hunched shape scuttling just out of the reach of his torch-beam. He shuddered. There it was again. Just out of sight like a glimpse of summer lightning. He began, unconsciously, to chew his fingernails.

In the light from the torch, a huge rent was visible in the mesh of the fence, the steel wire peeled back like the skin of an orange.

'Shaun?'

His voice sounded feeble and strained. The rain hissed back at him.

Vijay began to move back towards the station but didn't feel able to turn his back on the fence. The wind howled through the gaping hole.

There it was again. A definite shape this time, bunched up and knobbly. There was a strange smell too, like bad meat. Vijay turned up his nose and, without a second thought, ran back to the station. The darkness seemed to chase him all the way like the collapsing walls of a tunnel.

He pulled open the doors and stumbled gratefully inside. The klaxon was still blaring away.

'Can't we shut that thing up?' It was Dr Cooper's voice. Vijay was grateful she'd arrived, however bad-tempered, because she could always keep the loathsome Hawthorne at bay. He strode into the control room.

'Well?' said Hawthorne gruffly.

'The fence has been breached. Great big hole torn in it.'

Cooper looked up from the still-chattering computers.

'See someone?'

'I saw some*thing*,' said Vijay pointedly.

Cooper furrowed her brow and dug her hands into her pockets. She was a big, middle-aged woman with cropped, steely-grey hair and fearsome blue eyes. There was something very likeable about her no-nonsense manner to which Vijay warmed, although he often felt the rough edge of her tongue.

'Any sign of Shaun?' asked Holly. Vijay shook his head.

21

'Well, we might as well turn off the alarm, until we've found out what's going on. Shall I call the police?'

Holly turned off the klaxon and a blessed, peaceful silence descended like a blanket of rose petals on to the room. Cooper nodded absently.

'Er... yes, yes, you do that, Holly. We're all up and about now, anyway. Vijay, come over here and log these readings, would you? Incredible. I can't make head nor tail of it.'

Vijay slipped off his parka and picked up a sheaf of paper. Dr Cooper turned and beamed at her team like a successful football coach.

'Well, boys and girls,' she said. 'It looks as though our waiting has paid off.'

With theatrical timing, the chattering of the computers and the scratching of the ink tracers stopped. There was a slow, mournful whine as the machinery eased up. The harsh lights in the long room flickered briefly and then flared into full life again.

It was over.

Cooper laughed. 'Plenty to get on with, anyway!'

Vijay slid gratefully into a chair whilst Holly went to the phone. Cooper and Hawthorne were deep in conversation like schoolkids cramming for an exam. There would be time enough, Vijay decided, to get excited about all this. Time enough. In the morning. He felt his heavy lids closing.

The moor was still solidly shrouded in darkness. Only the brilliantly illuminated dish of the telescope, spreading its chilly glow in a wide circle, was discernible.

A good mile away from the station, on the old road which led to St Hilda's monastery, Billy Coote was beginning his day. He always got up early, even in this weather, folding away the stinking blankets and newspapers which had kept him warmish through the long night. He missed the old papers with their heavy broadsheets. The new ones might be easier for people to read but they weren't nearly as good cover. It was a shame more famous people didn't get shot, he thought maliciously. The supplement under which he'd slept after Bobby Kennedy kicked the bucket was so thick he'd hung on to it for weeks.

The soaked, peeling green planks of the old bus shelter hadn't been so uncomfortable after all, despite the draughts and the none-too-pleasant smell emanating from the corner. But as Billy himself had largely contributed to that, he wasn't about to complain.

He rummaged through his straggly grey beard and ran a hand through the remaining hairs on his sunburnt head. This was what he liked to call his 'ablutions'.

It was going to be freezing cold again, he could tell, with more rain or maybe even snow on the way. He sniffed the crisp air disdainfully.

In the summertime, he would watch the sun clawing its way over the horizon. He loved the way it came up behind the monastery. Made him feel all spiritual.

Perhaps it was just his wax-clogged ears playing tricks with him but, just at that moment, Billy Coote swore he heard a strangulated, grating whine like rusty chains being dragged across gravel. It seemed to be coming from quite close to the shelter. After a few seconds, the noise died away with a crump like the explosion of a Great War shell, and Billy looked about in confusion. He crept around the side of the bus shelter and peered into the darkness. There was something tall and solid, with a light flashing on top, standing there.

Billy walked out of the shelter and up to the structure which was barely visible in the murky darkness. As he drew closer, however, he recognized the thing as a police telephone box. This came as a great surprise because he was sure it hadn't been there the night before.

Intrigued, he looked the tall blue box up and down, gazed in at the frosted-glass windows and, after rubbing his grubby hand against the sleeve of his jacket, pressed his palm against one of the doors. He jerked back in shock. It was warm. And it was humming...

Morning came slowly to Crook Marsham, the monastery, the tracking station and, although no one knew it at the time, to the TARDIS, whose old blue paintwork glistened in the fine drizzle of new rain.

2

The Doctor, Ace decided, was in need of a change. Not of clothes, nor of face (she was beginning to understand something of his regenerative powers) but of environment. Of late, he had grown irritable and sulky, fond of pacing the console room and the corridors of the TARDIS with hands thrust deep in pockets, mumbling and sighing. From time to time his bushy eyebrows would twitch and his heavily lined forehead would crease into a thoughtful frown as if inspiration had seized him.

Ace had begun to retreat to her own little room, playing 'I wanna be adored' very loudly in the hope of stirring her strange companion into some sort of activity, however hostile. In all their adventures together she'd never known him so moody and sullen.

Having nothing to do, Ace's mind turned to the drab, roundel-indented walls of her own room. She'd never been one for feathering nests, even back on Earth, and the hectic pace of her life with the Doctor precluded any thoughts of making a real home in the TARDIS. But they hadn't been anywhere exciting since the Doctor had pulled his old ship back together again. These days he seemed happier playing scratchy old records on his gramophone than talking to her.

Ace had a thought. She'd never seen inside the Doctor's room. He seemed guarded and defensive whenever the subject was raised. Would it be full of mementos? Home? Childhood? Family? Or did the Doctor have too many memories to keep track of? After all, he did claim to be over nine hundred years old. You'd tend to amass quite a bit of junk after all that time.

Not for the first time, she speculated on how the Doctor coped with his frenetic, nomadic existence. On one of the rare occasions when she and her mum hadn't been at each other's throats, they'd talked about what it must be like to live forever.

'Couldn't bear it, Dory,' her mum had said. 'All those friends, all those people you'd love. You'd have to watch them all get old and die. And you'd just go on and on. Start all over again.'

Ace shuddered at the thought. She switched off her tape deck and gazed absently about the room.

She was a striking young woman with clear, soft skin and a heart-shaped, almost Edwardian face. Her thick brown hair flowed down the back of her T-shirt.

There were footsteps in the corridor outside. Ace jumped off the bed and threw open the door.

'Doctor?'

Ace glimpsed movement out of the corner of her eye and set off after it.

She came upon the Doctor in a little room off one of the main arterial corridors. He was lounging on a high, padded chair, staring into space. Cold, pale grey light from some hidden source reflected off his elfin face.

'Doctor?' said Ace in a quiet voice.

He was wearing a long, muslin nightshirt and a shot-silk blue dressing gown, but his legs and feet were bare.

'Running a bath, Professor?' said Ace cheerily.

The Doctor ran a hand through his tousled hair but gave no indication of having noticed Ace's presence in the room. She began to feel awkward and looked around the grey room which was full of dust and yellowing papers. The Doctor sat amidst it all like some somnolent Buddha.

'Well, if you're going to ignore me ...' she began.

The Doctor looked up at her and fixed her with a penetrating stare.

'What do you say to a bit of exploring?'

Ace was relieved. 'Anything's better than just hanging around inside the TARDIS.'

'Good, good. I think ... I think I can promise you something a little *recherché*.'

'Re ... what?'

But the Doctor was on his feet and off down the corridor without another word. Ace shrugged and walked after him, but he was covering ground at such an extraordinary rate that she found herself racing to keep up with the little man.

'Where are we going, Professor?'

'There's something I want you to see,' the Doctor called over his shoulder.

And so they plunged deeper and deeper into the heart of the TARDIS, taking in more shuttered rooms, alcoves and niches than Ace had seen in her short life. There were occasional delights and surprises: a big red room entirely full of hats, a patch of what appeared to be open countryside (which she could only presume the Doctor reserved for picnics) and a glimpse of the vast, mahogany-panelled TARDIS library. Ace stared in disbelief at the seemingly unending stock of bundled papers, scrolls and ancient, leather-bound tomes, all tied up with waxed string, piled against doors or sprawling like paper waterfalls down the library's spiral staircases.

'Books,' said the Doctor casually.

Reaching a junction point where four roundeled corridors branched off, the Doctor paused to get his bearings.

'We've been this way before,' sighed Ace.

'What?' The Doctor's tone was irritable.

'We've been this way already. I'm sure of it. We're lost.'

The Doctor bristled. 'Lost? Me! I know this ship like the back of . . . the back of . . .' He gazed distractedly up and down the corridor, '. . . beyond.'

Ace rolled her eyes and plunged her hands into her Levis.

'Maybe we should've left a trail like that Greek bloke with the minah bird.'

'Minotaur,' said the Doctor, sucking his finger. 'Anyway, we're not lost, I've found it.'

'Found what?'

Just to one side of them was a large, pearl-grey door, indented with the usual roundel pattern but possessed of a big, old-fashioned doorknob.

The Doctor bent down a little and slowly, almost reverently, opened the door.

Ace stepped back a little as a wave of icy air hit her face. Then another sensation seemed to steal over her. A deep and profound stillness. She was reminded of her first visit to church as a child when the sense of ritual and holiness almost over-whelmed her.

The room beyond the door had six crumbling stone walls, their solid roundels dappled by a warm green light. In the centre stood a massive granite console, elaborately carved like a Gothic altar. Nests of tiny, winking instrumentation crowded its pillars and panels.

'It's like sitting at the bottom of a swimming pool,' she said, gazing at the arched ceiling in awe.

The Doctor was already busy at the console, checking that the antiquated machinery was still operational.

'It has a certain charm, I suppose,' he said grudgingly. 'But it always seemed too tucked away for ready use.'

'What is it?'

'Tertiary console room. Not bad, eh?'

'Not bad? It's beautiful!'

The Doctor seemed to be warming to his theme which pleased Ace immeasurably.

'Oh yes,' he said, fussing over the console, 'a little spatial relocation and we can call this ...'

He paused and began to stare into space again.

'Home?' volunteered Ace.

The Doctor said nothing.

Ace turned her attention to the rest of the room. In a corner, where clumps of wisteria were winding their way up the wall, she discovered a full-length mirror mounted on a beautiful ebony stand. She grinned at herself in the mottled silver surface.

Hanging from and scattered about the old mirror were masses of clothes. This must be some of the Doctor's centuries of junk, thought Ace. She glanced over at him but he was absorbed in his work. Shrugging, she picked up a few garments and held them in front of her.

There was a big brown duffel coat of the type the Doctor was fond of wearing, a thick donkey jacket, a funny red thing which looked like a Roman toga (and probably was), several pairs of gloves, five collapsible opera hats and a tweed waistcoat splashed and stained with green ink.

Ace pulled a face. Then her eyes alighted on a rather drab grey tunic. There was a little badge embroidered on the apron and Ace smiled as she recognized it. As quickly as possible, she struggled into the garment and turned to face the Doctor.

'Ta, da!' she announced happily.

'Hmm?'

Ace smiled hopefully. 'Gross, isn't it?'

The Doctor's face set in a rigid frown.

'Take it off,' he said in a quiet, dangerous voice.

'What?'

'Take it off!' snapped the Doctor, swinging back to the console.

Ace stared dumbly at the Doctor's back. She took off the tunic in embarrassed silence and laid it down carefully by the mirror.

'Sorry,' she said in a hoarse whisper.

The Doctor's back remained obstinately turned towards her.

'If you don't want me to muck about, Professor . . .'

'*Doctor!* I'm the *Doctor!* How many times do I have to tell you, you stupid girl?'

Ace recoiled as if she'd been struck. The Doctor hovered by the console a moment, his face flushed with emotion, then he stalked from the room, his dressing gown trailing behind him.

Ace could feel a rising, numb pain in her throat and hands. Familiar symptoms for the onset of tears. Familiar symptoms which she'd convinced herself she'd outgrown.

No! she said to herself, angrily. No tears. Don't give him the satisfaction of seeing you cry. If he wants to treat you like this, that's his business.

She sat down on the stone-flagged floor and gently fingered the drab grey tunic. The embroidered badge stood out in red and gold: COAL HILL SCHOOL.

That was the place where they'd had that run in with the Daleks. So why was the Doctor so upset about that? And what was he doing with one of the uniforms anyway?

In an amazingly short space of time, the Doctor returned, now dressed in a chocolate-brown belted coat, russet waistcoat and checked trousers. Ace, feeling suddenly chilly, had struggled into the donkey jacket.

'Very fetching!' said the Doctor enthusiastically, as if nothing at all had happened. He spotted the brown duffel coat on the floor and put it on.

Ace glanced at the far wall as a roundel glowed into colourful life.

'Scanner?' she said, shakily.

'Yes. Neat, isn't it?'

The Doctor was all smiles now. What the hell was the matter with him?

A picture began to form on the scanner but it was vague and hazy.

'Reception's not so hot but then she hasn't been used in ages. Just getting used to it, I expect.'

It was obviously dark outside but Ace could make out a bleak, blasted landscape of moor and heather.

'Uggh.'

'Quite,' said the Doctor. 'Cold, wet and dark but at least you're home.'

Ace looked at him. 'Home?'

'Earth at any rate. Twentieth century. North of England. Plus a continuous precipitation of condensed oxygen and hydrogen compound.'

'Meaning?'

'Meaning it's chucking it down. Fetch another brolly, would you?'

A few moments later they stepped outside into the darkness. In front of the TARDIS stood the rickety structure of the old bus shelter, recently home to Billy Coote, who was now pelting like a madman towards Crook Marsham.

Over towards the east, the old monastery was etched against the threatening sky and the tracking station loomed like a behemothal saucer out of the purple heather.

The Doctor put up his umbrella, plonked his hat gracelessly on to his head and walked a little way forward to where a faded wooden road sign protruded like a lightning-struck tree from the sodden ground.

'Crook Marsham: one mile.' He turned to Ace and smiled. 'How about breakfast?'

The great black prow of the ship lurches sickeningly. There are already men in the water. Water like tar. Black, dreadful, fathomless.

A flare smashes into the sky and for a moment everything is clear. Stark. Vividly white.

Men in the sea. Life-boats. Empty life-jackets. The bulk of the ship slips under the waves. A mass of frothing foam as the sea covers her gun turrets. Then the awful, chilling moan as the protesting metal buckles and snaps. Panels burst. Black water floods her engines.

And then there is screaming. Men in white sweaters. Freezing. Saturated. Screaming as the ship's pull drags them under. Young faces blanched white by the flare. A few boats left. The tall turret of the U-boat slips under the water, its job done.

Silence. Men bobbing slowly in their Mae Wests. Most of them dead already, their faces turned down as if in penitence. Some are still alive, kicking their submerged feet. The great cold, marble-smooth expanse of the ocean is revealed as dawn comes.

Alfred Beadle. Thinking of home. Thinking of his mum and dad back in York, and Betty, his younger sister. Alfred Beadle, not yet nineteen, feeling the freezing water numbing his body. Staring out at a dozen of his comrades floating silently by . . .

Jackie Barrett, his big face turned towards the sky, quite dead. Eddie Turnbull. Always smiling. Always joking. Slipping under the waves as his life eases away.

Alfred Beadle. Thinking of home. Would Betty be making tea right now? He could do with some tea. Steaming hot. Strong and orange like it was on Sundays in his mum's best china.

Was it raining back there? He'd have liked to have seen the Minster in the rain again.

Something tugging at his leg. A sharp, clear cold pain like frozen needles. Blood pooling to the surface. And then the panic rising and his gorge rising as he sees the triangular fin break the water and circle. Circle.

Alfred Beadle. Screaming. Screaming for someone. The shark pulling blindly at him. Going down. Going under. Arms slipping under the life-belt. Pulling. Screaming for Betty. Salt water in his mouth. But soon it'll be over. Please Christ make it soon. Water in his eyes. Stinging. His hair spreading like weed under the water. Betty . . . Betty . . . Remember me, Betty . . .

'Betty, love. Are you all right?'

Lawrence Yeadon clicked on the bed-side lamp and put an arm around his wife who was sitting bolt upright in bed. Her nightie was soaked in sweat and there was an awful, haunted look in her red-rimmed eyes.

'Betty?'

She turned and looked distractedly at her husband. Then she nodded, slowly and deliberately. 'I'm all right.'

Lawrence eased her back on to the pillow.

'Another dream?'

She nodded again and reached for the little brown bottle of pills which stood on the cabinet.

'Your Alf again?' asked Lawrence.

She popped a couple of pills into her mouth and managed to swallow them.

'Yes. Alf again.' Her voice was dry as paper.

Lawrence sighed and switched off the lamp. The light of morning was already insinuating itself into the room. He put his hands behind his head and looked at the ceiling.

'You can't go on blaming yourself you know, love.'

How many times had he said that to her?

Betty Yeadon turned on to her side. She swallowed and tried to get a little saliva into her mouth. She couldn't close her eyes. If she did, she would see him again. Or what the sharks left of him. Bobbing in the water, his skin blanched and his eyes pecked out by gulls. The way the rescue ship had found him.

'I might as well get up,' she said, glancing at the clock. It was nearly half past eight. 23 December.

Lawrence closed his eyes. He felt terrible. They'd already been woken up once during the night by the siren from that bloody telescope on the moor. And now another of Betty's nightmares. Something would have to give sooner or later.

Betty slipped on her dressing gown and padded down the hall. She could hear her stepson, Robin, snoring gently in his room. Then his alarm clock clattered into life and she heard his frantic efforts to disable it. He moaned.

Placing her hand on the door, Betty closed her eyes and breathed deeply. It was as if she were drawing strength and comfort from Robin's presence. She opened her eyes and saw Nobby Stiles grinning toothlessly between her fingers. Robin's

31

giant poster of the World Cup winners stared at her, unseeing.

Suddenly feeling a fool, she pulled her hand away and walked off down the corridor.

A pair of football socks, stiff with sweat, lay discarded on the carpet like mummified earthworms. Betty picked them up and rolled them into a ball. She continued down the corridor and tossed them into the washing basket by the bathroom. Domestic things. Robin's washing. Lawrence's washing. That's what she needed to do. Comforting domestic things. Something mundane to keep her mind off it.

Betty entered the tap room of the pub. It stank of stale beer and cigarette smoke. She found a glass, helped herself to a triple measure of whiskey and selected a seat by the window. It was the same seat in which Jack Prudhoe had supped his solitary pint the afternoon before.

Betty glanced at the tatty Christmas decorations pinned across the bar and began to cry.

The Doctor was in voluble mood despite the driving rain and had discoursed on a variety of subjects, including Gothic architecture, his favourite angling flies and the importance of a clean collar, by the time he and Ace wandered into Crook Marsham.

It was getting light at last and the hotchpotch of houses and shops became distinct as they advanced up the main street.

'Bit bleak, isn't it, Doctor?'

The Doctor was gazing across the street at a rather dilapidated Saxon church.

'Bleak? No, no. It's characterful, Ace, characterful. Just look at that church. Eighth century, I believe, with Norman and Victorian additions. Look at the crenellations!'

Ace grimaced. She couldn't stand it when he became enthusiastic.

'Didn't you say something about breakfast?'

The Doctor sighed and turned away from the church. He spun his umbrella round like a water-dowser and pointed towards The Shepherd's Cross.

'Bit early in the day, isn't it?'

The Doctor grinned. 'Mmm, with the sun not even remotely

over the yardarm! ... Actually, I was thinking they might be serving refreshment of some sort. The TARDIS food-dispensers are all very well but sometimes you just can't beat a decent British cuppa.'

There was an upstairs light on but no sign of life. Suddenly, in a flurry of scarf, coat and bicycle, a young man came hurtling around the side of the pub, almost running the Doctor down.

'God, sorry. Are you OK? I'm a bit late for work. Are you sure you're all right?'

'I'll live,' said the Doctor, brushing himself down.

Robin jumped back on to his bike and grinned at Ace.

'I wonder if you can help us, young man?'

'Surely.'

'We'd like to know whether this fine establishment is open for some breakfast just yet?'

Ace found that she was staring at Robin as he spoke to the Doctor. There were disconcerting but very nice tinglings moving through her body.

''Fraid not,' said Robin. 'Mum's just up but the pub doesn't open till eleven.'

He was tall and slim with thick black hair and skin as smooth as soapstone. His eyes were an extraordinary green and his smile broad and cheeky.

'Try the café up the road,' he advised. 'Cheap and cheerful but it does the job.'

'Thank you very much,' said the Doctor.

Robin apologized again and then pedalled away like a madman. Ace watched him go all the way.

'Ace?'

Robin's slim form vanished around the corner and on to the moor track.

'Ace!'

'Hmm?'

'If you're still interested in breakfast . . .?'

Ace shook her head as if to clear it and smiled. 'Yeah, of course.'

The Doctor set off towards a flickering neon café sign about a hundred yards away. Ace followed close behind him, her head sunk thoughtfully on her breast.

'I wonder if we're anywhere near Durham. Have you ever seen the cathedral?' asked the Doctor.

'No,' said Ace distantly.

'You should, you know, you really should. Of course I remember the day it was finished . . .'

Ace looked up from her thoughts and smiled. She never knew whether the Doctor's tales were serious or not. At any rate, he certainly seemed to have snapped out of his depression. If anything, he now seemed a little too chatty. Almost as if he were trying to hide something . . .

Ace frowned.

Edmund Trevithick blinked into wakefulness. There was a band of cold winter sunlight streaming across his bed. He blinked again. For a moment he couldn't remember where he was. There was some fugitive memory prodding at his subconscious.

Lying there in the bed by the window, Trevithick began to think of his childhood. He remembered seeing the intense, thrilling white reflection off newly fallen snow as it peeked through the chinks in the curtains. And the joy of throwing back the heavy drapes to expose the acres and acres of land behind his father's parsonage, knee deep in wonderful snow.

His father (a completely different sort of chap out of church) would get into his 'civvies' and root out the old wooden sled from the outhouse. Then they would be off, Edmund, his father and Edmund's elder brother Maurice, speeding down the hill, bumping and smashing into little mounds of impacted snow or bruising their backsides on unexpected clumps of stubble, which protruded like yellow bristles from under the drifts.

The latter part of the year had always been his favourite. Better by far than the long, depressing summer evenings which stretched out like flavourless chewing gum. Better than the dull, in-between months with no special character. No, the end of the year it was, with the deliciously long run-in through the burnt turnip smells of Hallowe'en and dark smoke of November into the crisp, freezing, perfect-sunned days of early December.

And then Christmas! One huge red and green memory, packed to bursting with sensual delights. Pulled by his mother's hand into palatial department stores like castles of ice: twinkling lights, the hum of extortionately priced train-sets, the exciting smell of unfamiliar perfume, all mingling and bursting before his astonished little eyes. Going into these stores in daylight and the fantastic shock of emerging into wintry darkness − the reversal of the disappointment he felt coming out of a cinema into painful sunshine.

Trevithick recalled sitting with his father and brother in a wonderfully dark front room that smelled of tangerines. Dark as pitch. The corners of the room softened into abstraction by the orange light of the fire. His father helped him write out his list for Santa Claus and then tossed the small square of paper on to the fused knot of red hot coal. It spun briefly in the column of hot air, became temporarily transparent − he could see writing on both sides at once − and vanished up the chimney.

Then there would be tall tales from his father about winters so severe that houses vanished under drifts and match flames froze as they were struck.

That was back at the turn of the century. Then he'd seen really bad winters. The one in '47 . . . and '63, only five years ago. That had caught him short. He'd never last another one of those if it came, especially with the ancient heating in the Dalesview Home.

A bad smell, like rotting fish, dragged him back from his memories into reality. It was the same smell from the night before. Trevithick sat up in bed and looked around. The sight of the shattered panes and billowing curtains brought back his experiences in a rush of remembrance. He swallowed hard and pressed the buzzer which would summon Jill.

Jill Mason glared at the buzzing light by her bed. Edmund again. Was he never content? She knew already that whichever side of the bed she chose to get out of would be the wrong side. She'd slept badly and was in a rather foul mood. Trevithick's remarks of the previous night had touched a raw nerve. Yes, she would rather be with those 'bloody anarchists' in Paris than rot in this dismal corner of England. She'd received an exciting letter from an old university friend only the other day, extensively detailing the French students' pitched battles with the police on the Rive Gauche. It had been a magical summer, her friend assured her, getting stoned with her strange and interesting new French lover, trying to 'find herself' by looking inward.

Jill felt an almost painful sense of missing out on something huge and important. She should've been there too, challenging reactionaries like de Gaulle and Johnson just as she had at university, not locked up in an old folk's home. Sometimes she felt more of an invalid than her charges.

Trevithick's light buzzed. Jill sighed and threw on a heavily creased dressing gown. She padded down the corridor and threw open Trevithick's door.

'What is it, Edmund?' she yawned. 'Because if it can wait I'd appreciate it. It's not time for breakfast yet and Polly has her hands full with Miss Norton's drip . . .'

Trevithick didn't say a word. Instead he simply pointed at the window like some dying medieval bishop catching sight of the Grim Reaper.

Jill rubbed a hand across sleep-misted eyes and turned round. The sight of the smashed window turned her cold. She remembered the time her flat was burgled and how she'd thrown up at the sight of devastation. But it wasn't the financial loss, or even the mess, which had upset her. Rather it was the sense of invasion; the idea that some stranger had ploughed through her private things, destroyed the sanctity of her little nest.

She felt the same thing now and the same desire to vomit. Trevithick looked at her, a little fear in his eyes.

Jill then became aware of another sensation. An insistent, pungent smell wafting from the shattered window. It was like bad meat. Or the rancid smell of a dead animal in the road . . .

The Doctor and Ace had taken Robin's advice and were now warmly ensconced in Mrs Crithin's delightful café, a pleasantly cluttered room of red plastic upholstered seats and tarnished cappuccino urns. There was a heavy, greasy smell of bacon fat coupled with the not unpleasant blue haze of Mrs Crithin's eighth cigarette of the morning.

On the wall, Ace had found a calendar which, along with Mrs Crithin's splendidly boisterous decorations, told her it was almost Christmas. Christmas 1968.

She felt a little thrill run through her. So here she was at last. The real sixties. Not '63 where she'd seen little of England except Coal Hill School and the Daleks, but '68: time of the Beatles and the Stones, Martin Luther King and the Mexico Olympics, the Paris Riots and man on the moon. No, that was '69, wasn't it?

All she'd known of this time was her mum's enthusiasm and the evidence of faded home movies. Yet even these silent figures in vibrant colours mouthing and waving on warm beaches seemed to have something of the era's indefinable presence about them. Ace's mum with high, laquered hair and garish mini-dress laughing as Uncle Harry goosed her from behind. Harry's mint-green Hillman Minx with its Batmobile tail-fins gliding into the distance as the family waved him away. All this to the achingly comforting trill of the film projector.

The Doctor returned from the counter with two mugs of steaming tea. It was nice and warm inside the café and Ace took off her donkey jacket with some relief.

'Ta,' she said and took a deep draught of tea. It was a little too hot and burned the roof of her mouth.

The Doctor was staring into the middle distance, his inky black eyes distracted and fathomless. He drank some tea almost without thinking. Ace decided it was best to keep quiet. Mrs Crithin's tranny played a song which Ace could remember Uncle Harry humming in his familiar way. It drifted across the café as Mrs Crithin mopped up some spilled tea.

'Those were the days, my friend. We thought they'd never end. We'd sing and dance for ever and a day . . .'

Quite suddenly, the Doctor seemed to snap out of it and fixed Ace with his most charming smile.

'Well, Ace,' he mused, rubbing his finger around the rim of the mug, 'how are you keeping?'

It was such an odd question that Ace was momentarily taken aback. It was the sort of thing old aunts or distant cousins ask just before they remember they haven't seen you since you were knee high to a grasshopper.

'What d'you mean? You see me every day.'

The Doctor smiled, but it was a thin smile. 'I know, I know. But I mean . . . how are you? Really. In yourself.'

Ace frowned.

'Oh, I'm not putting this very well, am I?' said the Doctor, absently rummaging through the pockets of his duffel coat. 'What I'm trying to find out is ... well ... whether you're happy. Whether you don't think it's time to put down a few roots.'

Ace was shocked. The Doctor was full of surprises. She had a vague impression, too, that he was really thinking aloud, trying to vocalize a debate obviously raging inside his own head.

'What are you on about, Doctor?' She drank another gulp of tea. The burnt skin on the roof of her mouth was beginning to throb.

The Doctor sighed and gazed past her again, his eyes seeing different places, different people, different times ... 'I wonder if I'm not being a selfish old Time Lord. Keeping you from better things.'

'But Doctor, you're all I've got! I don't want anything else. Not yet. Where else could I go?'

The Doctor put up his hands. 'It's all right, it's all right. I'm not about to abandon you. I just thought ... perhaps ... perhaps it's time to stop all this aimless wandering. That's all.'

Ace nodded slowly. She'd been right then.

'I'm not daft, Doctor. You're talking about yourself, aren't you?' she said, cocking an eyebrow.

The Doctor looked at her in mock indignation and then his rumpled face collapsed into a resigned frown. 'Yes. I'm talking about myself.'

It had begun to rain again and Mrs Crithin switched on the dirty-yellow lights to brighten things up. Sheets of rain lashed against the big, plate-glass window. There was a quality of stillness in the air too, as in before a thunderstorm. Ace suddenly felt like a priest at confession.

'Go on,' she said quietly. The Doctor bowed his head and gazed at his mug of tea. In the garish artificial light he seemed much older, the lines on his wise face like the carving on some ancient crusader's tomb effigy.

'It's just that ... I've been thinking lately ... and if I've been difficult, then I'm truly sorry. Thinking ... whether I've really done any good. All these years ... all these years of roaming about. Righting wrongs. Interfering ...'

Ace felt an upsurge of tenderness inside her. 'But how can you say that, Doctor? You know you've done good. The whole world . . . Well, everyone is in your debt a hundred times over. You know that.'

'But have I the right to take it upon myself? To act as self-appointed judge and jury?' The Doctor looked Ace in the eye.

'You know you've done good,' she said, feeling that her attempt at reassurance was hopelessly inadequate.

'Have I, Ace? Have I?'

Ace looked away. Mrs Crithin was attempting to change the station on her tranny.

The Doctor rested his cheek on one hand and his deeply lined face rucked up against his fingers like ripples in sand.

'I'm so tired,' he said with a heavy sigh. His eyes flicked up at Ace. 'I've been thinking a lot lately. About the past. About my past, I mean.'

Ace suddenly remembered the incident with the grey tunic in the tertiary console room. The Doctor nodded as if he'd read her thoughts.

'Yes. The uniform. It was Susan's.'

Ace's ears pricked up. 'Girlfriend?'

The Doctor laughed almost scornfully. 'She was my first travelling companion. We were . . . we are from the same planet. I enrolled her in that school when I came to Earth with the Hand of Omega. We saw so much in our time together. But she left me. As they all do. As you will . . . And do you know, Ace, I don't think a day passes when I don't think of her.'

'What are you trying to say, Doctor?'

He shrugged. 'I miss her, I suppose. I miss . . . my family. In whatever sense of the word. There've been so many over the years. Ian and Barbara. Sarah. Jo. Dear Jamie . . . I whisk them up and give them a quick turn around the Universe but they all go in the end. And I'm left . . . ultimately alone.'

Ace found herself blinking back tears. He's just like the rest of us, she thought.

'Let me get this straight, Doctor. Are you talking about retiring?'

The Doctor smiled. 'I suppose I am, yes. Settling down some-where. For a few centuries at least. Somewhere away from death and disaster. Far from the madding crowd.'

'But where?'

Privately, Ace thought the Doctor was incapable of living a quiet life, like that old woman in the Agatha Christie books. Wherever she goes, people get bumped off.

'Perhaps it's time I went home. To Gallifrey.'

Ace was amazed. 'But you're always telling me what a dull hole it is. All those geriatrics swanning around doing nothing all day. Isn't that why you left in the first place?'

'One of the reasons.'

'So what's changed?' said Ace.

'I have. I mean ... all these years of poking my nose into other people's business. Perhaps I should try and sort things out back there. It's corrupt and it's a bureaucratic nightmare but its heart is in the right place. I think it's time I stopped shirking my responsibilities.'

For once in her life, Ace could think of absolutely nothing to say.

The café door burst open and a tall Asian man with shoulder-length black hair strode inside. Ace was struck by the appealing openness of his finely sculpted face but thought it a shame he masked his features with such an ugly moustache.

Vijay Degun ran his fingers through his soaking hair and grinned at Mrs Crithin behind the counter.

'Could I use your phone, Mrs Crithin? We had a bit of an emergency up at the station last night and it blew all our phone lines. I need to get through to Cambridge.'

Ace looked out of the window and noticed the big green Land Rover in which Vijay had arrived.

'There's a phone box down the road, you know, love,' said Mrs Crithin, 'but you're welcome to use mine.'

'I tried that one but it's out of order as well.'

Mrs Crithin frowned and led Vijay into the back of the café. Ace looked at the Doctor but he seemed disinterested and deep in thought. She crept up to the counter and leaned across. Vijay was just visible in a little alcove under the stairs, fiddling with the receiver of Mrs Crithin's phone. He frowned and tapped the instrument against his cupped hand. Something was wrong. He talked to Mrs Crithin for a few minutes and then ran back into the café.

'Thanks anyway,' he called behind him. 'All the lines must be down. Probably the weather!'

He almost ran into Ace as he barged towards the door.

'Oh sorry,' he said, his eyes already looking beyond Ace to the door. He paused on the threshold and the rain buffeted him. Then, wrapping his overcoat around him, he dashed from the café towards The Shepherd's Cross.

'Did you hear that, Doctor?' said Ace excitedly.

'Mmm?'

'All the phone lines are down. We're cut off!' Ace tried to sound bubbly in the hope of cheering the Doctor up.

'Er ... Ace,' he said in a quiet voice, 'I was wondering whether I could ask you a favour.'

'Yeah, of course. Anything.'

'I need some time to myself. To do some thinking. I was wondering — well ...'

Ace smiled. 'Here's two bob, get yourself to the pictures? Yeah, I understand, Doctor. I'll occupy myself for a bit. Where will you be?'

The Doctor stood up and put on his hat. 'I'm going to that monastery over on the moor. Good places to think, monasteries.'

'OK, Doctor.'

'I'll see you in The Shepherd's Cross this evening. Shall we say eight o'clock? Sorry to leave you in the lurch like this.'

'Eight o'clock, in the pub. Got you. Are you buying?'

The Doctor grinned, gripped her arm affectionately and stepped out into the rain. Ace watched his little figure, blurred by the downpour, as he walked out of the village. She sighed heavily.

Now what was she going to do? She had enough trouble keeping herself occupied in the middle of London, never mind in this hole. And this might be 1968 but she doubted whether Crook Marsham ever did much swinging. Still, there were compensations. That lad on the bike for one. She smiled.

There was a long-drawn-out grumbling noise and Ace looked down at her stomach.

Breakfast was a good place to start. She went up to the counter and beamed at Mrs Crithin.

'Three egg sandwiches and another cup of tea, please.'

'Betty?'

'Mm?'

'Customer, love.'

Lawrence Yeadon put down his tea towel and took his wife's hand.

'Are you sure you're all right?'

Betty smiled thinly at him. Her eyes were misting over. It was obvious she hadn't yet recovered from the night's tears.

'I'm all right. Honestly, Lol.'

Lawrence shook his head and moved to serve the old man who was impatiently tapping his ring finger against his empty beer glass.

'I'll serve Mr Medcalfe. You go and lie down.'

Betty protested but Lawrence held up his hand. 'Quite apart from the fact that I'm worried about you, you're not exactly presenting the image of barmaid of the month looking like that, are you?'

Betty shook her head, defeated.

'Now go on. Have a nap. You'll feel better for it.'

In truth, Betty was glad to leave the smoky bar and be alone with her thoughts. Robin wouldn't be back from work for a couple of hours and the upstairs of the pub was pleasantly quiet and warm. Betty glanced around the corner of Robin's bedroom and smiled at the devastated jumble of clothes and bedsheets. Not a stickler for neatness like his dad or his Uncle Alf.

Alf. Betty thought of her brother again and tears pricked her eyes. She fondled the silver photo frame which she kept on her dressing table. Auntie Jean and her mum, grinning falsely at a camera on some faraway summer holiday. Black and white seagulls circled in a black and white sky.

Why couldn't she stop thinking about Alf? He'd been dead for over twenty years. Guilt hung about her neck like an albatross.

Betty slipped off her shoes and walked across the thickly carpeted hallway to the bathroom. She turned on the tap and gorgeously hot water thudded into the pink porcelain. A few drops of syrupy bath oil completed the process and Betty felt a thrill of happy anticipation at the prospect of a restful soak. She stayed to watch the bubble bath froth from under the taps and then returned to the bedroom.

A mile away, at the tracking station, Dr Hawthorne stood up sharply as a fresh burst of data stormed through the room, sending computers and tracers haywire. He dashed to the internal phone in order to alert Dr Cooper. The line was dead. He cursed and ran from the room.

Betty took off her clothes with careful deliberation, as if she were engaged in some sort of ritual. The towelling bathrobe which she put on had been a present from Lawrence's sister Margie. It was a little too big but the freshly laundered, fluffy material made her feel warm and secure.

She still couldn't keep her mind off Alf. His image seemed to hover before her eyes like a projected film. She walked to the bathroom and stopped dead.

Under the frothy foam, seemingly deep, deep down in the water, something was moving.

Panic and a scream began to rise in her throat. A hand was fumbling its way out of the water: a vile, filthy hand, its flesh sunburnt and blistered, black scum and mould under its fingernails. And as it grasped the side of the bath, and an equally appalling body hauled itself out, Betty let go of her senses and slipped gratefully into a dead faint.

The thing in the bath hauled itself to its feet, sending water cascading on to the floor. It was a man, or the remains of a man, wearing a dark blue uniform and a filthy white sweater. The hair was lank and hung in a great wet slap over the mottled, fish-flesh white forehead. The lips were pulled back in a ghastly grin of decay beneath two empty, empty sockets, speckled and rimmed with black blood.

In her shock, Betty could have been forgiven for not recognizing the creature. But, in point of fact, over twenty years late, her brother Alf had come home to stay . . .

3

The Doctor held his umbrella like a shield before him as a fresh squall of rain tore across the moor. His feet squelched into the deep tracks which already pocked the moor path, their muddy outlines pooling with glutinous brown water.

He paused briefly and fumbled in his pockets as the wind flapped his coat against him. Pushing the umbrella under one arm he pulled on a pair of thick woollen gloves and wrapped his paisley scarf tightly around his neck.

It was terribly, bitingly cold and the Doctor could feel an aching numbness spreading across his exposed cheeks. He screwed up his eyes and peered at the gaunt tower of the monastery, now less than half a mile away, silhouetted against the gun-metal sky. Sniffing as a drew-drop formed on the end of his nose, the Doctor clapped a hand on his hat to prevent the wind from whipping it away.

His mind buzzed with a million conflicting thoughts but, in a cocoon of coats, the Doctor resolved to think only of his pressing need for warmth, comfort and a strong cup of tea.

He marched on, unwittingly ghosting the large, wellington-indented tracks of Jack Prudhoe.

Ace looked into her empty cup and then at her watch. It was past eleven and she was still Mrs Crithin's only customer of the day. The woman herself was engaged in a seemingly endless rota of table-mopping and washing up. She'd exchanged a few words with Ace, mostly about the 'shocking weather'. And wasn't it awful about Czechoslovakia? Ace had nodded with some gravity even though she hadn't a clue what Mrs Crithin was talking about.

Finally, the ever-smiling café owner had plonked her newspaper on to the table and Ace seized upon it, ravenous for distraction.

It was strangely fascinating to see what was to her old news presented on brand-new, creamy paper. Odd, she thought, that the reality of time travel with the Doctor really struck her only when she had a personal handle on it. Only a few hundred miles from where she now sat, her mum would be doing some of those things about which she was always reminiscing. Maybe planning which outfit she would wear and which of her fancy-men she would favour. Perhaps, on the dance floor of some sweaty, swinging nightclub, meeting the man with whom she would soon conceive little Dorothy. Little Dorothy felt herself shudder.

'You all right, love?' asked Mrs Crithin, leaning on her mop.

Ace nodded and smiled reassuringly. 'Someone just walked over my grave.' She turned a few more pages of the paper and paused at a picture which showed a small dark man and a leggy woman dancing at some delirious Californian festival.

'Lovely girl, isn't she?' said Mrs Crithin, looking over Ace's shoulder.

'Who?'

'That Sharon Tate,' trilled Mrs Crithin. 'I think she's ever so good. And it's nice to see them still as much in love.'

Sharon Tate? Ace's memory pulled up sharp at the naggingly familiar name. It was tied up somewhere in a kaleidoscope of images and half-recalled conversations. Then she had it. Sharon Tate: the beautiful wife of Roman Polanski, gruesomely murdered at the behest of Charles Manson and his 'family' of West Coast fanatics. Ace had read about it in one of her mum's grisly True Crime books. The title was something like *The Day the Dream Died*.

Ace looked into Mrs Crithin's eyes and felt suddenly uncomfortable with her knowledge of the future, like some ancient seer cursed with the gift of prophecy. She changed the subject with what she hoped was some nonchalance.

'What's your flying saucer thing up the road, then?'

Mrs Crithin stopped mopping and put her hand on her ample hip as if settling into a familiar routine.

'That's our telescope, love. Famous in the right circles. We have all sorts trooping up there. It picks up radio messages from outer space so I keep a table reserved in case we ever get any little green men.'

Ace grinned. 'And who was that bloke who came in a bit ago?'

'The darkie?'

Ace winced but sensed that Mrs Crithin's institutionalized racism wasn't intended to offend. She nodded.

'That's Mr Degun. Nice enough young man. Always got a word for you. He works up there at the telescope. Often comes in for his breakfast.'

Ace let her get back to her chores, folded the paper, thanked her for breakfast and paid with some uncertainty out of the heavy, predecimal coins the Doctor had left on the table. She stepped outside and was soaked in moments, her fringe hanging unpleasantly in her eyes as little drops of rain dribbled down her face.

Most of the shops had crawled into life and Ace hurried over to shelter under their dirty brown awnings.

A florid-faced man in a blood-stained white coat emerged into the dreary daylight, looked at the sky, grimaced and went back inside. There was a slightly sinister wooden sign in the shape of a smiling pig hanging on chains above the shop and it swung back and forth as the man slammed the door.

Ace dug her hands into her pockets, feeling her fingers numbing in spite of her gloves.

Rain bounced off the motley collection of boxlike cars, huddled against both kerbs like frightened sheep. Ace wondered how people could ever have fitted into such things, never mind think them classy. Most of them looked like old school radiators with pram wheels on each corner. She ran a finger across the shiny metallic paintwork of a Morris Oxford and gazed in at its snug interior. There was a pair of driving gloves on the dashboard and one of those wretched traffic-light air fresheners hanging from the mirror. Better than furry dice anyway, she thought.

Across the street stood Crook Marsham's little cinema, a tall, thin building sandwiched between a travel agent's and something which claimed to be a 'boutique'. A red-lettered ABC sign, fairly new, partially obscured the grimy shadows of the old name: The Plaza.

Ace laughed to herself. Old picture houses always had such

46

exotic names in spite of their locations.

This one was showing *You Only Live Twice* and there, under a chipped plate of glass, was a poster of Sean Connery, surrounded by Oriental women, and clutching a space helmet in one hand and a gun in the other.

When she'd mentioned going to the pictures she hadn't meant it literally. She'd seen the film half a dozen times on TV anyway. But it might while away the afternoon pleasantly while she waited for the Doctor. And at least there would be no adverts to interrupt it.

She was about to check the programme times when she noticed Vijay's Land Rover parked opposite the café. Stealthily she looked around and then, hunching her shoulders against the blasting rain, she crossed the street and looked into the exposed rear of the vehicle.

Inside, there were a couple of tartan blankets, some walking boots and a lot of fairly antiquated-looking machinery. Ace decided to have a better look and, again looking about her furtively, clambered into the back.

There was a distant clatter and she snapped up her head to look out of the tarpaulin-covered tail section. Vijay was leaving The Shepherd's Cross, warmed, no doubt, by a glass or two of brandy.

Without thinking, Ace flung one of the blankets over her head and crouched low amongst the machinery. One of the walking boots was jammed against her face and smelt none too pleasant but she ignored it and kept very still. Vijay clambered on board and slammed the door. Ace heard him cough, sigh and then start the engine. In a moment, the Land Rover pulled away and they were on their way to the station. Ace suppressed a smile. This way she got to see the only vaguely interesting thing in the whole place and could easily be back for her appointment with the Doctor.

'Sorry, Mr Bond,' she whispered as the vehicle sailed past the cinema.

The Doctor scurried under the impressive granite archway of the monastery entrance, furling his umbrella with some relief. In the shadows, he pressed himself against a wall and watched the rain coming down in diagonal slants.

The monastery was solid, imposing and stained with age, great mossy outcrops uglifying its splendid tower and porticos. The Doctor's gaze ranged about the place and he rapidly determined the period, picturing the positions of the open-air cloisters and dormitories in his mind's eye. Perhaps there was even a library. The thought of a peaceful afternoon out of the rain amongst old books gave him a little thrill of pleasure.

He walked through a covered colonnade towards the rear of the building. A huge, blank stone wall dominated this eastern side and above it all loomed the spindly tower, jutting like a tobacco-stained tooth into the eternally grey clouds.

The Doctor strolled on, careful to stay within the shelter of the walls, and soon came upon a rather forlorn-looking vegetable garden, dotted with cracked flower pots and plot markers which projected in some unfathomable pattern from the drenched soil. Like a graveyard for tongue-depressors, thought the Doctor idly.

At the top of the garden, jammed against a stone wall, stood a decrepit greenhouse. Its elaborate roof and once-elegant doorway suggested more prosperous days. Now several panes were blacked out and the woodwork, soaked, stained and peeling, buckled away from the glass. Inside, a large, black-robed man was bent studiously over a bed of soil.

Abbot Winstanley was enjoying the warmth of his greenhouse and had cheerfully abandoned his Gannex mackintosh and sou'wester hat in favour of the apron and battered panama he normally reserved for summer. Despite the ramshackle insulation, the greenhouse was as warm as any July day and, if he blocked out the hiss of the rain, Winstanley could almost hear the drone of pollen-laden bees as they flopped from one colourful bloom to the next.

A light tapping at the pane broke his reverie and he turned to see a blurred, duffel-coated figure grinning hopefully at him from outside.

'Just a tick!' Winstanley called chirpily, putting down his trowel. In an instant, he had flung back the door and revealed the Doctor.

'Good morning. I'm the Doctor. I wonder if I might ...'

'Come in, come in!' urged the Abbot, giggling unnecessarily.

48

'We can't let this horrid weather inside, now can we?'

The Doctor mumbled an apology and found himself steered across the greenhouse threshold. Winstanley slammed the door and sat the Doctor down in a striped deckchair which was as old and disreputable as the building itself.

Winstanley was a round-faced pudding of a man who cheerfully adhered to Friar Tuck clichés. His large shaved head was freckled and sunburnt and his grin split his face like a slice of overripe melon. The Doctor was struck, however, by the Abbot's watery blue eyes. Their melancholy aspect seemed at odds with his massive personality.

'Now then, my dear sir. Where were we? A doctor, are you? Well, well, we're all in good health here as far as I can recall.' He let out another peal of unnecessary giggles. The Doctor shrank back from the surfeit of good humour.

'I'm not here on medical matters,' he said soothingly, glancing about at the ripening tomato plants. 'I was wondering if you'd be willing to let me spend some time here. Away from it all. Time to think ...'

'Sanctuary, eh?' cried the Abbot, rubbing his hands together. 'Capital idea. We often get people popping in. More often to get out of the rain, though, I must admit!' His capacious frame shook with laughter.

With surprising deftness, the Abbot slipped into his mackintosh and floppy hat, ushering the Doctor outside into what looked like, at last, diminishing rain.

'I'm Mervyn Winstanley, by the way.' He grasped the Doctor's hand with his own sunburnt flipper and pumped it until the Doctor's knuckles ached.

As they negotiated the Somme-like garden, Winstanley related in a high, enthusiastic voice something of the monastery's history. At one time, it seemed, there had been almost four hundred brothers there.

'No call for it now, of course. There's just me and, oh, forty others. We have to make honey and novelty mugs just to keep the wolf from the door.' He disappeared through a low archway.

The Doctor hopped over one last muddy trench and then paused as he reached the archway, gazing back at the dish of the telescope which dominated the horizon. Something shivered up his back and the hairs on his neck rose in response. For a moment, he saw himself balanced on the slippery walkway of another telescope, the flat concrete hundreds of feet below. Saw himself falling, the world and his life rushing away from him.

He had come through that crisis, despite everything. Yet something of that fear and sense of doom seemed to hang about him now as he stared across the grey moor.

Rubbing his hand against the nape of his neck, the Doctor followed Abbot Winstanley through the alcove and was soon lost in the shadows.

Something cold pressed itself against Betty's cheek and her eyelids flickered. In the confusion of light and colour she picked out a dark shape bobbing about her face. Her eyes snapped open and she took in the terrible shape towering above her. A snow-cold, wasted hand held her chin so tightly that she could feel the skeletal fingers pressing into her flesh. She cried out and felt a wave of revulsion rising as her eyes flicked from detail to detail of the apparition before her.

Alfred Beadle's empty sockets gazed into Betty's red-rimmed eyes, his forced grin of decay seeming to grow even wider. He wagged a bony finger as if to admonish her and then let out a chuckle from between his teeth which blasted his sister full in the face. The vile head seemed to shudder its way towards her, black moisture and weed trickling from its hair.

There was a voice inside Betty's head and she shook herself to try to ignore it, to escape the awful pressure of his claws on her face, the proximity of his fleshless lips to her own mouth.

'What kind of a welcome's this?' the voice seemed to coo. 'Give your old brother a kiss . . .'

The face jutted forward. Closer. Rank, salty breath streamed across Betty's face. Closer . . .

She screamed so hard that she cracked her head against the side of the bath. For one long minute she lay panting and retching where she had fainted, glaring about the room as if the walls themselves were about to attack her. Then she felt the cold bath panel against her cheek and, in a rush of logic, connected it to the imagined icy grip of her late brother.

A deep, relieved sigh hissed from between her clenched teeth and she managed to haul herself into a sitting position against the bath. Blood roared in her ears. She glanced stiffly over her shoulder and realized the bathwater was about to overflow. Shakily, she got to her feet and turned off the juddering taps with some effort.

The rim of the bath was wet and warm. Betty sat down on it heavily, letting the edge of her dressing gown trail in the steaming water. Brushing a lock of damp hair from her eye she began to take long, grateful breaths. Then she glanced down at the carpet and started screaming.

She didn't stop, her throat and lungs aching with the strain, even when Lawrence came belting up the stairs, looking crazily about him as if trying to locate the problem.

'Betty! What is it? What's the matter?'

She flung herself, weeping, into his arms, her breath coming in huge, hysterical gulps.

'What is it? What is it?' Lawrence insisted, shielding his wife with burly arms.

But she was unable or unwilling to speak. Instead she allowed him to lead her from the bathroom and lay her down on the bed.

Lawrence looked down at her anxiously as she twisted and knotted the sheets between shaking hands. He stroked her forehead gently and made reassuring hushing sounds until she turned over on her side, eyes glaring fixedly at the wall.

After staying a few minutes, Lawrence decided it was time to call for help. Betty had coped with these nightmares long enough. He stood up and crossed the landing to the telephone.

'Dad?'

Robin's voice sailed up from the bar below. Lawrence paused with his finger on the dial and pressed the receiver to his chest.

'Up here, Robin!' he called over the bannister.

Robin was already on his way up, pulling off his coat and scarf in agitation. 'They said in the bar they heard ...'

'It's all right, it's all right. It's Betty. Another of her bad dreams.'

Lawrence dialled a number, listened, frowned and then dialled again. A dull crackling sound came from the receiver.

'No answer. Funny.'

Robin was making his way towards the bedroom. Lawrence

put a hand on his son's arm.

'She'll be all right with me, son. Could you go across and see if Dr Shearsmith's in? The phone seems to be playing up.'

Robin hesitated, glancing across the landing at the closed bedroom door. 'Well ...'

'She'll be OK with me.'

'Yeah. Yeah, of course. Whatever you think's best.'

Robin clattered away down the stairs and out through the bar. Lawrence sighed heavily and padded across the landing towards the bedroom. Passing the open bathroom door he failed to notice the large, wet boot marks rapidly evaporating from the carpet.

MRS CARSON: He's changed. Different somehow!

NIGHTSHADE: All right, Barbara, don't get hysterical.

(*Nightshade sits her down next to her unconscious husband and beckons Dr Barclay.*)

NIGHTSHADE: Any word on those meteorites, Barclay?

BARCLAY: Not yet, sir. But we've found traces of Enstatite.

NIGHTSHADE: Hmm. Normal enough. And the rocket crew?

BARCLAY: There's no trace of them. Anywhere.

(*The seated astronaut begins to moan, eyes staring ahead.*)

CARSON: Help me! Help me!

MRS CARSON: What is it? Robert? Don't you know me? Can't you say just one word?

(*Nightshade takes her to one side.*)

NIGHTSHADE: Leave him, Barbara. He'll come round. In time.

(*The telephone rings. Barclay answers.*)

BARCLAY: Yes? Yes, of course. Right away.

NIGHTSHADE: What is it?

BARCLAY: They've found something, sir. Down at the crash site.

NIGHTSHADE: Come on!

(*They run from the room. Fade to black.*)

Trevithick looked up from his perusal of the yellowing script on his knee. Jill stood by the window a few feet from him, letting the steam from her tea flood pleasantly into her face. She sniffed back shaky tears and looked at the bare brown poplars which lined the driveway. A fierce wind shivered through them.

'You know, I've always hated this time of year,' she said, without turning round. Trevithick merely grunted and toyed with his old script.

There was a car in the drive and Jill saw George Lowcock bending to retrieve something from the boot. He and the other policemen had been at the Home for several hours now. Hours, thought Jill, since she'd seen Edmund's shattered window and had, much to her own disgust, given in to her compulsion to vomit. The old man had been surprisingly tactful, considering the mess she'd made of his eiderdown, gently leading her to his chair next to the wardrobe with the broken door.

There was a short knock and Jill turned, smoothing the hair off her face in an effort to appear stoically calm.

George Lowcock, all overcoat, bulbous nose and whiskers, bustled into the room, flashing her one of his sweetest smiles.

'Well, love, nothing more we can do here.' He turned to Trevithick. 'You're sure there was nothing taken, sir?'

'Absolutely,' muttered the old man.

'Well, we know the glass was broken with some force. Apart from that, though ...'

'Just kids, then?' offered Jill without much confidence.

'Probably. Yes.'

Trevithick, however, knew his Sherlock Holmes and was not to be put off. 'No clues? The soil outside the window must be saturated. There have to be footprints of some kind.' His bushy eyebrows lifted expectantly.

Lowcock sighed. 'No sir. No footprints. No traces. Nothing.'

Trevithick grunted again and jammed his pipe into his lopsided mouth. Jill began to usher the policeman out.

Lowcock put on his hat. 'Naturally, we'll investigate as far as possible, miss. If you like, I'll leave one of the lads on watch for the next few nights. Might make the old folks feel a bit more secure.'

'I haven't told them yet,' said Jill.

'Oh well.' Lowcock beamed again. 'Probably very wise.'

He touched his hat and then, as he turned to the door, fixed Trevithick with a quizzical grin.

'Excuse me, sir. Have we met before?'

Trevithick rolled his eyes and adjusted himself in his seat. 'I don't believe so.'

Jill decided to mediate. 'This is Edmund Trevithick, George. he used to be . . .'

'No! Don't tell me . . . Hang on . . . Nightshade! That's it! Professor Nightshade! Eeh, we used to love that. Shepherd's Cross used to empty when you were on. Especially that one where you found those things in the ground.'

Trevithick smiled as if humouring a child. Lowcock fumbled in his raincoat and produced a battered address book. 'Would you mind? It's not for me, you understand . . .'

Trevithick scribbled his name on the flyleaf and Jill once again ushered out the beaming policeman.

'Well, you certainly made his day,' she said, sitting down and smoothing her skirt.

'Keep the punters happy, I always say.'

Jill looked at him keenly. 'Now, Edmund. Are you sure you've told me everything?'

'Stop treating me like a bloody child.'

'I'm sorry. But have you? Is there anything else I should know?'

Trevithick avoided her glance and contemplated his shoes. 'I woke up and the window was smashed. I rang for you. That's all.'

Jill stood up. 'Right then. In that case I'd better get on. There's some workmen coming to fix your window. I've got to get everyone ready who is going home for Christmas.'

Trevithick eyed her cynically. 'Catching one last Yuletide frolic before the cemetery, eh?'

'That's not very nice, Edmund.'

'Who's going where, then?' he asked brightly.

Jill looked up at the ceiling as if to conjure up a list of figures. 'Erm . . . the Rayner sisters are going to their family in Birmingham. Mr Dutton, Mr Bollard and Mr Messingham . . .'

'The Unholy Three?'

Jill laughed. 'Yes. They're going to Blackpool . . .'

'God help Blackpool.'

'And Mrs Holland is going over to Leeds.'

Trevithick pulled a face. 'You don't mean they're having her back after last year?'

'That was an unfortunate mistake.'

'Unfortunate mistake?' Trevithick mocked. 'I don't call peeing on the Christmas tree an unfortunate mistake. More like malice aforethought!'

Jill suppressed a smile. 'She was overwrought, poor dear. Anyway, the others are off to a hotel in Ilkley for the duration. We're taking a coach to York Station.'

'All except me.'

'All except you. And because of your bloody-mindedness I've got to spend my Christmas in Crook Marsham.'

Trevithick harrumphed but, in truth, he was rather looking forward to it. Now that he had no family. He thought briefly of his daughter's inert body on that wretched autobahn. And his granddaughter. Run off to join some hippy cult or other.

No, now it would be just him and Jill. Probably pulling crackers over a tin of Spam. He laughed lightly to himself.

'Well, my dear. 'Tis the season to be jolly.'

Jill smiled and placed a cool hand on his. He watched her leave the room and then turned back to the window. His mind began to race. He had kept quiet about what had really happened in his room. But what had happened? What could he tell anyone? That some strange voice had whispered the name of his old character out of the darkness? That there was that dreadful smell? Like the mass grave he and his men had come across in Poland during the war. Morbid, rotten, evil. Yes, that was it. There was something terrible about that smell. Something long-buried that should never have seen daylight again.

There was a commotion in the corridor and Trevithick raised himself a little unsteadily to his feet. Robin was beyond the door, his face flushed and his breath coming in gasps.

'Miss Mason? Miss Mason?' he called. Jill came down the corridor, her head cocked to one side. Trevithick shut the door behind him and joined them.

'You're Lawrence Yeadon's son, aren't you?' said Jill. 'What's up?'

Robin ran a hand through rain-glistened hair. 'It's my mum. She's not well. I tried to get Dr Shearsmith but he's not there.

Can you help? You are a nurse?'

Jill pulled a face. 'Well ... I'll do my best.'

She took down a heavy sheepskin coat from its peg and went to tell Polly what had happened. Trevithick walked up to Robin.

'You're from the pub aren't you, lad?'

Robin nodded distractedly, glancing up the corridor.

'Hmm,' mused Trevithick. 'I think I might accompany you. We've had a bit of trouble of our own up here. I could murder a pint.'

Robin smiled thinly. Trevithick went to fetch his coat and hat.

Realizing that Jill would probably be some time, Robin slid down the wall and relaxed. He couldn't work out what had happened to Dr Shearsmith. He was always in before four and had told everyone he was staying in Crook Marsham for Christmas.

Added to that, Robin had found the front door wide open and the record player on, struggling scratchily through 'That's the way it is' by the Ink Spots. There was an old photograph album, too, lying on the hearthrug and open to show faded, white-bordered pictures of Dr Shearsmith and his late wife on some long-ago Christmas Day. Some time during the thirties to judge from their clothes. There was a funny smell too. Like milk turning sour.

Jill strode towards Robin, a reassuring smile on her face. Trevithick appeared simultaneously, jamming a tweedy hat on to his head. Opening the front door, the three of them set out together into the gathering dusk.

Ace gazed down forlornly at the mud which caked her shoes. She'd watched Vijay open the security fence with some sort of electronic key and then crouched under the blankets again as they drove through into the compound. After he'd disappeared inside she'd waited and then hauled herself out.

The radio telescope was certainly impressive, she conceded: an enormous dish which towered over the E-shaped concrete buildings beneath. But once she'd walked around the thing twice she found herself at a bit of a loose end. It was also getting dark and was still freezing cold.

She thought briefly of barging through the big double doors

and announcing herself but didn't think this very wise. Finally, she decided to walk back to the village and set off for the perimeter fence, shivering as another blast of icy wind rippled over the moor. Little tufts of purple heather shuddered like dryland anemones.

The fence still sparkled with recent rain. Ace jumped a little as three arc lamps burst into life with a staccato clatter. Obviously part of the security set-up, she thought. Mind you, there hadn't been much evidence of restriction or surveillance so far. No knuckle-heads in peaked caps at any rate and years of petty confrontations with school caretakers and bouncers made her grateful for that.

It was only when she had traipsed forlornly to the exit gate that she realized getting out would be rather more difficult than getting in. There were two rows of barbed-wire ranged across the top of the fence and the gate itself was solid steel mesh. The square grey box into which Mr Degun had inserted his key winked its red light at her tauntingly.

'Oh brilliant,' she muttered.

Vijay, looking out of the window, failed to see Ace. Dusk was creeping into the periphery of his vision like spots mottling the edges of a mirror. The rich navy-blue colour of the sky took him back to Saturdays at home as a child. His father hunched over a pools coupon as Peter Dimmock read out the football results on *Sportsview*.

Vijay would be outside, relishing the thrill which the wintry darkness gave to his games to hide and seek. He'd press himself into dark corners or against midnight-black trees, watching the wind stir skeletal branches above his head.

Then air would burn his lungs as he pelted out of the wood, his friends in excited pursuit. After another adrenaline-powered race they would collapse on top of each other, giggling and hooting with joy.

A sudden flare of yellow light in the porch would signal the appearance of his father, coupon dangling from his hand, as he peered out into the darkness.

'Vijay? Vijay? Time to come in, now.'

And Vijay would bid a sulky goodnight to his friends,

dragging his heels in anticipation of the Saturday-night bath. He'd hug his knees to his chin, shrinking from the overly hot water which steamed around him and gaze at the black rectangle of night behind the flowery curtains.

He would hear his father pacing about downstairs, the television's sound an insulated mumble two floors below.

Occasionally, just occasionally, in those formative years, his father would pause after draping the big, rough towel around Vijay, look his son in the eye and say 'Bit of a treat tonight.' To Vijay that could mean only one thing. A new *Nightshade* serial.

So they would sit together before the tiny, flickering screen, Vijay's eyes wide with terror, his father pretending indifference whilst clutching the chair till his knuckles whitened.

Later, despite the excitement, Vijay would quietly wish he hadn't stayed up; his imagination transformed bedroom furniture or crumpled clothes into the bulky, crablike creatures which the Professor had so recently encountered. One night they had seemed so real. So real. He could have sworn the thing was advancing across the room towards him, mandibles swaying and dripping with fluid, eyes ticking and twitching as it bore down . . .

'All of them?'

It was Dr Cooper. Vijay turned from the window, once more conscious of the hum of the machinery around him.

'As far as I can tell, yes,' he said. 'I tried the café, I tried the pub, I tried the callbox. I even tried the surgery . . .'

'No joy?'

'Dr Shearsmith wasn't there and the phone was definitely out of order.'

Cooper sat down heavily. 'Maybe it's the weather.'

Vijay looked at his watch. Nearly four. Nearly time for Hawthorne to begin his shift. He blew air out of his cheeks noisily.

'Oh, this is outrageous!' cried Cooper, getting to her feet and thumping the bench. 'The biggest input of data, however confusing, that we've ever had and we can't tell anyone about it! We'd be better off sending HQ a postcard.'

'What about the radio?' asked Vijay, nervously stroking his

moustache.

'Hawthorne's fiddling with it. Looks like it's gone the same way as the phones.' She strode across the room and picked up a sheaf of papers which had fallen to the floor.

'Where's Holly?'

'Still sleeping,' said Vijay, and that was where he wanted to be right now. Or, at least, in Holly's embrace, resting his head on her breast as she soothed his fatigue away. Enjoying the sweet smoothness of her body against his. He blinked and realized Cooper was talking to him. 'Sorry, what?'

'I said it's past four. I'll cover for you tonight. Get some rest, you've done enough chasing around.'

Vijay grinned and thanked her warmly. Perhaps his dream wasn't so far off . . .

He passed Hawthorne on the way to his room and the rat-faced man shot him an inquisitive look. Cooper answered the unasked question.

'I'm covering for Vijay tonight. He's been out all day trying to find a phone that works. How's the . . . ?'

Hawthorne dropped a pile of electrical components on to the bench and several rolled to the floor.

'Buggered,' he said and sat down.

Ace had barked her knuckles for the fifth time trying to scale the perimeter fence when she noticed the hole. One of the arc lamps caught the outer edge of the torn mesh and she ran expectantly towards it, feeling the cold air rasping through her nose. The moor and sky, now just two broad strokes of darkness, bobbed around her as she jogged towards the fence. To her left, the parabolic dish blazed briefly as a circling lamp slid over its surface. Then she threw herself down by the hole.

The wire seemed to have been wrenched apart, razor-edges folded back towards the outside. She groped her way through, careful to avoid the edges, and felt her knees sinking into the peaty soil. Head through. She grasped a tuft of heather and pulled. Body through. Darkness pressed against her and she could feel hot, uncomfortable sweat patches spreading across her back and arms. Manoeuvring so that her feet wouldn't catch on the wire, Ace made a final effort and rolled through on to the moor beyond.

The black and purple landscape glowered at her like a bruised eye. She tried to ignore the mournful wind, stood up, put her hands in her pockets and started the long walk back to the village. Then she hit it.

Ace caught the thing with her foot and was flung headlong into the soil. She tasted mud and felt it soaking her clothes as she jumped back. The sweeping beam crept across the moor and Ace held her breath. The light came closer, suddenly illuminating the thing with horrible precision.

It was a uniformed man, his hands pulled back behind his head and broken at the wrists so that they hung grotesquely limp. He wore a black peaked cap above a face which might once have been youthful. But now it was foul.

The eyes were blank, sunk in their sockets and dulled to a strange grey colour above a mouth wrenched back in a snapshot of sheer fright. Livid purple weals and scratches crazed the pasty skin.

Ace cried out and stepped back, immediately feeling the treacherous mud slip beneath her. Before she knew what was happening, she was on top of it.

Howling in fear and nausea and disgust, she struggled to stand, to escape, but the thing seemed to erupt around her, belching out an unbelievable stink of corruption.

The station light swept back again and Ace saw the body expanding beneath her like a cast-off snakeskin, dark fluid draining away into the moor.

She threw herself clear and hugged herself. There was a rusty taste in her mouth and she realized she'd bitten her lip in agitation.

The beam came by again and this time there was no body. No uniform. Only a blackness like engine oil on summer grass and a lingering smell of decay.

Ace wasted no time. Urging herself to keep calm, keep calm, keep calm, she struggled back under the fence and sprinted the distance to the station entrance. Ignoring her earlier misgivings, she thrust out her hands and barged inside.

Cooper and Hawthorne looked up from their work and stared at her as if she were a gunslinger entering a saloon. Ace felt overwhelmed by the light and warmth, and staggered as coloured dots exploded before her eyes. She slid into a chair as a warm, thick comma of blood curled its way from her lips to her chin.

A man with arthritic hands, all bunched and knotted like rusty keys, was manning the bar of The Shepherd's Cross. Trevithick didn't know him but was enjoying the pint of stout he'd poured. Upstairs, Lawrence, Robin and Jill were ministering to Betty's needs.

Trevithick burped. It was getting on for seven o'clock and he would normally be settling down to watch television or read. He was halfway through *Bleak House*, always one of his favourites, loving the way Dickens drew him into that murky, fog-bound world.

Tonight, though, a long-forgotten excitement, something like the thrill of live performance, was flowing through his veins. There was the strange incident at the window, Mrs Yeadon's funny turn and his TV interview too. It was all very puzzling. And he liked a puzzle.

Lawrence Yeadon's jukebox was playing a particularly tacky version of 'White Christmas', all wispy soprano and electric piano, and the pub was crowded with ruddy-faced, laughing punters.

Trevithick finished his pint and looked up as the frosted-glass door opened. George Lowcock shuffled in, accompanied by a blast of cold wind and a little whirlpool of brown leaves. He rubbed his hands together rather theatrically and gave the pub one of his beaming smiles, nodding to all his old friends from the village. He spotted Trevithick at once.

'Hello, Professor!' he boomed, striding over to Trevithick's table. The old man flinched visibly and acknowledged the policeman with an embarrassed, lopsided smile.

'I gave your autograph to my wife. She was right pleased,' Locock enthused. 'Can I get you a pint?'

Trevithick perked up at this offer. 'Oh, that's very kind of you, Inspector.'

'Sergeant,' said Lowcock lightly. 'Call me George.'

'Er, thank you, George. A pint of Guinness, if you'd be so

kind.'

Lowcock stood up and did an elaborate mime to the man behind the bar. This was evidently understood as the barman shortly pushed his way through the crowd, holding two pint glasses in his crooked hands.

'I had no idea we had a celebrity in the village,' said Lowcock, after paying the barman.

'Oh, hardly that, George. It was quite a while ago.'

Lowcock beamed at him. 'Aye, but we all loved it. We'd never go out when you were on. How'd you end up in Crook Marsham?'

Trevithick didn't like the use of the expression 'end up' but smiled back regardless. 'Believe it or not, I'd planned to retire up here. Live with my daughter and son-in-law. But they were killed in a car crash in Germany ...'

'Oh, I am sorry.' Lowcock's heavy features fell sympathetically.

'Anyway, I'd moved all my stuff and couldn't really afford a place of my own. So the vultures got me.'

'Very pretty vultures if you ask me,' said Lowcock with a hearty laugh, 'if that Miss Mason is anything to go by.'

Trevithick laughed back. 'Hmm. Nice girl. Doesn't really belong with a load of old crocks though. She has ambition. I can see it in her eyes.'

They sat in silence for a while, sipping their drinks. A cheery hubbub of voices crowded around them and one or two couples began to exchange kisses under the mistletoe pinned above the bar. The red flocked wallpaper seemed to glow and blur as Trevithick gazed at it. He smiled, rather contentedly.

'So,' he said finally. 'How's business?'

Unexpectedly, Lowcock's face was rather solemn. 'Funniest thing really. I like to have a nice clean book at Christmas. Goodwill to all men and that. There's usually just a bit of rowdiness and the odd drunk.'

'But not this year?' asked Trevithick, eyebrows raised over the rim of his glass.

'Two missing persons,' said Lowcock gravely. 'Old bloke called Prudhoe been gone since yesterday afternoon and now Dr Shearsmith. His cleaning woman says he's vanished into thin air.'

'Yes, young Robin called to see him. Found the place empty and the door wide open, so he tells me.'

'Really?' Lowcock scratched his whiskers thoughtfully.

'And now the phones are out of order as well,' said Trevithick in the most mysterious voice he could muster. The one he'd used to great effect when he presented *Tales of Terror* for the BBC Light Programme.

'Yours too, eh? We've been trying to get the GPO in but . . .'

'The phones aren't working,' laughed Trevithick. 'Mmm, makes you realize how dependent we all are on our mod cons.'

They both jumped as a high-pitched scream rang out across the bar. The Christmas merriment froze like black ice. Lowcock was on his feet in an instant and Trevithick hobbled after him as he mounted the stairs.

They crossed the landing and threw open the bedroom door. Betty lay on the bed, struggling against the restraining arms of Lawrence and Robin.

Jill stood by the bed, a fearful look in her eye.

'Send him away!' wailed Betty, painful sobs breaking up her voice. 'Send him away!'

Robin managed to force her back on to the pillow and pressed a cold flannel to her forehead.

'What's the matter, Lol?' said Lowcock, furrowing his brow. Lawrence drew Lowcock to one side but Trevithick managed to overhear his desperate, unbelieving whisper.

'It's her brother.'

'Patrick?'

'No, Alf.'

'Alf?'

'Yes. She says . . . she says she's seen him again. She says he's come back for her.'

Trevithick frowned and looked down at Betty Yeadon, flailing and thrashing on the bed.

The Doctor was enjoying a simple meal of soup, bread and cheese in the Abbot's panelled study. Winstanley had made him extremely welcome, showing him around the well-preserved Norman cloisters and up the spindly black tower. The Doctor had been introduced to about ten of the monks, although he would have had difficulty telling them apart, so blandly unperturbed were their expressions. This, again, was in stark contrast to the Abbot, whose troubled eyes continued to undermine his determinedly cheery countenance.

Now the Doctor had been invited to a little late tea and had just finished the last of the soup when Winstanley came in.

'All done? Good. Excellent.'

'Delicious,' mumbled the Doctor, his mouth still stuffed with bread.

'I made the soup myself. Brother Jeremy made the bread. It's rather fine, isn't it?' Winstanley moved over towards the blazing fire and warmed his backside. 'Chilly places, I'm afraid.'

'I don't suppose they were built for comfort,' said the Doctor, settling into a studded leather chair. Winstanley poured two glasses of ruby port. The room glowed around them, a miasma of dancing shadows and reflected flame underscored by the reassuring tock of the Abbot's long-case clock.

The Doctor could see pictures in the fire. Shifting faces and events from long, long ago. Hadn't he once sat like this with ... Who was it? Victoria. Of course, Victoria. Outside the Cybertombs on Telos. Talking about his family. Sleeping in his memory. Sleeping ...

'Penny for them?' said the Abbot cheerfully.

The Doctor looked up, smiled. 'Hmm? Oh, just thoughts. Just thoughts.'

It was Winstanley's turn to look into the fire. 'You know, Doctor, I can't tell you how good it is to have a new face about the place. It can get awfully lonely up here. The moor ... the wind. It's not the most beneficial of environments.'

The Doctor turned interested eyes on Winstanley who avoided his gaze.

'You seem like a good listener, Doctor. Tell me ...' The Abbot rolled the stem of his glass between pudgy fingers. 'Tell me, do you have faith?'

'Faith?'

Winstanley nodded.

The Doctor inclined his head slightly, throwing his face into deep shadow.

'I used to think . . . I used to think I had faith. Faith in what was right and wrong. What was just.'

'And now?'

'Now I'm not so sure.'

The Abbot turned towards the fire, his eyes glistening as though he were crying. 'Yes. I believe I know what you mean.'

The Doctor sat up sharply as if to break the mood of melancholy. 'Tell me about your radio telescope.'

'Oh, that's a recent addition, Doctor. Five or six years old. We're tuned in to messages from the stars.'

'Have they had any luck?'

Winstanley chuckled. 'Not to my knowledge. They seem a nice lot up there, though. I've met Dr Cooper and Miss Kidd. And Mr Degun often pops in. I believe he's fascinated by our way of life. We could go over there tomorrow, if you like?'

The Doctor considered this, already feeling his insatiable curiosity rising. But then he remembered why he'd come to the monastery and set his mouth determinedly.

'No. Thank you, but no. I'm not here to get involved.'

'As you wish,' said Winstanley, pouring another glass of port.

The Doctor sipped his drink and returned to his contemplation of the fire. Winstanley began to hunt amongst his bookshelves.

'Perhaps you'd be interested in this, Doctor?'

The Doctor glanced at his pocket watch. It was a little after seven. He mustn't forget his appointment with Ace.

A small, vellum-bound book, dwarfed by the Abbot's sausage-fingers, was pressed into his hand.

'Local history,' said Winstanley. 'And decidedly colourful too.'

The Doctor began to turn the brittle yellow pages which were crowded with crabbed print. Wide-bordered pictures appeared every once in a while, showing Saxon serfs labouring in the fields or building rudimentary houses on the moorland. The Doctor recognized the village church, without its later embellishments, and finally came upon a splendid print showing a large, heavily fortified Norman castle, narrow flags spiking its battlements.

'Marsham Castle,' said the Abbot over his shoulder. 'Built

65

by Sir Brian de Fillis in — let me see now — 1156. Yes, 1156.'
He ran a hand over his shaved head. 'Gone now, of course.'

'One of the ruins that Cromwell knocked about a bit,' said
the Doctor smiling.

'You're closer than you think. Read on.'

The Doctor settled back, holding the small volume between
his hands.

*This great victory upon the moor of Marston, given unto
Parliament by the grace of our Lord Jesus, did result in the
rout of Prince Rupert and his men. God did make them as stubble
to Cromwell's sword. Brave Ironsides, notwithstanding a grave
injury, beat the Prince's horsemen into retreat and sent Captain
Phillip Jackson in pursuit.*

*Coming upon a troop of the Royalists in the castle of
Marsham, in the county of York, Jackson reported that the
King's Men did experience such ghastly terrors and phantoms
that they cried aloud to heaven.*

*Upon surrendering themselves to Parliament's mercy, the
castle was consumed by a strange fire and all were glad to return
to their camp. This place has long been notorious for weird
happenings ...*

The Doctor looked up from his book and chewed his lip
thoughtfully.

4

In Phillip Jackson's view, the day had already dragged on long enough. Now the night was hot and still, the cloying perfume of wild summer flowers mingling with wisps of gunsmoke. Overhead, the sky, smooth and unperturbed as an upturned tea cup, was a rich collage of dark blue and sunset crimson.

He laid back his handsome head and enjoyed the soft pressure of the heather tangling in the shining black locks of his hair. It had been a good day.

Jackson's belief was strong: to fight for true democracy, the freedom to worship as he chose, and not to labour under the tyrannical rule of an unworthy king. Today's victory had been sweet indeed but Jackson knew well how soon he would be called upon to fight again. Had he not promised Cromwell to pursue the Royalists to perdition if needs be?

1644, however, had not been a good year for Parliament. King Charles stood firm even with the war two years old. Then had come a morale-crushing blow, only the previous day, as Prince Rupert entered the city of York unopposed after crossing the north bank of the Swale. Sniping attacks by Rupert's men had followed and Jackson saw Cromwell's face darkening with anger.

'We must stop and fight!' he had bellowed at the Earl of Manchester. 'Else lose all to that puppy Rupert.'

Manchester had sat long and thought hard, fingering the delicate embroidery of his collar. Then he nodded his assent.

They had drawn up on the long ridge of open plain that stretched down to Marston Moor, Cromwell's force of twenty-seven thousand against Rupert's eighteen thousand. A line of hedges and ditches separated the two armies. Six miles due west stood York and four miles to the east the little settlement of Crook Marsham, dominated by its ruined Norman castle.

Jackson had seen its sun-shimmered battlements hovering on the horizon.

Before battle could begin, Parliament had observed its traditional good grace, allowing Rupert to await the Earl of Newcastle and his men. The day had worn on, the mood of impatience spreading from the florid-faced Cromwell to his troops. At around four in the afternoon, Newcastle's men finally arrived. To Jackson's disbelief they had retired for supper, as they believed the hour too late for fighting that day.

At around seven in the evening, with the pleasant smell of woodsmoke drifting across the plain, Cromwell had come into view, massive and inspiring astride his horse. He narrowed his eyes, watching the distant enemy figures moving like indistinct ink-blots on a purple canvas. He caught Jackson's eye, smiled slightly, and then bellowed the command to charge.

With a great whooping cry, Parliament's horsemen thundered across the moor, scattering the surprised enemy like frightened sheep. The night was suddenly alive with the yellow sashes of the Roundheads and the Royalists' vivid scarlet.

Cromwell's dragoons, three thousand strong, attacked Lord Byron and the Royalist right wing, decimating them. Jackson hacked away with his sword, a rush of grotesque faces flurrying past him.

A musket ball whistled past his ear and he felt himself twist and fall awkwardly from his horse. The ground raced up to meet him, iron hard, and he lay there a moment, winded and sick as booted feet staggered past. Then there were strong hands under him and he opened his eyes to see Cromwell himself lifting him bodily on to his horse.

'Thank God we've not lost you,' he said with a smile, the fire of battle shining in his eyes.

Jackson pulled on the reins and charged again. A Royalist soldier, his face already streaked with mud and dark blood, launched himself at Jackson's flank. The captain heaved his massive sword and took off half the soldier's face in one movement. The body fell under Jackson's horse and the captain rode on, shouting in exhilaration.

There was another salvo of musket fire and Cromwell reeled in his saddle, his warty face contorting with pain. Blood pumped from a wound in his neck. Jackson reigned in his horse and called above the din of battle, 'We must get you to the field hospital, sir!'

Cromwell shook his head, wiping the soil-caked wound as if to dismiss it. 'The second charge, Phillip, the second charge!'

Jackson nodded worriedly and followed his brave leader back to the ridge. After organizing the second charge, Cromwell had finally assented to treatment and retired.

Jackson and his men swept back on to the moor, Rupert's routed cavalry fleeing before them. The fighting became desperate, the iron stink of blood mingling with powder smoke as the two forces waded into each other. Then with a terrifying cry of triumph, Parliament's reserve of three thousand Scottish cavalry tore into the Royalist right wing which broke and fled.

'Is this not a sight to behold!' cried Cromwell, returning from the field hospital sooner than he ought, with his neck haphazardly dressed. At once, he declared Parliament's centre and right to be in a hellish state and, thrashing his horse, swept behind the enemy to his men's assistance.

How much longer the fighting had continued, Jackson couldn't be sure. If he closed his eyes he saw only anguished faces and glittering swords. He let his eyes roll back and gazed up at the darkening sky, the summer scents of the moor stirring around him. Then, with a groan, he sat up, eased off his boots and pulled down his stockings which were blackened with leather stains and mud. A leg of roast chicken was thrust into his hand and he ate ravenously, pausing only when he saw Cromwell striding towards him out of the darkness.

'Your wound, sir?' said Jackson, wiping greasy hands on his tunic.

Cromwell shrugged lightly. ' 'Tis little. A scratch. A far greater wound was Valentine Walton's boy. I have written to the father, God grant him mercy.'

Jackson nodded sadly. The boy's death that day had been a great blow to them all.

'But the victory is ours, Phillip. By God it is!' cried Cromwell, his heavy face suffusing with passion. 'Of twenty thousand the Prince hath not four thousand left. Colours, muskets, men. All are ours.'

'And Rupert?'

Cromwell sighed. 'Fled. Vanished. The jackanapes has the devil to protect him.'

Jackson unbuckled his belt and sat back on the warm ground. Cromwell changed tack.

'But still there is more to do. The battle has fatigued thee, I know, but I must return to the Eastern Association. The war is not yet won. I am relying on thee, Phillip, to remain here and hunt down any of the king's men who linger.'

Jackson sighed inwardly. He was exhausted. All he wanted now was to bathe and sleep. He looked down at his aching feet and nodded. 'I am, as always, at your service, sir.'

'Not mine, lad. The Lord's,' said Cromwell with a smile, clapping the young captain on the shoulder. 'Take your men and circle a few miles hereabouts, but tax them not too severely. Bring back Rupert and I'll make a general of thee.'

Jackson watched Cromwell disappear into his tent. He was right, of course. There might still be a few Royalists hiding in the surrounding countryside. Perhaps even Rupert himself. It was worth sacrificing a few hours to find them.

Wearily, Jackson pulled up his stockings and forced his sweat-soaked boots on to his feet. Within half an hour he had rounded up a dozen unwilling soldiers and had begun to trot away eastwards.

He felt curiously drawn towards the fires of Crook Marsham with its great ruined castle. On that fine, balmy July night, the old black towers were virtually indistinguishable against the wine-dark sky.

Sad, tired eyes gazed across the moor towards the cheery orange glow of Cromwell's camp. Sir Harry Cooke rubbed a wounded hand against his brow and sat down heavily against the crumbling castle rampart. Routed, by Christ. Routed!

He boiled with frustration. Why did the King allow his armies to be led by such incompetents? Rupert, the arrogant fool, had calmly taken supper though Cooke had warned of impending attack. 'They have not your sensibilities, your Highness,' he had insisted through clenched teeth, 'and care little for the lateness of the hour.'

And then stupid sulky Newcastle, retiring to his carriage to smoke a pipe!

Cromwell's men, sitting in their corn fields, had begun singing psalms, their rousing, passionate voices drifting through the summer haze.

'Is Cromwell there?' Rupert had asked anxiously. Aye, he was there, as they had discovered all too soon, caught unawares, their senses dulled by inertia.

Cooke and six or seven of his men had eventually fled the carnage, skulking to the old castle like disgraced dogs. There were men stationed on the far ramparts, looking down into the tiny settlement below. It was important they were not seen. Cooke knew from experience that loyalties were uncertain in this conflict and that the inhabitants of Crook Marsham might welcome them with open arms, only to betray them to Cromwell's militia. Better to hide out in the old ruin where no one was likely to pry and then slip away at some more opportune moment.

Ralph Grey, his fine-boned face drawn and weary, shambled along the battlements towards Cooke, who sensed he was troubled.

'What ails thee, Ralph?'

Grey glanced down at the decrepit main hall in which the men were huddled.

'They're out of sorts, Sir Harry,' he said with a sigh.

Cooke grimaced. 'We've suffered a great defeat, Ralph. I would expect no less.'

Grey shook his head slowly. 'No sir, 'tis this place.'

'This old ruin? What of it?'

Grey ran a finger across his beard. 'The men are afraid, my lord. They feel there is some evil at work here.'

Cooke snorted.

'They say they would rather face Cromwell than the Devil,' Grey continued.

'Much the same thing,' laughed Cooke, his portly frame shaking. 'Come, Ralph, we're too old and wily to believe in such nonsense.'

Grey made a little signal with his hand. 'There is a man, sir . . .'

71

A slight figure stepped out of the shadows, his uniform caked with mud and gashed at the sleeve.

'This is Will Todd, my lord,' said Grey, ushering the youth forward. 'A local man. Tell Sir Harry what you told me, Will.'

Todd shifted uneasily, like a guilty child.

'I was born in Crook Marsham, my lord. But my family went to York some years ago, my father being a skilled mason and work there plentiful...'

'Yes, yes...' said Cooke impatiently.

'This castle has stood since William of France came here and has been a ruin all that time.'

'What mean you by that?'

'Only a few years after the castle was built there were queer tales about the place. People spoke of the dead rising at night and all manner of things...'

'Phantasmagoria,' said Cooke, waving his hand dismissively.

Will Todd clenched his fists uncomfortably. 'Sir Brian, the Norman who built the castle, went mad. They say his wife came back from the grave to haunt him. After that no one would live here. No one.'

Cooke eyed him severely. 'And this prattle of yours has put the men into a ghastly humour, eh, Todd? I should have you horsewhipped for spreading such discontent. You're no better than a gossipy old woman.'

'I never meant...' pleaded Todd weakly.

'No, but the damage is done. We would do better to go to our beds and forget these tales of yours. Off with you, now.'

Todd made a little bow and clattered down the stone staircase to the ruined hall. Grey turned to his superior.

'Don't you feel it too, sir?'

'Nay!' barked Cooke. 'And, mayhap, if your mind were turned more towards soldiery than witchcraft we should not have been trounced on the moor today!'

Grey flinched and stepped back.

Cooke sighed and looked at Grey more kindly.

'I am sorry, Ralph. We lost many good lads today. If any man is out of sorts then it is I. To your bed now, old friend.'

Grey bowed slightly and disappeared down the steps, his boots echoing hollowly around the stones. Cooke rubbed his tired face with his injured hand and looked down at his men as they wrapped horse blankets around themselves. The tiny fire they had lit was flickering into extinction and, within minutes, the cold stone walls were plunged into midnight blackness.

The high, roofless castle beams loomed above them like the ribs of a long-dead beast. Cooke glanced about him in the whispering night at the deeply shadowed niches and empty fireplaces which might contain all manner of secrets. He shivered and, drawing his cloak around his shoulders, made his way stiffly down the stairs to his men. He looked at their troubled faces as they drifted into sleep. Despite his bluster, he rather wished Will Todd had not told him those tales about the old castle. He screwed his eyes tightly shut.

Jackson let his horse trot quietly along the well-trampled path that led to the castle. His men trailed in a silent, weary procession behind him, their shoulders bowed with fatigue. Jackson himself found that the gentle rocking motion was lulling him into sleep when a hissed whisper startled him awake.

'Captain!'

Jackson turned. A soldier behind him, obviously more alert than his comrades, was pointing towards the castle.

'What is it?'

'There's someone there, sir. I swear it. Down there, by the gates.'

Jackson strained his eyes. Was that a figure — no, two — in the shadows by the castle's sturdy entrance? He sat up in his saddle but whatever had been there was lost in the deep blue shadows.

'I see nothing,' he said wearily. 'But we'll stop here and rest awhile.'

His men flopped gratefully from their saddles and led their horses to a little circle of trees. Within moments they were stretched out on the hard ground, asleep.

Jackson himself stayed in his saddle for a time, gazing over at the darkened battlements some five hundred yards distant. The night was warm, silent, expectant.

Sunlight streamed through the children's hair as they jumped and capered about. Harry Cooke watched their smiling faces and felt himself laugh silently. His daughters, Bridget and tiny Mary with her big brown eyes, so happy and content in the gardens, hiding in the old stables and amongst the fragrant bushes.

Then the sky seemed to darken. A solid, warty face loomed out of the shadows, casting gloom over the happy scene. The children turned and screamed, running to their father for protection. Cooke held out his arms but his daughters seemed to make little progress, as though they were wading through molasses.

The ominous face seemed to swell, blotting out the sunshine. Cooke narrowed his eyes and glared at the apparition. It was Cromwell.

Of course, it was always Cromwell.

Now there were soldiers in the garden, faceless Roundheads in dull, pewter-coloured armour. Light flashed on their swords as they raised their weapons high in the air.

Cooke tried to scream but could feel only a silent tightening in his chest. Mary looked up at the shimmering blade and shot a desperate look at her father. The Roundhead stepped forward, his dark figure a hazy silhouette against the white light of the sun. The sword crashed down. This time, Cooke screamed and felt the air vomiting from his lungs in an unstoppable screech.

The night exploded around him like a dam-burst. He sat up, shaking with fear and grief, looking about him like a startled animal. Dark ruins. Sleeping men. Warm night breeze. He sighed. They were still in that damned castle.

He rubbed his face and neck, already feeling the sweat growing clammy on his flesh. Ralph Grey was asleep nearby, his blanketed form undisturbed.

Cooke let his head sink on to his chest. Why had he dreamed about them tonight? It was two years now since they'd been taken from him, and by brain fever, not the sword of some treacherous Roundhead. He thought once again of his daughters' golden ringlets and their clear, smiling faces.

Something moved on the battlements.

Cooke craned his neck and got to his feet, groaning with effort. He picked his way through the sleeping soldiers and dragged himself up the stone steps to the battlements. The night was silent now, save for a distant rustling as if the breeze were stirring the blossom-laden branches of distant trees.

He could see no one on the walkway. As he turned to make his way back into the ruined hall, there was a soft giggle from the shadows. Cooke seemed to recognize it at once and spun round.

'Who's there? Come out!'

Now he could hear a gentle voice ringing in his ears. Some sweet lullaby he remembered his wife singing to the children. The sound seemed to buzz around his head, making him swoon and tremble. It was beautiful. And so sad.

Two shapes detached themselves from the walls and stepped out before him. There was no moonlight to reveal them in detail but Cooke recognized them at once. He sank to his knees and cried out.

Bridget and Mary walked towards him, their perfect, heart-shaped faces smiling delightedly.

'Papa! Oh, Papa!'

Their voices were like a balm to his grief.

'Oh my little pretties!' he cried out, his voice cracking with emotion. He stumbled towards them across the walkway.

'Sir Harry!'

Cooke looked down. Ralph Grey and two other men were gazing up at him in horror.

'Sir Harry, this is the Devil's work!'

Cooke fell to his knees again, gazing appealingly at the little figures before him as if willing them to be real.

'But my daughters...' he said desperately.

'Your daughters are dead, my lord.' Grey kept his calm, though fear was coursing through him.

'Dead?' Cooke looked at his daughters with sad, exhausted eyes.

'Come away, Sir Harry. I beg you. Come away.'

Cooke glanced down at Grey and then at the happy, smiling faces in front of him.

'Come, my dears. Come to your father,' he said hoarsely.

'No!' Grey cried out, bolting for the steps.

The little girls grinned and moved swiftly to their father with outstretched arms, their skirts whispering over the floor.

Cooke opened his arms to embrace them and began to squeal horribly as their little faces fell inwards, smiles turning into glistening maws. He began to thrash at them desperately. Prickles of yellow light shimmered over the apparitions' surfaces as they blurred and shimmered into one, drawing Cooke's screaming body into them. Grey got to within a few yards of the horror and then flung himself back against the walls.

'Get out! Get out!' he screeched at the men below. 'For Christ's sake! Or we're finished!'

Cooke was merging with his daughters now, forming a column of blazing light in which shapes seemed to twist like monstrous embryos.

The men hesitated below. Grey shielded his face from the intense light before him and bellowed at the soldiers.

'We are bewitched! Go! For your souls' sake!'

The terrified men scrambled at the heavy doors and flung them open. Outside, the night was strangely calm. They ran at full pelt away from the castle, lungs and legs searing with pain.

Grey knew that his position was hopeless. His idea of rescuing Sir Harry was impossible; the knight he had served so faithfully had vanished into the ball of fire before him. Grey began to heave himself over the battlements, his tired hands gripping at the ancient stonework for support. Tendrils of energy whipped and crackled about him as the column of energy slid nearer. He paused briefly on the ramparts, the world spinning dizzily about him. He wouldn't survive the fall, he knew, but there were worse things than death. The nebulous thing which had been Sir Harry lapped at the stonework like hellish flotsam. Grey closed his eyes and threw himself into space.

Jackson saw them first, racing across the moor as if the devil were at their heels. He looked up from his recumbent position as terrified cries echoed through the night. In an instant his men were alert and on their feet.

'I knew it!' he cried delightedly. 'I knew they were here-abouts!'

But the smile froze on his lips as he saw the gibbering men tumbling through the undergrowth towards him.

'Take your prisoners, lads!' Jackson ordered, jogging up to Will Todd as the young man collapsed on to the ground. The Roundheads laid hands on the fleeing enemy as they staggered into the circle of trees.

'Sweet mercy, save us!' cried Todd, pawing at Jackson's legs.

'What is it! What ails thee?' Jackson laid a kindly hand on the boy's shoulder.

Todd looked up fearfully. 'We are bewitched!'

Jackson frowned and then turned swiftly to his subordinates, ordering them to treat their prisoners with care and kindness. Then he mounted his horse and set off at a gallop for the castle.

Within minutes, the skeletal towers loomed above him and he slowed to a gentle trot. The doors were wide open and horribly inviting. His horse snorted and pulled back a little. Jackson glanced down and gasped as he saw Ralph Grey's broken body staring up at him, neck lolling to one side.

Jackson dismounted and stepped over Grey's body. The hall before him was silent and dark. He glanced around, trying to pick out shapes from the confusion of black shadows. Up on the battlements, there seemed to be the faintest trace of light, like the dying embers of a fire.

Cautiously, Jackson mounted the stone steps and emerged on to the walkway.

Sir Harry Cooke lay sprawled on his back with a look of abject horror on his face, his limbs smashed and broken. Jackson walked slowly towards the corpse, stretching out a gloved hand to touch the purple face.

He cried out as his fingers pushed straight through Cooke's forehead as though through rotten fruit. He shuddered and felt bile burn his throat as the body crumbled to greasy dust before him.

Outside the gates, the horse began to snort and stamp, unnerved. Jackson looked at the creaking beams and black stonework. They seemed to quiver and distort as though he were drunk, swooping, blurring and bending out of shape.

The air was charged. Jackson shuddered.

A vast tendril of boiling energy began to crackle around the battlements like St Elmo's fire, seeping down the stained walls and licking at the edges of the gateway. Every stone in the castle shone with unearthly radiance.

Jackson lost no time, staggering down the steps and across the empty hall which was bucking like a ship in a storm. He pounded through the gates, dodging to avoid Ralph Grey's body, and threw himself on to his horse, flogging at it madly until he had put half a mile between himself and the castle.

Light began to rip and twist at the stonework. Jackson cast back glance after glance, urging his horse onwards with stabs of his spurs.

His men and the prisoners were gazing at the castle in awe.

Jackson's horse thundered into view and he thrashed his arms about in frustration.

'Down! Get down! Lest you lose your wits!'

Great pulses of energy seemed to flood across the moor from the castle which blazed like an Armada beacon against the night sky. Jackson threw himself clear of his horse and rolled under the trees, tucking his head under his folded arms. The soldiers followed suit and scurried for shelter, crying out in distress as a tumultuous explosion stunned their senses. Then the sky seemed to split apart as though the sun had disintegrated.

The original castle, which had stood empty for many hundreds of years, was eventually destroyed during the Civil Wars, just after the battle of Marston Moor. The cause of the fire was unknown but contemporary reports speak of a conflagration so terrible that not a stone remained come the morning. Certainly there is no trace of Marsham Castle today but the visitor may enjoy a fine view of the ancient battlefield from the hill which remains.

The Doctor closed the second book which the Abbot had given him and frowned deeply.

'Interesting?' said Winstanley, still pottering about the shelves.

'Arresting,' said the Doctor. 'Tell me, what's become of this . . . hill that the castle stood upon?'

Winstanley ran his hand along a line of gilt-embossed books. 'Oh, it was just a local beauty spot for years . . .'

'Is that all?'

Winstanley looked up from the brown pages of a spineless

tome and thrummed his fingers against his side.

'Well, until they built the radio telescope on it.'

5

Thomas Edward Hawthorne liked order. Trains that ran on time, freshly rolled cricket pitches, neatly pressed suits and folded handkerchiefs. He had lived his whole fifty-five years according to an ordered pattern: passing from a straightforward childhood to a straightforward school and a straightforward double First in Mathematics and Physics.

Above all, he loved the order of numbers, that indefinable, near-poetic quality which abstract higher maths could achieve. Sometimes he would sit alone in his sparsely furnished flat and simply let his mind wander, drift and twist along the mental pathways he had created out of beautiful numbers. Those who knew only the cynical misanthrope would never believe the smile of sheer pleasure which inevitably crept across his face.

He had risen quickly in his chosen field, joining Frederick Storey and his team of radio astronomers, first in Cambridge and later in the famous New South Wales experiments of the late fifties. Those embryonic days had been exciting and fulfilling, Hawthorne and Storey making a strong team. After his mentor's retirement, Hawthorne had been confident of promotion, believing himself to be Storey's natural successor. To his chagrin, the power vacuum had been filled, not only by a stranger, but by a woman. His working relationship with Dr Christine Cooper was always tense but he found himself thriving on the frisson between them. Before long, the ebullient scientist commanded his respect and loyalty.

Now they were together again, in what Hawthorne was sure must be the bleakest corner of England. Nevertheless, it was *England*.

He had hated Australia. Hated the flies, the heat and the irritating good humour of the locals, forever slapping him on the back or pressing gnat's-piss beer into his hand.

He had returned to London with great relief, relishing the drizzle, the smell of damp earth and the sound of cabs slicing through rain-puddled streets. It had been good for a while.

But London had changed. As the weeks went by, Hawthorne found himself experiencing something like culture shock. Men who looked like girls paraded up and down the streets, wearing embroidered Indian frocks and their hair down to their shoulders. Young people were in open rebellion against authority, organizing 'sit-ins' at the LSE or even dropping out of society altogether to live in miserable hippy communes. Next best thing to anarchy in his opinion.

One aspect of British life, however, needled him like no other, just as its threatened arrival had back in the thirties. *There were blacks everywhere.*

Manning the building sites, crowding the labour exchanges and positively overrunning London Transport. It was unbelievable.

He thought of the friends who had died in the War, died to preserve a country and a way of life which they revered. Now it was polluted by the dregs of Empire. By God, it was a sad time to be an Englishman.

As a young man, he had walked a hundred miles to hear Oswald Mosley speaking. He could taste the atmosphere even now: thousands of like-minded men, splendid in their black shirts, listening to that incredible orator denouncing the coons and the yids and all the other scum that were sapping Britain's strength.

But Hawthorne was no longer a young man. He had watched his dream of a racially pure country vanish in a wash of feeble liberalism.

Somewhere, deep in the shadows of his complex mind, Hawthorne kept his own private bogey-man. An image from his childhood half-wrapped in fear and half in nostalgia, bringing with it memories of his mother as she sat by the bed reading stories. Even as a child, Hawthorne had possessed a rational mind, his imagination balking at the obvious conceits of the fairy story. How could a carpet fly? How could a genie fit inside a bottle?

Only one story fascinated him and he would urge his mother

to read it over and over again. It was a little Uncle Remus tale concerning Brer Fox's plan to ensnare Brer Rabbit in a thorny bush by means of a sticky facsimile child called the Tar Baby.

Hawthorne had never been afraid of the nasty fox, never really cared whether Brer Rabbit would escape or not. It was the image of that sightless, dripping black baby in its cage of prickles which haunted him. He would check under his bed every night, fearful that a tacky black paw would clutch at his ankle.

Without really knowing why, he still connected his fear of outsiders with that terrifying childhood memory. Like the Tar Baby, they were dirty, unnatural, somehow less than human. And Hawthorne was still checking under his bed.

The phone call from Cooper inviting him to join her in Yorkshire had been all the excuse he needed. Leaving London was like recovering from a long illness and the further north he travelled, the more certain and traditional things seemed to become. But then he had arrived in Bradford, realizing with sick certainty that he had swapped one wave of immigrants for another. There to meet him at the station was his new colleague: young, handsome, intelligent and brown as a berry.

Hawthorne found himself flinching whenever Vijay came near him, the boy's cultured, almost too English accent annoying him intensely. It seemed unnatural and forced, like a chimp at the zoo dressed in human clothes — an analogy which pleased Hawthorne immensely.

He was glad to work with Cooper again. She brought back some of the certainties of before, her no-nonsense attitude a sturdy rock upon which to anchor his future. The Kidd girl was all right too, if a bit cocksure and modern in her thinking. She was a friend of Jocelyn Bell, the postgraduate down at the Mullard observatory who had discovered the first pulsar earlier in the year.

But now there was this flood of bizarre, unfathomable data, none of which made any sense. And the telephones were out of order. The only certainty seemed to be that the double star Bellatrix, in Orion, had just gone nova. The signals were just discernible amongst the nonsense which had overwhelmed their systems the previous night.

Thomas Edward Hawthorne liked order. At twenty-six

minutes to eight on 23 December, a chunk of disorder called
Ace came into his life.

'What the hell...?'

Cooper scurried towards Ace and managed to prevent the
girl's head from hitting the console. Ace flopped weakly into
Cooper's arms, sucking her cut lip and mumbling insensibly.

'Trespassers,' sighed Hawthorne. 'That's all we need. What's
happened to the bloody security guard? It's outrageous.'

'Gone AWOL,' said Cooper, prising open one of Ace's
eyelids.

'It's outrageous.'

'All right. You've made your point. Help me get her into the
chair. She's in a state.'

Gingerly, Hawthorne took Ace's arm and dragged her over
to a padded chair, noting her curious clothes with some distaste.

'Locals wandering all over the moor. You'd've thought they'd
be used to the telescope by now.' He pushed his glasses back
up the bridge of his nose and ran a hand through brilliantined
hair.

Cooper wiped the blood from Ace's mouth with a handkerchief.

'Look at her clothes. They're a conservative lot in these parts.'

'She looks like a dustman in that jacket. The things they wear
these days.'

Hawthorne turned his attention to the data chattering before
him. The green display flared light across his gaunt features.

'Bellatrix again. Hell of a nova. I just wish we could sort
out the real signals from all this... dross.'

Cooper frowned thoughtfully, sat back on a bench and looked
at Ace's sleeping form.

'Well, young lady. What are we going to do with you?'

The night had become dry and frostily clear. The Doctor,
strolling into Crook Marsham with his umbrella hoisted over
his shoulder, looked up at the bone-white moon on its bed of
brilliant stars. He breathed in deeply and enjoyed the cold air
which flooded his lungs.

Leaving the moor path, the Doctor rounded the corner of the
Post Office and walked up the main street, his shoes crunching

smartly on the frost-crazed pavement.

There was a soft chime from his coat pocket and he noted with some satisfaction that he was almost exactly on time. The Abbot's books, intriguing though they were, hadn't delayed him unduly. Strange coincidence, that. The telescope being built on the site of the old castle. A castle reputed to be haunted and destroyed by a mysterious fire.

The Doctor smiled. Every old building had its echoes, every battlefield its mournful piper or whey-faced soldier. Ten a penny.

No, it was time to face the future. Act on his impulses and do something positive about his resolution to... How had Ace put it? Retire. Yes. There was something comforting about that word.

I have done enough.

It was good to be here in a tiny, dull corner of his favourite planet with nothing to distract or entice him. He glanced back across the moor and saw the telescope dish, illuminated by its arc lamps, shining brilliantly in the dark night.

I have done enough...

Warm colours and a babble of excited voices washed over the Doctor as he pushed open the door of The Shepherd's Cross.

The room was packed. Alcohol-flushed faces bobbed amongst a mist of cigarette smoke. Trevithick and Lowcock were pressed into a corner, speaking in urgent whispers.

'She needs a doctor,' Trevithick urged. 'We have to get the phones working.'

The Doctor pushed his way through the crowd to the bar and ordered a glass of ginger beer. Ace was nowhere to be seen. He clicked his tongue in annoyance. Trust that girl to get herself lost. No, not a girl any more, he reminded himself. A woman now, even if a little pig-headed and immature.

'Miss Mason has sedated her,' said Lowcock. 'She'll be all right till we can get proper help.'

The Doctor glanced across the room and caught the eye of Mrs Crithin, now looking quite glamorous in a tight-fitting minidress. She gave him a kindly smile and called 'Evening, Doctor.'

Trevithick and Lowcock turned simultaneously and looked

the little stranger up and down.

'A doctor, are you? Smashing. Would you mind...?'

'Ah well. I'm rather busy...'

'It's just that we're having trouble with our phones and our own doctor can't be found.' Lowcock looked appealingly at the Doctor. The Doctor opened his mouth to protest and then sighed. He could give a little of his time to helping these people. It wasn't really getting involved at all...

'Very well.'

'Wonderful. This way please.'

The big policeman took the Doctor's arm and led him up the stairs, Trevithick trailing behind.

'It's just up here, Doctor er...?'

'The patient?' said the Doctor quickly.

'It's Mrs Yeadon,' called Trevithick from behind. 'The landlord's wife. Seems to be in a state of shock.'

Inside the bedroom, the Doctor was introduced to Jill and Lawrence and reacquainted with Robin, who apologized again for running him down that morning.

The Doctor removed both his coats and rolled up his shirt sleeves.

Betty Yeadon was semiconscious, her eyelids twitching as if desperate to spring open. Robin sat by the bed, holding his stepmother's hand.   ·

'What happened?' asked the Doctor.

'She's been having nightmares.' Lawrence's voice was thick with fatigue and emotion. 'This afternoon I heard her screaming and found her in the bathroom. She didn't say anything for ages, but...' He hesitated, looking from his wife to his son and down to the floor.

'But?'

'She's been dreaming about her brother, Alfred. He was killed during the War. She... feels guilty about his death.'

Robin looked up. 'Why, though? She's never explained it. Uncle Alf knew what he was doing. It wasn't Mum's fault he got killed.'

Lawrence thrust his hands into his pockets and sank his head on to his chest. 'She thought it was her fault, Robin. Your Uncle Alf was a conscientious objector. He refused to fight. At least, at first...'

'So?' Robin's question hung in the air.

'Betty was just a teenager then. I don't suppose she really understood the issues. Anyway, her friends began to taunt her about her brother and she started to get at him. The whole white feather bit. Eventually he caved in. Joined up. Three months later, he was dead.'

'How did it happen?' Jill's face was a mask of sympathetic concern.

'His ship was torpedoed in the Pacific. Half the crew survived the sinking but the sharks got most of them, Alf included.'

'God.'

Lawrence sat on the edge of the bed and took Betty's feverish hand in his. 'She reckons he'd be alive today if she hadn't interfered.'

The Doctor had taken Betty's pulse and temperature.

'What did you give her?' he asked Jill.

'Just some of her own sleeping pills.'

The Doctor nodded, producing a tiny green bottle from his trouser pocket. There was a soft plop as he unstoppered the bottle and waved it under Betty's nose. For a moment, everyone was aware of a sweet, heavy odour, and then Betty seemed to sink into a deep sleep, her agitated limbs settling on to the blankets.

'She'll sleep properly now,' said the Doctor, straightening up. 'The nightmares have become much worse, then?'

'Progressively,' said Lawrence. 'But today... today was something different. I couldn't make it out at first. But she says she's *seen* Alf. His ghost.'

'Ghost?' The Doctor's eyes flicked up.

Lawrence nodded and shrugged his shoulders. 'I want her to have professional help. I'm going over to York tonight. I can't get anyone on the phone. Would you come with me, Doctor?'

The Doctor looked about evasively. 'Unfortunately, I have a prior engagement. Perhaps your friend here...?'

Lowcock nodded. 'I'll come with you, Lol. I'm sure they can manage at the station for a few hours.'

Lawrence thanked him and then showed out Jill, whose mind

was already full of her old charges and their Christmas destinations. 'Thanks for your help, Doctor . . . ?'

'Don't mention it.' The Doctor smiled.

'Any word on Jack Prudhoe?' asked Lawrence.

Lowcock shook his head. 'No. Nor Dr Shearsmith.'

Lawrence sighed. 'Robin, can you stay with your mum while we're away?'

Nodding, Robin resumed his place by the bedside. Lawrence and Lowcock left the room, discussing the relative merits of the infirmary and the general hospital.

'Fancy a pint?' said Trevithick as he and the Doctor descended the stairs.

'Perhaps another time.'

'Not seen you around here before, have I?'

'No. My friend and I are just travelling in these parts.'

Back in the bedroom, Robin's ears pricked up as the Doctor's words floated up the stairs. His friend? That girl he'd been with earlier. The one with the long hair and the lovely eyes. Robin smiled slightly to himself and looked down at Betty's peaceful form.

Trevithick had persuaded the Doctor to stay and returned from the bar with a ginger beer and a frothy Guinness.

'I say, Doctor, I wonder if I might ask your advice. I need an objective opinion on all this.' Trevithick raised his glass. 'Cheers.'

'Cheers. All what?' The Doctor sipped his ginger beer and sat down.

'There are some funny things going on in this village, Doctor. I can't quite put my finger on it but I have this feeling . . . Good Lord, how rude of me. I haven't even introduced myself. I'm Trevithick.'

'The engineer?' said the Doctor brightly. 'Oh, my dear fellow, I've always wanted to meet you . . . No. Wait. Wrong century, isn't it? Different chap.'

'Edmund Trevithick,' said the old man, rather crestfallen. 'The actor. I used to be Professor Nightshade. D'you remember?'

The Doctor gave another of his evasive smiles. 'I get about a bit.'

'Well, never mind. The thing is, last night, at the old folk's home where I'm billeted, someone broke in. Someone or something.'

'What are you getting at?'

Trevithick gazed down at his pint. 'I saw a figure. In the lamplight outside. Just for a moment. But it was familiar. And then, when I found my window smashed, there was a terrible smell. And the voice...'

'Voice?'

'It said my name. But not Trevithick. It called me by the name of my old character. It called me Nightshade.'

'What did you do?'

The old man harrumphed a little. 'I'm ashamed to say I passed out.'

The Doctor looked up as the door opened and a small, red-haired man came in. Still no Ace. 'And you think this has something to do with Mrs Yeadon?'

'I don't know, Doctor. But now the phones are all out of order and two people have gone missing. Lawrence told me that Jack Prudhoe came in here yesterday afternoon. He saw something out of the window and just ran outside. No one's seen him since.'

The Doctor looked away. 'I'm sure there's a perfectly rational explanation,' he said unconvincingly.

Trevithick looked disappointed that his new confidant wasn't more enthusiastic.

'Excuse me a moment,' said the Doctor, standing and crossing to where Mrs Crithin was sitting, her mouth open in mid-anecdote.

'Hello, love,' she said as the Doctor raised his hat.

Unseen by both, Robin crept to the bottom of the stairs.

'I was wondering whether you'd seen anything of my young friend?' said the Doctor.

Mrs Crithin pulled a face. 'Not since this morning, love. She stayed a good while after you left and we had a chat. She did seem interested in the telescope, though, if that's any help?'

'Ah,' said the Doctor. 'No doubt she's got ahead of herself

again. Thank you very much.'

Mrs Crithin smiled and turned back to her audience, already geared up for another saucy Christmas tale.

The Doctor threaded his way through the crowded room to Trevithick. The old man drained his pint and looked at the Doctor expectantly.

'Any luck?'

'It seems my friend may have gone up to the radio telescope. I'd better go and see.'

Trevithick nodded and shook hands with the Doctor effusively. 'Thanks again for your help with Mrs Yeadon. Hope to see you again soon.'

'Yes indeed.' The Doctor was already turning for the door.

From his crouched position on the stairs, Robin watched first the Doctor and then, after a protracted struggle into his coat, Trevithick, disappear into the night.

Robin glanced up the stairs at his stepmother's bedroom door. She was sleeping peacefully now. She'd be all right. If he could just have a word with the Doctor. Find out where he and the girl were staying and get a chance to talk to her. Interesting women didn't often come to Crook Marsham.

With one last, guilty look up the stairs, he pulled on his coat and pushed his way outside into the freezing night.

'*Ace?* What kind of a name is that?' said Hawthorne witheringly.

'Does it matter?'

Ace was alert now, her eyes flashing in agitation. Cooper and Hawthorne stood before her with arms crossed like angry parents.

'What does matter, young lady, is what you're doing in this compound. Suppose you tell us that?' Cooper's face was set in a stern frown.

'Look, I told you. I was in the village with my friend...'

'This... ''Doctor''?'

'The Doctor, yes. He went off to the monastery and I got bored. I sneaked in here for a look around. That's all.'

'That's all?' Hawthorne's narrow eyes dwindled into furious slits. 'This is a government installation, young lady. We can't just let all and sundry traipse through!'

'Look...' said Ace.

'What I can't understand is what's happened to our supposedly brilliant security system...'

'Look!' cried Ace angrily. 'That's what I've been trying to tell you! I found a body outside.'

'A *body*?' said Cooper incredulously.

'Yes! Outside the fence. It was in uniform. Could've been a security guard.'

'What did it look like then?' Hawthorne cocked his head to one side.

'I don't know. He was all rotten. Decomposed.'

'We're wasting our time.'

'Now look,' said Cooper sternly. 'If you think you can get out of trouble by making up cock-and-bull stories...'

'I saw it!' yelled Ace.

'Well, let's go and have a look, shall we?' Hawthorne pushed his glasses up the bridge of his nose.

'We can't,' sighed Ace hopelessly. 'It melted away.'

'Came and went like a summer cloud, did it?'

'All right, Tom, Leave it. Something's obviously happened.' Cooper turned and looked Ace in the eye. 'If the phones were working I'd call the police. As it is, just think yourself lucky...'

There was a deafening screech as the entire room flooded with power. The strip lights flickered, died, and were replaced by orange emergency lamps. Data screed across the consoles, forcing gauges and needles into irrational regions of the scale.

'Here we go again!' cried Cooper, hands flapping at her sides. 'Quick, you — Ace — make yourself useful. Go to the living quarters.'

'I don't —'

'Left, left, then right,' called Hawthorne, throwing himself into a swivel chair as paper poured from the printout to the floor.

'Get Vijay,' said Cooper, 'and Holly if she's awake. Their rooms are marked. No time to explain!'

'But...'

'Go!'

Ace scrambled to her feet and dashed off into the interior of the building.

Emergency lights flashed around every blank wall, heightening the hectic atmosphere. She raced past lockers and storerooms, even a TV lounge, before she spotted a door marked 'H. Kidd'.

Ace paused, panting for breath, knocked and threw open the door. Empty. She cursed.

The next door bore the legend 'Vijay Degun' and a sign cannibalized from a cardboard 'Fragile − With Care' notice which now read 'agile − Wit...'

Ace didn't knock this time.

Inside the room, Holly and Vijay lay curled naked against one another, a mess of blankets pulled haphazardly around them.

Ace cleared her throat in embarrassment and Vijay sat up sharply, his thick black fringe obscuring his eyes.

'I'm sorry,' she said quietly. 'They want you in the control room. There's some sort of emergency.'

Vijay looked momentarily nonplussed and ran his hand through his hair as if to wake himself up. 'Right,' he said at last.

'Her too.' Ace indicated Holly with a nod of her head.

Vijay jumped out of bed, clutching a blanket around his waist and scanning the room for his discarded clothes. 'That's OK. She needs the rest. I don't want to wake her. You can go now − er?'

'Ace.'

'Right.' Vijay smiled. 'Thanks.'

Ace let her eyes linger briefly on his finely muscled chest and then, mentally admonishing herself for her wandering thoughts, exited.

She ran all the way back to the control room where Cooper ushered her into a chair. Both she and Hawthorne were totally engrossed in the eruption of data which crackled like a bonfire around the huge room.

Sleep was a beautiful release and Betty Yeadon, for once free of her nightmares, wallowed in it. Muted colours flashed across her closed lids as her breathing settled into a soft, regular pattern.

The room around her was empty, Robin's vacated chair pushed back against the wall. The frosty night outside whispered around the drawn curtains.

Betty turned over in her sleep as a bubble of memory floated to the surface of her unconscious.

There was a dull thud somewhere below.

Plash

The curtains stirred slightly and there was another smaller sound, as if bare winter branches were scraping at the window.

Plash

She opened one eye, feeling the weight of drowsiness gushing through her brain like thick soup.

Thud

She opened both her eyes and felt suddenly alert. The bedside clock ticked loudly.

Plash

Plash

Betty pulled herself back to the headboard and dragged the blankets around her. The rustling sound came again and she glanced feverishly around the room.

Thud

Thud

She gazed at the closed bedroom door. There were four panels in it. A white, glossy door.

Silence hissed about her.

Thud

Plash

Thud

There was something coming up the stairs. Dragging its feet.

Thud

The other sound reminded her of rain-soaked shoes.

Plash

She knew who it was. What it was. The dream that wasn't a dream. The wet footprints in the carpet. The terrible skeletal grip on her cheek.

Plash

Thud

Thud

The rustling came again. Betty jammed her fist into her mouth, eyes bulging in naked terror. Where was Lawrence? Where was Robin? Where *were* they?

The footsteps stopped. The door seemed to loom before her,

heavy with the presence behind it.

Betty looked at the bottom of the door. A four-panelled, glossy white door, under which a pool of black sea-water was slowly forming.

She tried to speak, call, scream, but her throat tightened into a rasping croak. All that came out, in a whisper so low she scarcely heard it herself, was a name.

'Alf?'

From behind the door came a soft, low chuckle.

'Doctor! Doctor, wait!'

Robin called after the little figure who'd made amazingly rapid progress across the coal-black moor. The moon bled pale light on to the Doctor's face as he turned and looked back. Robin ran to catch up with him, feet sinking into the mud.

'Hello again,' said the Doctor as the boy reached him, out of breath. 'Shouldn't you be with your mother?'

'It's OK. She's sleeping,' said Robin. 'I — I just wanted to...well, your friend, the girl...'

'Ace?'

'Is that her name? Ace.' He turned the name over on his tongue like an unfamiliar delicacy.

'Her real name's Dorothy but she wouldn't thank me for telling you.'

'Well, I just wondered whether...'

'Yes?'

The Doctor raised an eyebrow, enjoying the young man's discomfort.

Robin was saved by a terrible, whooping scream which echoed across the moor like the howl of a wolf. Both he and the Doctor jumped in alarm. There was movement about a hundred yards ahead and they turned to make it out. A small, silhouetted figure was stumbling about, making incomprehensible gurgling sounds in its throat.

'Come on!' cried the Doctor, grabbing Robin's arm.

The figure was stationary now, swaying a little in the moonlight and sobbing uncontrollably. The Doctor pulled out a torch from his capacious pockets and swept the beam on to a blanched, panicky face, the stern mouth flecked with spit, the eyes two

93

perfect circles of fear like bullet holes in ice.

'It's Mrs Prudhoe!' hissed Robin.

'The missing man's wife?'

Robin nodded vigorously. The Doctor placed a reassuring hand on the old woman's wrinkled brow. 'All right. It's all right now, Mrs Prudhoe. Mrs Prudhoe? What's wrong? What happened?'

She stared at the Doctor but seemed to look right through him, struggling against the firm grip of his hands, her mouth working away in silent protest.

Sensing his ministrations were futile, the Doctor let Mrs Prudhoe go and she shambled off into the darkness, weeping.

'Doctor! Over here!'

Robin was some way off now. He had found the little enclave in the rocks surrounded by stubby trees. The Doctor picked out the area with his torch and the beam bounced over black moor and grey stone as he advanced. He could feel Robin's breath by him as he turned the beam into the hole.

'Jesus,' cried Robin, taking a step backwards as the torch revealed the appalling sight within.

Jack Prudhoe lay in a heap, legs and arms snapped, paunchy skin streaked with purple scratches. His face was pressed flat so that his mouth and nose were just two gory holes, as though he'd been flung against plate glass.

The Doctor moved towards the body and gingerly touched Prudhoe's arm. There was a horrible crack as tissues split apart and clouds of opaque vapour flooded the little niche. The Doctor gagged as the smell engulfed him. Robin turned and ran outside, hurling himself down on the heather.

Pushing a handkerchief into his mouth, the Doctor forced himself to watch and shuddered involuntarily as the body rippled and fell inwards, trickling away into the ground.

The Doctor remained a few minutes more and then stepped outside, drinking in the frosty air with relief. He patted Robin on the shoulder as the boy knelt there, doubled up.

'What . . . what happened to him?'

The Doctor shook his head and looked up at the sky above them. He sighed heavily. Would there never be an end to it?

* * *

Trevithick turned up the collar of his coat as a chilly wind from the moor shivered through the village. It was bloody cold. He rubbed his gloved hands together and grumbled a little under his breath.

Christmas Eve tomorrow! In all the excitement, he'd almost forgotten. But now he could sense that lovely, indefinable crispness in the air. Was it snow? Would they have snow for Christmas? He looked forward to that beautiful, serene quiet which heavy snow always brought to the world and the satisfying crump his steel-toed winter boots would make in virgin drifts. Nothing quite like it.

If memory served, they'd finished the last *Nightshade* around Christmas. December 1958, wasn't it? Only ten years, yet it seemed like a lifetime. He could remember the producer's party afterwards: the usual mix of sentiment and jollity, too much booze and too many false promises to keep in touch. He'd walked home that night knowing it was the end of an era. Things were never quite the same again.

But at least his public remembered him! Perhaps they were planning a reunion. Or a new series? Or (he pulled up sharp at the thought) *This Is Your Life*!

By God, they'd have to do some detective work to find all the old buggers he'd worked with.

William Jarrold had nipped off to America to take Hollywood by storm. Went down like a lead balloon, according to the papers.

Poor Jimmy Reynolds was dead, of course. Tragic really. But only the good die young. That's why I've lasted so long, the old man laughed to himself.

There was a scuttling sound nearby and Trevithick stopped, his ears pricked.

'Hello?'

There was another sound, so like wind-rattled branches that he turned to the high hedge which grew by the pavement.

'Who's there?'

His heart pumped a little faster. George Lowcock had said it might be kids who'd smashed the window. There were all sorts of lunatics about these days and if they could tear up Grosvenor Square, why should they hesitate at attacking an old codger like him?

'I know you're there,' he said firmly. The scuttling sound came again, like claws on glass.

Trevithick caught a smell on the breeze, recognized it and felt his stomach heave. He turned and ran. About fifty yards from the Dalesview Home, something stepped out into the road.

It couldn't be. It couldn't be.

It was under the yellow streetlamp just as it had been the night before.

'No!' Trevithick gasped, his lopsided mouth falling open.

The creature was almost seven feet tall, a shiny, black-carapaced body like a cockroach mounted on grasshopper legs. Its massive bristly head rolled back and forth inquisitively as its mandibles juddered and clicked before it.

Trevithick gawped, feeling his heart knock against his ribs like a racing engine.

It was impossible.

He pressed himself back against the hedge and yelled as the creature lunged at him.

It pulled back, the muscles of its neck bulging through its skin. Trevithick threw himself to the ground and rolled over, repeating the fall he'd learned for *The Sword of Araby*.

Surprised at his own agility, Trevithick struggled to his feet and pelted back the way he'd come. He could taste rust in his mouth and a crippling stitch beginning to develop in his groin as he clattered and slid across the icy pavement.

The creature scurried behind him, its great muscular legs rippling with effort.

It wasn't true. Couldn't be.

Trevithick saw the pub, lights ablaze in the taproom. There were still people in there. Had to be. Had to be.

He was a few feet from the door when a brittle mandible wrenched him backwards, slicing through his jacket and waistcoat. He fell heavily and lay there, winded, as the creature reared over him, its head thrashing about as if in triumph and sticky fluid pumping from its maw on to his face.

Trevithick screamed.

The creature flared with light as Lawrence Yeadon's car swung crazily around the corner. Trevithick took his chance and rolled again. The car seemed to be almost out of control and screeched across the pavement, lurching to a stop inches from the pub door.

Trevithick looked up. The creature was gone. He got shakily to his feet and stumbled over to the car. The doors opened simultaneously, Lawrence and Lowcock almost falling out of their seats on to the frozen ground.

There were people emerging from the pub. The two men gripped the car for support and took great gulps of air. Trevithick wandered up to them, feeling his exposed chest where the mandible had seared the skin.

'Did you see it? Did you?' he begged.

Lowcock turned his pale face to the old man. He looked confused and frightened.

'We couldn't get out of the village. Couldn't get out...'

The Doctor approached the perimeter fence with Robin scurrying behind him.

'What happened to him, Doctor? What's going on?'

The Doctor waved his hand airily. 'I don't know, I don't know. We must find Ace. Make sure she's all right.'

Robin eyed the squat grey box which controlled the security system. The red light winked in the darkness.

'You need a special key to get in there,' said Robin.

The Doctor looked at him impatiently, prised off the front of the box, rethreaded two blue wires, pulled out a third and jammed the end of his torch into the box which exploded in a flurry of sparks. The fence slid slowly open. The Doctor smiled, lifted his hat and ushered Robin through. 'After you.'

Robin looked up at the dish dominating the sky above them. He felt an unpleasant sensation of falling backwards, the kind of insecurity he suffered crossing suspension bridges or gazing up at skyscrapers.

The Doctor pushed open the double doors and they found themselves in a featureless corridor, its cold walls stained orange by the emergency lights. Through the glass of the inner door they could see the frantic activity within the control room. A deafening chatter of machinery and computer printouts seeped from under the door. The Doctor paused on the threshold.

'Now, Robin. Circumstances like these demand tact and patience. Understand?'

Robin nodded dumbly, then the Doctor barged through the door, doffed his hat and said, 'Good evening, I'm the Doctor. Hello, Ace. Having trouble?'

Robin didn't think much of the Doctor's ideas on diplomacy.

Cooper and Hawthorne barely looked up from their work. Vijay looked at the Doctor in blank astonishment.

'Come in! Come in!' called Hawthorne. 'The more the merrier!'

'Your friend, I presume?' Cooper looked up from stabbing a row of buttons. Ace ran to the Doctor and gave him a hug of welcome.

'Are you all right, Ace?' he said, furrowing his brow. She nodded and smiled. Robin hung awkwardly to one side and then offered his hand in greeting.

'Hello again.'

'Hi.'

They grinned at each other and looked at the floor simultaneously.

Ace was reminded a little of Mike, the young man who had wooed her and, ultimately, betrayed her in their battle against the Daleks. Robin had the same cheeky smile, the same sort of piercing eyes, although green rather than blue. There was also the suggestion of something dark about Robin, some indication of deep currents under the still surface. Ace looked forward to exploring.

The Doctor was already at one of the consoles and ripped off a printout as it pooled at his feet.

'White dwarf. Double. Hmm...you've got an exploding star on your hands.'

'Now look here...' began Hawthorne.

'Oh shut up, Tom,' barked Cooper. 'We need all the help we can get just now. We know about the star, Doctor...'

'It's a big one, isn't it?'

Cooper nodded. 'It's the only bit of solid information we have. It's the rest of this stuff that doesn't make sense.'

The Doctor joined her by a row of display screens and gazed down at the fluctuating figures.

'Massive energy levels of some kind.'

'It's flooding the systems. We can't cope with it. We can't trace it.'

Vijay joined them. 'But it has to be coming from the same sector as the nova. We've had the telescope trained on the same area since all this began.'

The Doctor drummed his fingers on the console. 'And where's your nova located?'

Vijay didn't have to consult his figures. 'It's the Bellatrix double in Orion. 24τ. We've been monitoring the whole constellation for four weeks now.'

'But the other signals are completely different,' continued Cooper. 'Just a stream of nonsense. It can't be coming from Bellatrix.'

'Possibly not, possibly not,' mused the Doctor. He looked about the room, eyes flashing. Ace knew this expression.

'He's thinking,' she said to Robin.

The boy nodded. 'I'm Robin, by the way.'

'Ace.' She looked at him inquisitively. 'So... how did you meet up with the Doctor again?'

'I think you were supposed to meet him in the pub...?'

'I got held up.'

'Anyway,' Robin continued, 'my stepmum's been taken ill and the Doctor lent a hand.'

'I didn't know he was that kind of Doctor,' said Ace, grinning.

Hawthorne was still looking daggers at the Doctor, obviously displeased at the way the little stranger had insinuated himself into the proceedings.

The clock which Holly had so patiently watched the previous night ticked loudly to a quarter past ten. Once again, with startling speed, the instruments whined to a halt; gauges and monitors shuddered back to their normal, quiet watchfulness.

Ace was reminded of the atmosphere in a launderette when all the machines finish their washing cycle.

The strip lights faltered and then sprang back to life, allowing the orange emergency lamps to shut down. Everyone looked around as the unaccustomed silence returned.

'Same as before,' said Cooper. 'How long did it last?'

Hawthorne glanced at the monitor and pushed back a strand

of greasy hair. 'Just under three quarters of an hour.'

'Longer than last night,' said Vijay.

The Doctor tossed his duffel coat on to Hawthorne's chair and plunged his hands into the reams of paper which had tumbled to the floor.

Cooper sighed heavily, thrust her hands into the pockets of her lab coat and cleared her throat.

'I'm Christine Cooper. This is Tom Hawthorne. Vijay Degun. Your friend here tells me you're a scientist?'

The Doctor didn't look up from his scrutiny of the papers.

'Doctor!' urged Ace.

'Hmm? Oh yes. Scientist, explorer, philanthropist, general do-gooder. That's me.'

'Well, as I said, we'd be grateful for any help.'

The Doctor gave her an intense look, took off his hat and sat down in a swivel chair. 'Help? Yes. . . I'll help. I always do.'

'Doctor. There's something going on. . .' began Ace.

'Yes. I know.'

'What d'you mean?' said Hawthorne, plucking the Doctor's coat from his chair with distaste.

The Doctor crossed his legs on the console. 'Telephones that don't work. Energy from space. People seeing ghosts. That sort of thing. Now young Robin and myself have come across a body on the moor.'

'A security guard?' asked Cooper.

'What?'

'This young lady claims to have found the body of a security guard. We seem to have lost one.'

'That's very careless of you.'

Robin looked up. 'No, it was Jack Prudhoe. An old bloke from the village. His wife found him out there. When the Doctor touched him he just sort of. . . melted away.'

'There, you see. Just like I told you!' cried Ace triumphantly.

'Massive tissue collapse,' said the Doctor gravely. 'I've never seen anything quite like it and I've seen a few things in my time.'

'And the smell. . .' Robin sat down heavily.

'Yes. That too.' The Doctor sat up and placed his hands on the console before him. 'Whatever happened to Mr Prudhoe triggered some sort of instantaneous corruption. Like exposing

100

a sealed coffin to the air.'

'Does anyone else know about this?' said Cooper, frowning.

The Doctor shook his head. 'No. But your friendly local bobby and Robin's father have gone off to get help for Mrs Yeadon. If they can sort out the communications problem too we might start to get somewhere.'

Hawthorne grimaced and started to clean his glasses with the hem of his cardigan. 'Well, I for one reckon we should think pragmatically and try to make some sense of this data. Bodies or no bodies. There's nothing much else we can do.'

Vijay shrugged. 'I agree with Dr Hawthorne.'

It was probably the first time he ever had.

Holly felt as if she'd been drugged. Sleep hung heavily about her, plucking her back into blissful unconsciousness whenever she stirred. Until her head hit the downy pillow, she hadn't realized how totally exhausted she was. There'd been a full day on duty followed by her sympathetic relief of Vijay. Then the crisis had kept her up until almost seven in the morning. Sliding between freshly laundered sheets, she had fallen almost instantly asleep.

At some time during the day, she'd been aware of Vijay getting into bed beside her and had snuggled up to the warm pressure of his body. Now he seemed to have gone again but Holly couldn't be sure. She was dreaming or remembering or both.

Uncle Louis was there, his face stern, his arms folded. Holly was grinning sheepishly, James by her side. They were both seventeen.

There had been some sort of fuss about them going off together, James's mum ringing up Louis to enquire where the 'young lovers' had got to. James, she explained, had his exams to worry about and couldn't waste his time dallying with girls.

In truth, they had been down by the brook, enjoying the forbidden thrill of first kisses. The air was summer sweet. Holly had let James's fingers trace the outline of her eyes, lips and slim neck. They were young, in love, and, that night, in trouble.

Louis had shouted at her, worried about local gossip and how a young girl could get herself a reputation. It might be 1957 but there were still standards to maintain. Adolescent anger boiled within her, pouting her lips, quickening her breathing.

But, against all the odds, it had worked out. Holly and James went on seeing each other all through the summer. The months lengthened to years. University and separation seemed only to deepen their affection. She felt incomplete without him.

Holidays became times of unadulterated joy, brimming over with silly talk, passion and the indefinable pleasure of sharing. Sometimes she felt her love for him like a hot physical weight, pressing through her ribs, and she would smile without quite knowing why.

By the spring of 1962 they were contemplating marriage. Holly had graduated with honours from Cambridge and was considering a research post at a physics lab in Scotland.

James, ever the optimist, was using his English degree to bludgeon his way into a position as junior reporter on a Northumbrian paper. They were scouting for a house on the Scottish border and it looked as if they would see each other most weekends and alternate Wednesdays for the first few months.

Holly had just arrived in Scotland when she got the call from Louis. She was so pleased to hear his voice that she babbled on for a full minute before registering the heavy silence at his end. Then it came. A simple, leaden sentence.

'Listen, love. I've got some bad news. I'm sorry. I don't know how to say this. It's James. There's been an accident...'

She knew at once that he was dead and felt numbness rising through her. There were no tears, not then, just a hot, dry emptiness. The phone had hung limply in her hand for hours as the room darkened around her.

Well, that was over now. Six years gone. She had managed to continue at the lab. Pushed herself into her work. Done well. Very brave. Everyone had said so.

In the last year or so, she had finally started to relax again, making new friends and generally enjoying the loosening up of society which the decade was bringing. Now there was the tracking station. And Vijay...

She did love him, she knew that. But it was a different sort of love than the sort she'd felt for James. Perhaps a little more spiky. A little less sure. But different...

Something tugged at her foot.

Holly blended it into her dream and imagined herself tripping over a paving stone. She jumped and was awake.

The room was overwhelmingly dark. No light peeked under the door from the corridor beyond and the heavy curtains were tightly drawn. She glanced at the luminous hands of her alarm clock. A quarter to eleven.

There was some pressure on her feet. She stirred her legs under the blankets, thinking, for a moment, that a cat must be lying there. But there were no cats in the station. And the weight was too heavy.

She felt her heart rate increase. The pressure on her feet shifted slightly.

If only she could make out something in the darkness. Her mouth went dry. She swallowed.

There was a sound, very close by, as if someone were breathing in her ear. Or stirring fallen leaves.

Holly reached out and found the trailing cord of the lamp switch. She pressed the button and a little sun of weak orange light exploded in the room.

There was a man sitting on the end of her bed, dressed in a sports jacket and tapered trousers. He had short, blond hair, finely chiselled features and his broad hands were folded neatly across his lap. He was smiling.

Holly drew back with a startled cry, her mind spinning in disbelief. She tried to form words. But the man just put his finger to his lips and smiled benignly.

It may have been the shadowy light, but there was a disquieting blankness in the man's gaze; his eyes were black and opaque like unpolished jet. He reached out and took Holly's hand in his, the palm warm and reassuring. Then he giggled.

6

Billy Coote was snoring loudly, an old grey army blanket slung over his skinny form. The monk's cell in which he lay was bare and functional, although someone had once had the presence of mind to install a radiator in the far corner: a fussy thirties thing convoluted like intestines and painted a depressing cream colour.

Billy snorted and coughed loudly in a hacking spasm, what his dad always called 'the workhouse cough'. Too many Wood-bines and draughty bus shelters, some doctor had once told him. But never mind that, he'd had some good times on the road. No responsibilities, nobody trying to tie him down. It hadn't been so bad...

That morning, he had run down into Crook Marsham full of tales about a funny police box — tales that had been greeted with the usual mixture of scepticism and amusement. Somewhat forlornly, he had wandered over to the monastery where he knew he was guaranteed a bed and a free meal once or twice a month, sometimes more if he pushed his luck.

The Abbot always treated him kindly but didn't like to see him hanging around. Not very Christian of him in Billy's opinion. No, his true friend there was Brother Alec, a former soldier who had spent a good while sleeping rough in his time.

He understood Billy's way of life, letting him stay in the monastery and doling out some of the monks' leftovers.

'As long as you don't make a *habit* of it,' he would always say, laughing at his feeble joke.

Tonight, Alec couldn't really turn him down. It was freezing cold (Billy had chuckled at the conspicuous corduroys showing beneath Alec's robes) and looked like it might snow. He could hear the wind from the moor now as he drifted in and out of sleep, the thin, arrow-slit window rattling in its frame.

There had been a time when his opinion counted for something in Crook Marsham and the surrounding districts. Right up until the War he had been a bit of a local celebrity, consulted on all manner of things from the possibility of a dry summer to the sex of unborn children. After all, he *was* the seventh son of a seventh son. More or less.

Well, he had the 'gift' certainly, even though it was a bit erratic at times. His weather forecasts in particular brought down the wrath of local farmers and, after predicting a mild winter in '63, his services had been spurned in favour of the BBC's.

Sometimes, though, an image so pure and unsullied would spring into his mind that he could announce with certainty its coming to pass. It had been that way over the Abdication crisis (Billy had heard the King's departing speech in his mind a whole year before its broadcast), Churchill's death, and even the date of the last election (which had won him ten bob).

In the village, however, he was relegated to the position of local idiot: someone with whom to pass the time of day, buy a drink for at Christmas and use as a bogeyman to frighten errant children.

Get to bed now, or Billy will come and get you!

He was happy, though, happy enough. If it wasn't for the headaches.

They'd first appeared some months previously: sick, dull, thumping pains at the base of his skull, sometimes accompanied by blinding lights.

He was seeing things too. Nothing he could get a grip on. Colours and places, lit up like Christmas trees, that swam and shuddered in his mind.

After the attacks he would feel hollow and utterly miserable, a profound, stomach-deep depression which took days to lift. It was all very worrying. He would talk to Brother Alec about it in the morning.

Abbot Winstanley heard it first, a low, low moan, drifting down the corridors of the monastery. He opened his eyes and listened intently. The sound came again, haltingly — a desperate, shuddering wail like the cry of a lost soul or the mournful song of a whale.

Winstanley remembered childhood stories about — what were they called? — yes, the Gabriel Ratchets. A celestial horde of wretched spirits forever doomed to walk the earth. This was how they might sound, he thought. Desperate, hopeless, forgotten.

He got up and padded to the door of his cell, pressing his hand against the dark wood.

It came again, more substantial this time, like a breath of wind blowing suddenly fierce. Winstanley slipped on his shoes and opened the door. The corridor beyond was completely empty.

He looked up the passageway towards the Great Hall and then down towards the kitchens. Nothing. Only a hollow, silent darkness.

He caught his breath sharply as the moan sounded right by him, fluttering the hem of his habit and creeping down the back of his neck. He shivered, wishing he were not alone in that sad corridor. If only the Doctor had returned. Winstanley had derived great comfort from the newcomer's arrival.

Somewhere, deep in the monastery, a heavy door creaked and slammed shut. Winstanley jumped out of his skin and ducked back into his room, shutting his own door with sweaty hands.

Billy Coote's door swung shut of its own accord and the old man's face jerked in response. The air about his sleeping body seemed curiously stirred, whispering around the grizzled locks of hair, teasing at the wide-open, staring eyes which had turned as black and opaque as coal in a snowman's face.

Holly felt herself falling. The man's grip on her arm had become intense, painful; his hand felt hot and searing as if it were burning into her skin. His face seemed to balloon before her heavy eyes, the mouth expanding into a gaping hole.

Holly could see things in his opaque eyes and felt strangely comfortable. It would be so easy just to let go. So easy...

The man's shape seemed to shift and change, his skin blurring and glittering like burnished metal. Light began to trail from his hands and eyes.

Holly turned leaden eyes to gaze into his face. The mouth

was huge now, red lips and teeth glistening with spit.

'Holly!'

She turned. Vijay had strolled into the room and was staring in disbelief at the miasmic cloud into which Holly seemed to be sinking.

'Holly!' he called again, desperately thrashing his arms at the insubstantial entity. There was a crackle of energy and Vijay was tossed across the room, hitting the wall with tremendous force. He picked himself up, clutching his bruised chest, and stumbled towards Holly. He called her name again and again, his voice rasping with despair.

Eventually she turned her sleepy head.

'Vijay?'

The cloud seemed to retreat; its staggering brightness dimming like a sputtering candle.

Holly forced herself to think of Vijay, their first meeting, their first kiss. He was solid, concrete, substantial. Her wavering consciousness strained to lock on to his image as he swam at the edge of her vision. She was suddenly paralysed with fear, her eyes bulging.

Vijay waded across the room, the pulsing cloud wrapping diminishing tendrils around him. A thick, viscous fluid settled on his skin, running in rivulets into his nose and mouth. He spat disgustedly and wiped at his coated eyes.

Holly could feel a dull pulsing in her head and pressure on her skull as if an unseen hand were forcing her down.

It was too late, she told herself. She was lost.

Vijay's face rose before her like a painted mask, furrowed with concern and anxiety.

Too late.

She was suddenly alert and gulping air with pistol-shot clarity. Vijay was holding her tightly in his arms and she blinked over his shoulder at the room, now partially lit by the corridor lamps. The man was gone.

'Are you OK? Holly? What happened?'

She shook her head. Slowly at first and then with unnatural speed, she began gabbling a stream of incomprehensible words.

Vijay's hand cracked across her face and she fell, sobbing, into his embrace.

Vijay picked her up bodily, forced her into some clothes and managed to struggle out into the corridor. He threw her over his shoulder and began to walk back to the control room. But Holly pulled away and slid to the floor.

'All right, Hol. It's OK now,' said Vijay soothingly.

She raised bloodshot eyes to him.

'It was James! It was him!'

'James?'

She grabbed Vijay's hand.

'My fiancé. You remember?'

Vijay nodded dumbly.

'He died. He's dead,' Holly cried, her voice hoarse. 'But he was there in the room. And he wanted me. I could feel it!'

Vijay sighed heavily and folded her into his arms, cooing softly.

'All right, Hol. Don't talk now.'

She flashed angry eyes. 'I want to! I want to talk! James is dead. How could he be here? How could he?'

Hot tears welled in her eyes and rolled down her flushed face. 'I love you,' she said simply. 'But he meant so much to me. You must understand.'

'I do,' said Vijay, stroking her hair. 'I do.'

Whatever he had seen in the room was certainly unearthly. A cloud of light and energy, like a delicate sea creature, trailing crackling fronds. It had terrified and astonished him. And, just for a moment, he'd made out a human face, its features writhing and twisting in fury.

Vijay put his arm around Holly and together they shambled down the corridor.

The gaudy wallpaper in the TV room was, Ace surmised, an attempt to bring a touch of homeliness to the otherwise sterile station. There were a few cheap prints pinned to the walls and a dog-eared poster of Che Guevara. Skinny Christmas streamers pocked with drawing-pin holes were ranged haphazardly across the ceiling.

After the crisis in the control room, Ace and Robin had been allocated the TV room as their billet for the night. Vijay had been very kind, helping with bedding and refreshment, although he still seemed a little embarrassed in Ace's company. She thought of that old gag, 'I didn't recognize you with your clothes on'.

For a while, she and Robin had watched TV, or rather, Robin had watched TV and she had watched him. Blue light from the screen bounced across his features as he sat entranced by a programme bravely entitled *Colour me Pop!*.

Ace liked the curve of his jaw in the moody light and the way his Brian Jones fringe hung untidily in his eyes.

A youthful strutting figure had popped on to the screen and Ace laughed out loud.

'What is it?' asked Robin, smiling.

'Is that who I think it is?'

Robin frowned. 'Mick Jagger? Yeah.'

'You should see him now. He's well past it.'

'What do you mean?'

Ace bit her tongue. She had forgotten where she was. And when.

'Nothing,' she said quietly.

Sometime after eleven, they had settled down for the night, their beds separated by a pile of coats, boots and Ace's rucksack. Robin clicked off the light.

Ace heard him undressing in the darkness and grinned to herself. His teeth chattered as he plunged beneath the thick blankets.

Ace was dog tired but her brain refused to quieten down. An image of that vile corpse out on the moor sprang into her mind and she shook her head to get rid of it. She didn't want to think about that.

Instead, she thought about the nameless excitement she was experiencing. The gentle sound of Robin's breathing sent a tingle of pleasure coursing through her. She could hear the ticking of his eyelashes and knew that he was as wide awake as she.

'I know this sounds a terrible cliché...' Robin announced suddenly.

Ace put her hands behind her head. 'Try me.'

'You're not like any other girl I know.'

Ace barked a laugh.

'Sorry,' he grinned.

'No. Don't apologize. I like you too.'

There was a deep and satisfying silence.

A thick mist hung about the base of the Minster, gathering in eddies inside the crumbling yellow niches.

Tim Medway strolled to his car, rubbing his hands together to keep warm and looking around him at the awakening city. He smiled.

Daylight was bleeding through the dark blue of night and milk bottles greeted the morning with a chorus of chinking.

Coloured bulbs hung across the street like strings of paste jewellery, swaying slightly in the cold wind.

This was Medway's first time in York. Arriving mid-afternoon the previous day, he'd found himself so enchanted by the labyrinth of winding streets and tea shops that he'd decided to postpone his appearance in Crook Marsham. Old Trevithick could wait for his interview. Probably had nothing better to do anyway.

Instead, Medway had buttoned up his overcoat and thrown a long scarf around his neck, enjoying the undercurrent of Christmas which bubbled within him.

Bay-windowed shops glittered with antiques and wooden toys, motley collections of old ship's instruments, Victorian dolls, angels, rocking horses and merry-go-rounds.

It was like some childhood ideal, he thought to himself, grinning in excitement: a composite of Dickens, John Masefield and C. S. Lewis, resonant of a kind of Christmas he had never known yet seemed to remember all the same.

His reflection, tall, tanned and good-looking, stared back at him from every window.

He'd eaten well, drunk just a little too much and stumbled to his hotel through streets bunched so close together the buildings on either side almost touched. There was a frost ring sparkling around the moon and the distant, brassy music of a Salvation Army band drifted towards him. He had wished everyone and anyone a *very merry* Christmas.

Now it was Christmas Eve and he had woken early, crisscrossing his hands behind his head and listening intently to the peal of bells.

When he found the car, it was rimed with frost and he had scraped away at the windscreen with a little plastic spade until it was clear.

He let the car tick over for a while, warm air blasting through the interior, and took out a brand-new map from the glove compartment.

Crook Marsham was six miles to the west. Shouldn't take him long. Time for a nice leisurely breakfast in the village before he made his way to the − what was it called? − the Dalesview Residential Home.

Medway switched on the windscreen wiper and pulled out Trevithick's file from his briefcase.

'Edmund Trevithick,' he announced to himself. 'Born 12 May 1898. Educated Repton School, blah, blah . . .'

He turned a page and pulled out a couple of photographs of the young Trevithick.

'No formal training. Joined Acton Rep. 1923. Went to Hollywood in the thirties. Came back for WWII. Distinguished Service Medal.' Medway pulled a face, surprised.

'Films include: *Flames of Passion* (1946), *Sword of Araby* (1949), *The Man from the Ministry* (1951), *There's Someone in My Trousers!* (1965). Best known for his TV work in the last years of his career, especially the popular *Nightshade* serials (1953−58). Retired in 1966. Family: Married Margaret (d. 1956), one daughter Paula (d. 1967) and granddaughter.'

Medway closed the file, put the car into gear and reversed into the misty street.

When the confirmation had come from Jill Mason he'd watched some of the old man's work. *Nightshade* he remembered well, of course, but he was most impressed by Trevithick's tremendous output of television plays and his delightful sparring with Gilbert Harding on *What's My Line?*

All in all, he was rather looking forward to the interview. It would certainly bring a touch of excitement into the old boy's retirement.

Edmund Trevithick picked up his umpteenth glass of whiskey with a shaky hand. Early light blotched the taproom carpet in pools of milky blue.

Lowcock and Lawrence Yeadon lay sleeping in the positions they had assumed upon entering The Shepherd's Cross the previous night. Both had collapsed as if utterly exhausted, causing grave concern amongst the remaining customers. They had fallen into a deep sleep, resisting all attempts to get them to bed. Trevithick had taken charge, bringing blankets and pillows from the airing cupboard and sending the old man with the arthritic hands to check on Betty. He had returned, saying her door was locked and it seemed wise not to disturb her.

Trevithick himself, however, had not slept well. His mind fizzed with unanswered questions. Events had been curious enough before but now! That creature... It was fantastic.

He heard a mumbling groan behind him and turned to see Lowcock stirring in his blanket-covered chair. The policeman's lively, humorous face now seemed heavily jowled and tired. He rubbed his eyes and looked blearily about him.

Trevithick pushed a whiskey into his hand and he drank it gratefully.

'What happened out there?' said Trevithick, immediately pouring another drink.

Lowcock gulped it down and waved his hand about. 'Don't know. How long have we been out?'

Trevithick looked at his watch. 'It's a quarter past eight. You got back about half past ten last night and you've been asleep ever since. We couldn't wake you.'

Lowcock shook his head and rubbed his face, his cheeks making a slapping sound like wet liver.

'We got as far as the moor road,' he said at last, cradling the whiskey glass in his hands, 'and we were just talking about who we should contact in York. Then...'

Trevithick looked up expectantly.

'Then?'

'I felt it first. Sickness. Nausea. Waves of it. Like we were on a rolling ship in a storm. I felt awful. And I could see Lawrence did too. He almost lost control of the car. We stopped for a bit and then tried to carry on but it was no good. It was like a physical barrier stopping us getting out. We were both sick in the car.'

Trevithick frowned. 'Anything else?'

112

Lowcock nodded slowly. 'Oh aye. Plenty. That's why we came tearing back here like a couple of nutters. We both felt this... terror.' He threw up his hands hopelessly. 'That's the only way I can describe it. Overwhelming terror. Hysterical we were. As if something was coming over the moor to get us. I've never been so scared in my whole bloody life.'

He finished off the whiskey.

'George.' Trevithick put a hand on the policeman's arm. 'There's something happening in this village. I think it's beyond any of our understanding, but we've got to do something. Pool our resources. Get all the facts together.'

Lowcock grimaced. 'What facts? What do *you* think is happening?'

'I don't know. Listen. I know this is going to sound incredible, but, last night, when I was walking home...'

'How's Betty?' said Lowcock suddenly. 'Christ, I forgot all about her. How is she?'

Trevithick put up his hands. 'It's all right. I sent someone up to relieve young Robin but he'd locked the door. We didn't want to disturb her. She's fine, I'm sure. But listen, last night...'

Lawrence sat bolt upright in his chair, blinking his eyes in confusion. He looked at Lowcock and Trevithick with a puzzled frown as if unsure of who they were. Then he threw aside his blanket and clattered across the room to the stairs.

'Lol, it's all right!' called Lowcock, getting to his feet.

There was grim determination in Lawrence's tired face as he sprinted up the stairs to the bedroom. He glanced down absently at the carpet which seemed to be wet through.

'Betty?' He hammered on the door. 'Betty? Are you all right, love?'

He tried the door. It was locked.

'Robin?'

His shoes squelched on the sodden carpet.

'Betty? Robin? Come on, son. Open the door.'

He could hear the alarm clock's muffled ticking. Lowcock and Trevithick appeared behind him.

'Betty?'

His voice was tinged with panic. He put his shoulder to the

door and the frame cracked, sending paint flakes to the floor.

Lowcock leant his shoulder against the panels and the two men slammed against the woodwork with all their strength. The door split from the hinges outwards and they almost fell into the room.

Trevithick hovered in the doorway and stumbled as Lowcock backed into him, pressing his sleeve to his mouth. The room smelled rank. Furniture and clothes lay scattered and the window was missing entirely, as if punched out cleanly by an unseen hand.

In the centre of the devastation stood the double bed, tilted slightly towards the wall. The thick eiderdown was pulled up to the pillows, completely covering the shape underneath. A wide green stain like fruit mould was spreading across the embroidery.

Trevithick held his breath and crossed the threshold. He noticed at once that the door had not been locked; rather the woodwork seemed to have expanded, sealing the door like the entrance to a tomb.

Lawrence sat down calmly on his side of the bed and folded back the eiderdown. Betty Yeadon glared back at him, her features horribly contorted and stretched back like perished rubber. Broken capillaries zig-zagged across her flattened face.

Lawrence let out a howl of grief and made to grab his wife's shoulders. He jerked back in abject horror as her body shattered in his hands, the skin falling away in brittle shards. For one awful moment he could feel the bones in her wasted arms but then they too shuddered into nothingness beneath his fingers.

Lowcock and Trevithick pulled him off the bed and stared in revulsion as the sheets stirred before them. There was a brief, shocking crack and then the body disappeared in a cloud of noxious vapour.

Lowcock took charge. 'Get him out! Edmund! Out! Quick!'

Trevithick dragged Lawrence from the room whilst the policeman managed to pull shut the remains of the shattered door. Kicking open the door of Robin's room, Trevithick laid the sobbing man on the unmade bed.

Lowcock scrambled across the landing, picked up the phone, dropped it and then clapped the receiver to his ear. There was complete silence. He swore loudly and threw the phone aside.

'I'm going to the station. Look after him. I won't be five minutes.'

Trevithick nodded quickly. 'Righto.' He put a comforting arm around the weeping man beneath him.

Posters of unfamiliar footballers and pop stars grinned in innocence at him from the walls. Trevithick felt his breath coming in painful gasps.

What the hell was going on? And what should he do now?

Events seemed to slipping out of everyone's control. He looked down at Lawrence and suddenly decided he should pay a little visit to the Dalesview Home. If he could find the fella with the arthritic hands and leave Lawrence in his care for a while...

There was something in the top drawer of his dressing table which just might prove useful...

The tracking station control room was silent save for the occasional oath of exasperation as the Doctor attempted to repair the radio.

Beside him sat Holly, now dressed in ski pants and one of Vijay's crewneck sweaters. Her eyes were wide and red with crying.

Vijay had tried to persuade her to return to her bed but she wouldn't hear of it, preferring to sit awake and aware through the long night.

'Blast!' cried the Doctor, throwing aside a delicate arrangement of wires.

Cooper was blearily contemplating her first coffee of the morning. 'What d'you reckon then, Doctor?'

The Doctor sighed and sat down on the end of the bench.

'It's useless. Blown out.'

'Then we're cut off,' said Hawthorne flatly as he strode into the room.

'Don't be so melodramatic, Tom,' said Cooper. 'Vijay can drive over to York and even if the phones aren't working there, we can get through to Cambridge somehow.'

Hawthorne shrugged.

The Doctor glanced across at Holly and then walked over to

her. He sat down on his hands and smiled.

'How are you feeling now?'

Holly nodded as though shaking a loose thought. 'OK. I'm OK, thanks.'

The Doctor chose his next words carefully. 'Vijay said . . . Vijay said you'd seen something in your room. What, exactly?'

Holly looked down and sighed. 'I know it sounds silly, impossible . . .'

'Never mind how it sounds.' The Doctor put his hand on hers. Holly took a deep breath.

'I saw my fiancé. He died six years ago. I saw his ghost.'

The Doctor considered this. 'How did he appear?'

'What do you mean?'

'Was he as you remembered him?'

'Oh yes! Very much. He was so alive. I could feel it. It was like he was drawing me into him. It would've been so easy . . .'

The Doctor looked straight at her. 'But you didn't?'

'There was something wrong. I felt him beginning to change. I went all sleepy. I could see Vijay coming into the room and I knew I had to get back to him. It was like one of those nightmares where you're running through treacle.'

Vijay came in with some freshly made toast and tea. He put his arm round Holly.

'And what did you see?' asked the Doctor.

'I don't know,' said Vijay. 'Not a person really. A sort of cloud. Colours. Trails in the air. Like I was tripping.'

'Tripping?' The Doctor raised his eyebrows.

Vijay cleared his throat. 'Drugs. You know. Acid. It was like that.'

'I see,' said the Doctor with mock gravity. He smiled warmly and left them together. Vijay lifted up Holly's face to kiss her but she pulled away.

'Don't,' she said simply. Vijay sighed heavily and looked glumly at the floor.

The Doctor checked the correlation receivers and turned to address Hawthorne. 'What's the tolerance of your safety cutouts?'

Hawthorne sniffed. 'That's what's very odd. They should've cut out way before the levels they reached. Luckily, we've sustained no damage so far.'

'Hmm,' the Doctor mused. He looked around the room. 'Where's Ace?'

It had been a long night. Ace had finally managed to cool down her excitement sufficiently to get some sleep, although she'd been aware of raised voices in the corridor at some point. A woman's voice (hysterical) and what sounded like Vijay's (placating).

Ace had been awoken by the tuneless squawking of a rook somewhere outside. The sound made her think of bleak, frosty Sundays in the park as a child; bare, black trees against a snow-filled sky.

She became suddenly aware of Robin watching her and inclined her head on the pile of stuff which had served as her pillow.

'Morning,' she said softly.

'Morning.' Robin smiled his cheeky smile.

Ace ran her tongue around her mouth and silently wished she had a bottle of mouthwash. It tasted like the bottom of a birdcage in there.

Robin reached out his hand and softly touched her face. She closed her eyes, enjoying the sensation, and then delicately took his hand in hers. His gentle breathing sounded closer as he moved his head towards her face.

'Come along, Ace. We have to be going!' The Doctor's voice carried down the corridor from the control room. Ace opened her eyes sharply. Robin pulled away.

'*Ace!*'

'All right!' she bellowed.

She looked fondly into Robin's eyes and then gave him a light peck on the cheek. 'Come on, sunshine. Plenty of time. Let's see what the Doctor's got planned for us.'

He smiled contentedly. Ace bounded from beneath her blankets, unconcerned by her seminakedness. Robin blushed in spite of himself.

'Oi,' Ace warned, laughing. 'Close your eyes.'

'If you insist.'

* * *

117

'All I'm saying,' whispered Hawthorne, 'is that the girl is obviously unstable.'

Cooper stared at him. 'What d'you mean, unstable?'

'I need hardly remind you that she has been seeing things. And that wog boyfriend of hers...'

'I've told you before. I won't have that kind of abuse in my station!' barked Cooper.

The Doctor looked across to where the two scientists were sitting and raised his eyebrows. Hawthorne was keen to keep this conversation quiet.

'All right, all right. I'm sorry. But the boy freely admits to taking hallucinogenics. You heard him. Whatever Miss Kidd saw was obviously some drug-induced fantasy...'

Cooper ruffled her grizzled hair. 'I'm not so sure.'

'Well, whatever the reason, do you really think we should have such people working here?'

'Tom!' Cooper slammed her fists down on to a bench. 'If ever any of my staff sufficiently compromise themselves so as to prove unreliable I'll take direct action. Until then, we have a bit of an emergency on our hands so can we *please* get on?'

Ace and Robin walked into the room grinning. The Doctor looked at them almost coldly. 'Ah, there you are. I need to see the Abbot again up at the monastery, if you'd care to accompany me?'

Robin looked at Ace. 'I really should be getting back.'

'Oh.' Her face fell.

'It's my mum.'

Ace nodded. 'They can be a pain in the arse, can't they?'

'Look, if you're going to the monastery, I can meet you there. I'll only be a couple of hours.'

The smile returned to her face. 'All right then. It's a date.'

Robin grinned and shrugged. 'Yeah. I suppose it is.'

He kissed her quickly on the cheek and, waving goodbye to the rest, left the room.

'Ready?' said the Doctor.

Cooper began to fumble under a bench. 'Hang on a tick, Doctor. I'll need to get in touch with you if there's another energy surge.' She popped up again. 'Here.'

She tossed a small black box across the room to the Doctor,

which he caught nimbly.

'Walkie-talkie,' she said. 'Not much of a range but that might work in our favour. It may have survived the blowout. Anyway, if you hear from me, then we'll know.'

'Thank you.' The Doctor slipped the device into his already bulging pockets. '*Au revoir*.' He marched out. Ace gave a general smile to the room and dashed after him.

'What a funny little man,' said Cooper.

Outside, the day was fine and cold. The Doctor yawned and strode on, Ace struggling to keep up.

'Doctor! Hang on!'

The Doctor didn't stop.

Who rattled his cage? thought Ace.

She sighed. He was keeping something from her as usual. Why did she always let him treat her like this? She thought of the feel of Robin's hand against her face, his lips on her cheek. He was real, uncomplicated, human. Until then, she hadn't realized just how much she'd missed that quality.

On the radio, The Move were urging everyone to call the fire brigade. Medway hummed along tunelessly until static crackled across the frequency.

With one hand still on the steering wheel, he fiddled with the dial and cursed as the reception broke up completely. He clicked the dial to 'off' and the car was silent except for the gentle hum of the heating.

The road ahead emerged on to the moor and he pulled up the car a moment to check his bearings. The windscreen wipers thrummed repeatedly as a fine drizzle swept across the land.

Medway craned his neck and saw the old bus shelter with the road sign by it.

'Crook Marsham. One mile.' He smiled to himself, pressing down on the accelerator.

The road across the moor was narrow and black, rain glistening on its old surface. Black and white posts studded with hexagonal reflectors appeared every few yards. They were quite tall, in order to project, Medway assumed, above the deep snow which doubtless struck the area.

119

He fumbled in the glove compartment and pulled a succession of keys, loose change and chocolate wrappers on to his lap before finding a crumpled packet of Camels. He clamped his lips around a cigarette and struck a match off the dashboard, drinking in the smoke hungrily.

Shame he wouldn't be in London for Christmas. It was always the best time to be there. Anyway, what did he have to go back to now? Since Julia left him he'd spent two Christmases alone with the dog, falling asleep in front of Alastair Sim on the box and a bottle of whiskey on the table.

It was a terrible time to be alone. And no one, he thought, ever thinks it can happen to them. He certainly didn't, not after the Christmases he used to have.

Relatives crowding the kitchen which steamed with pudding smells. His father, breath reeking of booze, becoming overly affectionate and shaking him by the hand as though he were grown up. Then out would come the beer and attempts would be made to introduce Tim to the serious business of alcohol.

When Christmas Day dawned, young Tim and his brother and sisters would wake ridiculously early, creeping into their parents' room and jumping on the bed. Then there were rituals to be observed. First, the Christmas morning cup of tea (an annual treat this; probably the only time the kids made their parents one). They would stand on the freezing kitchen lino in their pyjamas, hopping from foot to foot and willing the old kettle to boil. Pans of vegetables, sliced and put in water the night before, already crowded the cooker.

Tim would peek through the closed doors of the living room where the piles of presents had magically appeared. Even the skinny, tinselly artificial tree, normally a poor relation of other families' real ones, was imbued with the special aura of the morning, glowingly lit by the light filtering through heavy, gold-coloured curtains.

At last, the tea would be ready and presented, with some gravitas, to his parents.

After deliberately stalling, Medway's mother would say 'All right then' and they would line up at the top of the stairs, squealing with excitement.

'Go!'

And, in a flurry of loosening pyjamas, the two girls and boys would hurtle down the stairs, fling open the living-room door and fall upon the mountain of parcels like vultures.

Medway smiled to himself. He always meant to get back home for Christmas but somehow never got round to it. Only one of his sisters still lived near to his parents and she would dutifully stay over on Christmas Eve, even obeying the old tea-making ritual.

But he imagined it a lonely Christmas now, the echoes of their frantic race to the presents replaced by a grown-up shamble downstairs at ten or eleven o'clock. Slippers and hankies instead of toys and magic.

Of course, when Julia came into his life, all the old joys returned. He found himself staying up late on Christmas Eve, wrapping tiny presents in expensive paper. Buying a huge, fragrant tree as a deliberate antidote to the pallid one of yesteryear.

Then he and Julia would stroll along the banks of the Thames, hugging each other in affection as lights shimmered on the water.

Once, they'd made love during the Queen's speech, giggling and grinning the whole time, ignoring the pine needles which insinuated themselves into their buttocks. He'd never quite been able to take Her Majesty seriously again.

Medway glanced in his rearview mirror and caught sight of the monastery for the first time. Grim-looking place, he thought to himself.

The car crunched over broken glass and he slammed on the brakes as a coach loomed into view. It had swung diagonally across the road, its smashed front end jammed into a dry-stone wall. Clouds of steam billowed from the engine. Medway's blood ran cold as he saw the limp body of the driver hanging through the shattered windscreen.

He pulled the car on to the side of the road and jumped slightly as bewildered figures began to emerge from the steam. They were old, staggering from the shelter of the bus like desperate ghouls.

He was relieved to see a young woman running towards him. She was attractive but in some distress, locks of her lacquered hair falling into her eyes.

'Thank God,' Jill Mason gushed, putting a protective arm around Mrs Holland who was wailing softly in a fractured voice.

'It's awful. Awful,' intoned Mr Messingham, his thick round glasses hanging off his nose.

Jill managed to steer her charges away from the sight of the dead driver.

'What happened?' said Medway, opening the boot of his car and producing a blanket.

Jill shook her head. 'We were heading for York. They're all going home for Christmas. *Were* going home.' She sighed. 'Some of them said they felt queasy. I thought it must be travel sickness but then I felt it too. And the driver.'

Medway wrapped the blanket around Mrs Holland. There were now about fifteen old people grouped around his car.

'It was this awful sickliness,' Jill continued. 'Got worse the further we went. They got hysterical. Then the driver just let go of the wheel...' She looked over at the driver. 'Poor sod.'

Medway regarded the shivering group before him. 'Well, you can't stay here. I can drive you down to the village in shifts.'

'No. I've got a better idea. The monastery's closer. They're all in shock. I'm sure the monks will help. You could take the frailest in the car. I'll walk the rest. It's not far.'

'Right.'

'Thanks, er...?'

'Tim Medway.' He offered his hand. Jill reacted.

'From the BBC?'

He nodded. 'You're not...?'

'Jill Mason. It's my Mr Trevithick you've come to see.'

'Is he...?'

Jill shook her head. 'No. Stubborn old goat refuses to go anywhere for Christmas. Probably very wise in the circumstances.'

Medway helped four old people into his car. 'Are you sure you can manage?'

Jill nodded. Medway got into the driving seat. Mrs Holland sobbed quietly in the back.

'Can I call the police from the monastery?' Medway asked through the window.

'I doubt it. All the phones are out of order.' Jill stopped as if struck by a thought. 'Mr Medway?'

122

'Yes?'

'Did you feel anything? When you were coming here?'

Medway shook his head. 'No. Nothing.'

Jill waved him off and the car moved slowly on to the rough track to the monastery which branched off the main road.

She gave one last look at the dead driver and then set off in the same direction, herding the old people before her like wayward sheep.

Abbot Winstanley was glad the morning had come. He had lain awake half the night anticipating the return of that mournful wail, eventually succumbing to sleep in the early hours.

Now, despite his exhaustion, he was up and about. He had already observed the usual patterns of prayer, spoken at length to Brother Alec about letting that awful old tramp into the monastery again and outlined his plans for the Christmas Day menu to old Minnie the cook.

He was supposed to be finding a relevant biblical passage to read for his fellow monks but instead was sitting in his study, staring at the previous night's fire.

Terrible doubts gnawed away at his mind. How long had he been in this wretched place? Twenty years? From novice monk to Abbot. Twenty years of kneeling and praying and abstaining in the service of his faith. He laughed a little to himself. Faith in what? An increasingly godless generation locked on a course of self-destruction? A youth culture which worshipped sexual ambiguity and promiscuity? Or was it faith in the God who had created them all?

Well, that was the problem, he thought to himself. He didn't really have faith at all. Not any more.

He wanted to. Oh, how he wanted to. Faith like the burning sense of right and fulfilment he had once possessed, the faith which had sustained him through a turbulent youth.

What was left now? He was as old and hollow as the monastery itself, running a cottage industry that saved money, not souls.

He glanced through the latticed study window and saw the Doctor and Ace heading towards the entrance. His heart leapt. If anyone could help him with his crisis of faith it was the

123

Doctor. He seemed so wise, so much older than he appeared. Like a man standing on the bank of time, unconcerned by the furious flow of the years.

A few moments later, Ace and the Doctor were shown in.

'How do you do,' said Winstanley warmly as the Doctor introduced Ace. 'Your friend and I have been having some very interesting chats.'

'I bet,' said Ace, glancing round the room at the bookshelves. 'Quite a library you've got here, vicar.'

'Er. Abbot. Yes, yes, it's a bit of a hobby of mine.'

The Doctor spread his hands on the desk before him. 'I won't beat about the bush, Abbot. There are some very curious things happening here. I'd like to see some more of your history books, if I may?'

Winstanley clapped his hands together delightedly. 'Of course, of course.'

He pulled out an elegant mahogany stepladder from a niche in the wall and bustled up to the top shelf. 'Particular period?'

'Any,' said the Doctor airily. 'As far back as you can go.'

Within minutes, Winstanley was handing down volume after volume — pamphlets, guide books and hefty histories.

'Ace. Get looking,' the Doctor instructed, throwing half a dozen books over the desk.

'What for?'

'Anything unusual.' The Doctor's head disappeared into a pile of papers.

Ace sighed. This wasn't her idea of a fun morning. Sorting through historical junk was too like a school lesson. She'd seen history, real history, past and future; and academic substitutes were bound to pale beside that.

She glanced at her watch. 11:30. Still a good hour and a half before Robin would get there.

Ace let his image swim into her mind as she carelessly leafed through the documents on her knee. She saw him on his bike, just as he had been when she'd first seen him. That smile had said everything...

'If you're not going to concentrate then you're no use to me.'

Ace looked up, stung. The Doctor was regarding her with inky eyes.

'Sorry.' She looked down at the papers and books, dense with old print. One book, far more modern than the rest, caught her eye at once.

'Doctor?'

He raised his eyes from the book in his hands.

'Is this any good?' she said.

The Doctor moved around the side of the desk and peered over her shoulder.

'What is it?' called Winstanley, still perched up his ladder.

The Doctor took the slim volume from Ace's hands and scanned a few pages. 'It's an archaeological work. It seems there was an expedition here in 1919. A dig. They found remnants of Palaeolithic quarrying.' He cast his eyes over the dust jacket. 'Seems it was abandoned. Under mysterious circumstances.'

'Where was this, then?' said Ace.

The Doctor looked at her steadily. Ace nodded. She knew where.

7

Medway left the car in a side road adjoining the main street and walked towards the police station. He didn't notice the disturbed bushes growing by the pavement, nor the other faint traces of Trevithick's encounter the previous night. But he felt distinctly uneasy.

There was a chilling wind blowing off the moor, stirring bare branches and discarded newspapers. Telephone wires swung like slack skipping ropes against the white sky, sighing as the wind blew over them.

Jangling his keys in his pocket, Medway began to whistle 'We Three Kings' without much enthusiasm, glancing about nervously at the clusters of nineteenth-century cottages which dotted the road.

The local pub seemed a more enticing prospect and he could have done with a little something after his experiences that morning. Ferrying hysterical geriatrics was not his thing at all and his supply of small talk had run very low indeed. Still, the monks had been kindness itself, saying all the right soothing things in that pleasant, bland monotone beloved of men of the cloth.

Now he had to do his bit and report the accident.

Funny how such a big thing could go unnoticed. In fact, the whole village was terribly quiet. More like a wet Sunday in March than Christmas Eve. Already missing York's wonderful festive air, he made a mental note to spend some more time in York before returning to London.

Medway pushed his hands into his pockets, overcoat tails bunching behind him, and mounted the steps to the police station.

'Have you seen this man?' announced a poster by the entrance. Medway hadn't. He pushed open the door and was taken aback by the scene which met his eyes.

In contrast to the quiet of the village, the police station was in turmoil. The front desk was piled with papers. Uniformed men scurried to and fro. One man, at the back, a look of hopeless resignation on his face, was constantly dialling and redialling a heavy black telephone.

'Excuse me...' announced Medway.

The bustle continued. Medway rang the desk bell.

George Lowcock appeared from his office, jamming his hat on to his head. A smaller, rosy-cheeked man scurried behind him.

'Just try, Albert, that's all I ask. We've got to find a way out somehow.'

'Excuse me,' said Medway again. Lowcock looked at him briefly and then made for the door.

'Yes, sir?' sighed Albert wearily.

'I've come to report an accident. A coach... on the road out of the village.'

Lowcock turned in the doorway. 'Coach?'

'Yes. A party of old folks and a Miss Mason.'

Lowcock approached him. 'Any hurt?'

'The driver. Dead, I'm afraid.'

Albert licked a pencil and pulled out a note pad. 'And you are?'

Medway puffed out his cheeks. 'My name's Tim Medway. I'm a BBC reporter. I'm here to interview Mr Edmund Trevithick...'

Lowcock raised an eyebrow. 'Are you now? Well, laddie, you stick with me and I'll take you to him. Mind you, after what we've all been through I doubt he'll be in any state...'

Medway frowned. 'What d'you mean?'

'Never mind now. This coach...?'

Medway leaned against the desk and shrugged. 'They were heading for York. Miss Mason said they were overcome by some sort of sickness and the driver lost control.'

'Sickness,' said Lowcock thoughtfully.

'Think it's the same thing, George?' said Albert, pushing the pencil behind his ear.

Lowcock pouted his lower lip. 'Could be, could be.' He

looked Albert in the eye. 'Do you remember that pollution scare a few years back?'

'Oh aye,' said Albert brightly.

Medway was getting interested, his journalistic nose sensing a story. 'Pollution?'

'Oh, nowt much,' said Lowcock dismissively. 'There was a fire at a chemical plant a few miles off. I was just wondering whether it could be something like that.'

'That doesn't explain Mrs Yeadon, George. And what about Jack Prudhoe and Dr Shearsmith?'

'Mmm. You're right. "It is fatal to theorize without facts", eh Watson?'

Lowcock turned to Medway. 'Come along then, I'll introduce you to Professor Nightshade.'

He took Medway by the arm and led him outside. Albert leaned over the desk towards one of the young constables. 'Peter, get over to the York road, will you? Report of an accident.'

The Doctor rubbed his fingers across weary eyes. The print on the books before him was beginning to swim and centuries of reading in diverse libraries across the galaxies told him it was time to call a halt. He slammed shut the massive tome before him.

'I think we've found out as much as we can from here,' he said, glancing over at Ace. She looked at her watch. Just after midday and still a while until Robin would arrive. She smiled at her companion.

'Look, Doctor. I'm sorry if I haven't been much help so far. What with everything we talked about before...'

The Doctor cast his eyes downwards. Ace continued, 'I had a pretty rough day yesterday. Finding that stiff...'

'I know,' said the Doctor. 'I'm sorry.'

'I just want you to know that even if I'm not with you, I am... in spirit.'

The Doctor gazed at her sadly. 'I understand. Thank you.'

How many times had he been here before? With Victoria on the gas platform. Jo in Llanfairfach. Tegan in London.

She'd grown up before his eyes; this funny misfit, changing

from a little bundle of venom with more chips than a Monte Carlo casino into a confident, maturing adult. It had been a struggle though. He had hated the lies and the half-truths he'd felt compelled to create in order to protect her from the future. After Fenric and more recently their adventures battling the Timewyrm, he'd hoped to have put all that behind them. But now there were other considerations...

Ace jumped as the walkie-talkie in the Doctor's pocket squawked into life. He produced it with some relief.

'Doctor?' It was Cooper's voice, distorted by static.

'Yes, Dr Cooper? Over.'

'Bloody hell. It works! Erm... We're monitoring a slow build-up. I'd like you here. Over.'

'On my way. Over and out.'

He stuffed the black box into his coat and picked up a pile of selected books which he'd tied together with string. 'Coming?'

Ace shuffled uncomfortably. 'I thought I might hang around here for a bit. If that's OK with you?'

The Doctor nodded a little stiffly. 'Whatever,' he said and left the room.

Ace sat down in the Abbot's chair and chewed her lip. There was a funny sensation churning in her stomach, a kind of nervous anticipation mingled with sadness, like the first and last days of school combined.

The Doctor left the Abbot's study and traversed the narrow corridor which led to the open cloisters. He paused a moment, gazing at the hard white sky which was once more threatening snow, then he turned the corner towards the Great Hall.

He found the room buzzing with noise and confusion. A dozen or so monks were helping the coach party into hastily improvised beds, nursing sprains and applying poultices. Jill Mason stood to one side, banging the last dregs from an ancient tea urn. Mrs Holland was still moaning softly to herself in the corner.

'It's these blackie postmen,' announced Mr Peel to no one in particular.

The Doctor approached Jill. 'Hello again. What happened here?'

Jill sighed, pushing the annoying curl of hair from her eyes. 'We had an accident out on the moor. All very peculiar.'

The Doctor mumbled something sympathetic and then reeled as a small shambling figure almost knocked him off his feet. Billy Coote glanced at him for a moment, biscuit-brown teeth protruding aggressively, then shuffled towards the twisting stone steps which led to the tower.

Jill explained what had happened, proffering a mug of strong tea which the Doctor declined.

'Did you all feel this?'

'Yes. But Mr Medway, the one who helped us, must've been driving in the same conditions as us and he didn't feel a thing. I thought it might be something in the air...'

'Gas?'

'Something like that. But what Mr Medway says rather rules that out.'

'I'm not so sure,' said the Doctor darkly. 'He was coming *into* the village.'

'What d'you mean by that?'

'Where's Abbot Winstanley?'

Jill looked around at the chaos in the room. 'He was here. Can't see him now.'

The Doctor turned towards the door. 'Never mind. Just tell him I've gone back to the telescope, would you?'

He gave her a little smile and left the room through the big double doors.

Jill carried two mugs of steaming tea over to Mrs Holland. She sat down and sipped one herself, letting the old woman cradle hers like a security blanket. 'All right now, Esmé?'

Mrs Holland looked at her blankly, her toothless mouth champing in agitation.

'Wilfrid?' she called weakly. 'Oh, it's you. I was just recalling...'

She looked down and frowned. 'It's all changed now, you see. All changed. I used to have such lovely long hair. My mother used to sit and brush it by the fire. Like spun gold she always said.'

Mrs Holland put the mug on to the arm of her chair and held out her hands before her. The skin was tight and wrinkled like a chicken's, large liver spots speckling every finger. She turned to look at Jill, her eyes full of regret and what could only be bitterness.

Robin enjoyed the walk into the village, despite the cold. This wasn't his favourite time of year by any means. He was a summer boy, content to potter around in his T-shirt and shorts during the dog days of July and August, playing football with the lads from work well into the balmy night. Sometimes he would put in a few hours behind the bar at the pub and this, in addition to his wage from the newspaper office in York, usually meant he could save enough for a holiday. By the summer of 1969 he hoped to have enough to get to Italy. Or maybe Brazil for the World Cup the year after.

But now things had taken an unexpected turn. This girl, Ace, whom he'd only known a day or so, had totally floored him. And, wonderfully, she seemed to feel the same way too. It was early days, of course, and he wasn't getting his hopes up, but maybe he was on to something good here.

She had balls. Not real ones, of course (though he suspected a few of his previous girlfriends had). No, it was her zest he liked, her spontaneity and sparkle. That and her rather appealing face. He smiled. Maybe she could come to Italy with him. Maybe they could go away sooner . . .

Slow down. Slow down. You hardly know her yet.

He thought of Ace's words: 'Plenty of time, sunshine' and beamed.

Still beaming, he walked through the door of The Shepherd's Cross. Trevithick looked up from a table where Lawrence sat, head in hands.

'Robin! Oh, thank God!' cried Lawrence, springing to his feet and scooping up the boy in his arms.

'What's wrong, Dad?'

'Thank God. Thank God,' Lawrence muttered, burying his face in Robin's coat.

'Where's Betty?'

Lawrence drew back a little and Robin saw the puffy redness of his eyes for the first time.

'What happened up there? Did it get you too?' Lawrence said

131

in a gabbled shriek.

'What?'

'How come you're all right and she's...'

Robin took him by the shoulders and shook him. 'Where's Mum?' He looked Lawrence straight in the eyes. 'She was sleeping when I left her.'

Lawrence's face fell. 'You *left* her?'

Robin licked his dry lips. 'I had to go. The Doctor...'

'You left her? How could you do that? How *could* you?'

Robin shook him desperately. 'What's wrong? Where is she?'

Lawrence turned on him. 'She's dead, you selfish little bastard!'

'What?' Robin's voice was leaden.

'I left you in charge. I thought I could trust you!'

'I've got to see her...'

Trevithick laid a hand on the boy's shoulder. 'No, son. It'll do no good. You'll only upset yourself.'

Robin shrugged him off angrily. 'Get off me!'

Lawrence grabbed Robin by the shoulder, spun him round and cracked him across the face. A ribbon of blood trickled from his nose. He looked at Lawrence and then down at the floor.

'How *could* you?' hissed Lawrence. 'How *could* you?'

Robin marched towards the stairs.

Trevithick sat Lawrence down and pushed the inevitable glass of whiskey into his hand. He could hear Robin's footsteps above. There was a long, pregnant silence followed by a dreadful, hollow moan. Moments later, Robin clattered unsteadily down the stairs.

'Hardly anything left of her,' he croaked, running his hand over his face.

Trevithick nodded sadly. 'We don't know what happened, son, but the police are doing everything they can.'

Robin looked dazedly at the old man. 'I've seen it before.'

'What?'

'I've seen it before. Out on the moor. Me and the Doctor. We found Jack Prudhoe. He's dead. Same... same thing.'

Trevithick felt suddenly scared.

Lawrence looked at Robin. 'I'm sorry. I didn't mean...'

132

Robin looked blank. 'I've got to go,' he stammered and ran from the room.

Lowcock and Medway stepped back as the pub door burst open and Robin dashed past them towards the moor path. Grimacing, Lowcock stepped inside.

'Everything all right?' he said quietly.

Trevithick shrugged helplessly. 'Listen, George, we have to talk...'

'Hang on a minute, Edmund.' Lowcock turned to Medway who was hovering by the door. 'Edmund Trevithick, this is Mr Medway of the BBC. Come to see you.'

Trevithick frowned, as though annoyed that something so trivial should get in his way now. 'Hmm? Oh, yes, yes. Pleased to meet you.'

Medway sat down, smiling in a baffled sort of way.

'Listen, George,' continued Trevithick. 'Robin says that he and that Doctor fellow found Jack Prudhoe's body out on the moor.'

'Good Lord.'

Trevithick moved closer to the policeman and whispered. 'Died the same way as Betty, it seems.'

Lowcock sat down heavily. 'Whatever next?' He took off his hat and laid it on the table before him. 'There have been... further developments, Edmund. Your Miss Mason and her coach party have had an accident.'

Trevithick gasped, his lopsided mouth falling open.

'It's all right. They're all fine except the driver, poor devil. Isn't that right, Mr Medway?'

'Yes. They're all up at the monastery.'

Lowcock puffed out his cheeks. 'It seems they experienced the same symptoms as you and I yesterday, Lol.'

Lawrence turned his head and raised raw, exhausted eyes.

'Sickness. Nausea,' continued Lowcock. 'Driver lost control.'

' "Like we couldn't get out of the village" ,' said Trevithick quietly.

Lowcock started. 'Eh?'

'Isn't that what you said this morning? About last night?'

Lowcock sat back, frowning, and then roused himself. 'Anyway, this won't get the washing done!' he said cheerily. 'Lol,

133

I want you to come with me to Mrs Bass's B and B. No sense you staying here and upsetting yourself.'

Lawrence nodded dumbly and allowed himself to be led from his chair to the door. Lowcock turned to Medway and Trevithick. 'I'll leave you two to get acquainted.' He tipped his hat and helped Lawrence outside to the car.

Medway looked at Trevithick rather uncomfortably. 'I . . . er . . . I seem to have come at a rather bad time.'

Trevithick chuckled. 'You can say that again.'

'Of course, I won't detain you any further. We'll arrange to meet some time in the New Year.'

Trevithick stood up and pushed the whiskey bottle towards the newcomer. 'Nonsense,' he cried, pulling two glasses from the bar. 'I won't hear of it.'

Medway looked at the bottle gingerly. The old boy was probably half cut already. 'Well, I'll help if I can.'

'That's it exactly,' said Trevithick, a little unsteadily. He felt in his pocket for the old army service revolver which he had retrieved from his room. He was rather glad, now, that he had bothered to keep it in good condition. That creature wouldn't catch him napping again.

'First of all,' he said to Medway, 'you can sit there and listen. I want to tell you what's been going on . . .'

Vijay was having trouble concentrating. Every few minutes he would cast an anxious glance across the control room to where Holly was sitting, seemingly absorbed in her work. Vijay suspected that she was just functioning automatically in order to blot out her recent experiences.

Cooper was running around the room like a thing possessed, ruffling her hair perplexedly as fresh data came through. Hawthorne was absent, something for which Vijay was hugely grateful.

The double doors opened and the Doctor strode into the room. He nodded to each of them and put down his pile of books on a bench.

'Ah, good,' cried Cooper, joining him.

'Steady signals,' said the Doctor, casting a glance at the console screens.

'Yes, but not from the nova. Something else.'

'A build-up of some kind. As if it were gaining strength.'

'As if *what* were gaining strength?' said Vijay, looking up.

'That's what we have to find out.'

He sat down in a swivel chair and cleared his throat. 'I think it's time we examined a few facts.'

Holly rose from her chair and sat next to Vijay, allowing his arm to snake around her shoulders.

'Go on,' said Cooper, folding her arms.

'Firstly, this station is not the only thing to occupy this site. There was quarry work here, thousands of years ago, and a twelfth-century castle too. The castle was unoccupied for most of its life because it was reputed to be haunted.'

'Oh come on, Doctor. We have enough problems in the material world ...' began Cooper.

The Doctor held up his hands. 'Bear with me, bear with me. During the English Civil Wars, the castle was occupied by a small troop of Cavaliers who saw something that terrified them. Afterwards, the castle was destroyed by fire.

'In 1919, an archaeological expedition was launched, ostensibly to dig up the ancient quarry. But it was abandoned after several prominent members disappeared.'

Cooper harrumphed. 'I still don't see what you're getting at.'

'I would've dismissed this stuff as superstition just as readily as you were it not for some striking parallels. Two people have died, that much we know. A third, Dr Shearsmith, is missing. Mrs Yeadon at The Shepherd's Cross has been confined to bed after claiming to see her brother's ghost. Miss Kidd's experience we all know about.'

Cooper turned to Holly kindly. 'Holly's been working very hard ...'

'I know what I saw!'

'So do I,' said Vijay.

Cooper bit her lip and changed tack. 'You said parallels?'

The Doctor pulled at the string tying together his books. 'I didn't notice it at first. Ace found it.' He scanned the closing pages of the book which Ace had given him and gave a little cry of satisfaction.

' ''Further investigation into the disappearances'',' he read

135

aloud, ' "was hampered by a breakdown in the telephone systems and a mysterious outbreak of sickness which afflicted any who strayed on to the moor. Although later attributed to a form of water poisoning, no concrete information has ever become available".'

He clapped the book shut and gazed at his little audience. 'I need hardly remind you of our communication difficulties. And, this morning, a coach party from the old people's home was unable to leave the village after the driver crashed the vehicle. They all complained of a terrible sickness.'

There was a slow handclap from the far wall. They all turned to see Hawthorne, a sour smile on his face. 'Very good, Doctor. Keep this up and you'll have them believing in Santa Claus.'

'All right, Tom,' said Cooper quietly.

'Well, what is he trying to suggest? That we're being plagued by demons?'

'Look, Tom, we've all been under a lot of stress...'

Hawthorne stalked across the room, eyes blazing. 'No! I'm sorry, Dr Cooper, but I think I've been quiet too long. We let this — this *person* and his freakish friend waltz in here without so much as a by-your-leave! Within five minutes he's telling us what to do...'

'Story of my life,' said the Doctor.

'And now,' roared Hawthorne, 'now you're sitting here listening to him tell ghost stories!'

'Dr Hawthorne...' put in Vijay.

'And as for you,' Hawthorne stepped back disgustedly, 'I'm going to make sure you're off this project by the New Year. I don't intend to have my work jeopardized by an hysterical girl and a stupid bloody nigger!'

Vijay shot to his feet and caught Hawthorne by the lapels of his lab coat. For several seconds they glared at each other. Then Vijay let go, a protracted, angry hiss escaping his nostrils.

'I believe I'm a Paki to you, Dr Hawthorne. You might at least get your terminology right.'

Hawthorne glared at them all in contempt, turned on his heel and disappeared into the interior.

'Tom!' called Cooper. 'Tom, for God's sake!'

She threw up her hands helplessly. 'I'm ... so sorry, Vijay.'

Vijay shrugged. Holly forgot her own troubles for a moment and kissed him fondly.

The Doctor looked down, a little embarrassed. 'Well, whatever Dr Hawthorne's opinion, I urge you to take this seriously. I can't explain what's happening but we must all be on our guard.'

'Hang on!' said Cooper suddenly, her eyes darting to the consoles. 'It's starting again!'

The afternoon was wearing on and there was still no sign of Robin. Ace had wandered around the monastery, trying to interest herself in the tapestries and carvings. She found a small, wizened gargoyle which reminded her a bit of the Doctor and laughed. But then she recalled their conversation in Mrs Crithin's café.

Retirement! He really seemed serious. And where did that leave her? She needed to convince him that he really had been doing good all these years, that the Universe needed him.

Ace sat down on the sill of a glassless window which looked out on to the cloisters. She had thought that their terrifying experiences inside the Doctor's own mind during the final battle with the Timewyrm had exorcized the Doctor's angst. Obviously she had been too optimistic. Although, she thought carefully, it didn't seem to be guilt over any past actions which was haunting the Doctor. His malaise seemed to run very deep, seemed to be a profound dissatisfaction and loneliness, a yearning to belong.

Ace thought of her Auntie Rose, always bemoaning the youth of today and saying how much nicer everything used to be. That was what was wrong with the Doctor. He was trapped in the past. Remembering happier times which probably weren't that much different to today.

She looked about at the crumbling stones.

How many lives had this place seen come and go? How many people who thought themselves so important?

Ace smiled to herself. And how many young women had sat here thinking exactly the same thing?

It was like the sixties, she thought. Everyone was always going on about how brilliant they were. Admittedly, she wasn't exactly in the best place to observe things. Crook Marsham wasn't Carnaby Street. But things probably weren't so different to her own time. People were a bit happier. There was more sex all of a sudden. Things were colourful and fun after the drabness and austerity of wartime. But it was more than likely that the decade was fondly remembered because everyone was so much more optimistic about the future. A summer of love that would go on forever. It they'd known what was coming, just how much fun would the sixties have been?

Ace had risen from her seat and looked up at the already darkening sky. She turned and caught sight of the cheerful glow coming from the windows of the Great Hall. Strolling up to the big wooden door, she heaved it open and stepped inside.

The room was a forest of candles. They protruded from every available surface: long, stout church specimens in waxy puddles spreading a cheerful and cosy yellow light around the place. A blazing fire crackled in the hearth.

Jill Mason was walking between the chairs like a miniskirted Florence Nightingale. Most of her charges had dropped off to sleep although the Rayner sisters and Mr Peel were mumbling quietly to themselves. Three or four of the monks had lingered too, leaning against the walls or staring into the fire.

Ace felt a little thrill of pleasure run through her. It would be good to be here with Robin, somewhere so festive and cosy. She walked towards Jill, her shoes making a satisfying clop on the stone-flagged floor.

'Everything OK?'

Jill turned round. 'Er, yes. Do I. . .?'

'Ace.' She extended a hand. 'I'm a friend of the Doctor's.'

Jill smiled. 'Of course.'

Mrs Holland jerked into wakefulness, blinking about herself in confusion. Jill laid a soothing hand on her brow.

'It's all right, Esmé.'

'Wilfrid? Is that you?' The old woman grasped Jill's hand and touched it to her wrinkled cheek.

'It's Jill, Esmé.'

'Jill? Oh.' Mrs Holland frowned. 'Oh, yes. Of course. I was just thinking. . .Wilfrid. He's gone now, you know.'

Jill stroked Mrs Holland's hair affectionately. 'I know.'

'Nineteen-fifteen. I can remember the day. He was first in the queue at the recruiting office, you know. Oh yes. He used to parade up and down in front of that mirror with his big boots on and all his buttons shining. "I'll be back for Christmas," he said. But he wasn't. I knew there was something wrong but ... but you were supposed to get a telegram. There was a bit of a mix-up. All I got was a brown-paper parcel. His uniform. His boots. And his little pocket book.'

She turned tear-misted eyes to Jill. 'There was a bayonet hole through it. The pages were all stuck together, all ... stiff with blood. I remember. I just stood on the step and cried.'

Mr Messingham shifted in his chair and cleared his throat. Then he began to sing in a high, tuneless voice.

'Pack up your troubles in your old kit bag...'

'And smile, smile...' joined in Mr Dutton.

'Smile...' finished Mrs Holland.

'While you've a lucifer to light your fag...'

'Smile boys, that's the style,' croaked Mr Bollard, grinning.

Jill and Ace began to join in as best they could. Mrs Holland looked around at her friends. Their expressions were strangely melancholy, betraying the wealth of emotion stirred up by the old song. Mr Peel rubbed a hand across his eyes. He seemed to be crying.

'What's the use of worrying? It never was worthwhile, so...!'

Ace began to gravitate away from the group, feeling a little uncomfortable. She'd always hated singsongs, right from school assemblies to New Year revelling. They smacked of people trying too hard to enjoy themselves.

'Pack up your troubles in your old kit bag and smile, smile, smile!'

Ace stepped through the door of the Great Hall and found herself once again in the chilly cloisters. Evening had drawn about the monastery now. Where was Robin?

Mr Dutton raised his hand, a wicked smile cracking his face as he launched into a discordant rendition of 'We're Gonna Hang Out the Washing on the Siegfried Line'. Jill looked on benevolently. This was just the thing to get their spirits up.

Later, she would reflect on the irony of that phrase.

She looked across at Mrs Holland and her smile froze. The old woman was sitting bolt upright, transfixed by something she had spotted in the corner.

'Esmé?' called Jill.

Mrs Holland peered into the candle-lit gloom, her mouth champing in agitation. Jill looked again. There was a man standing in the shadows by the fireplace. Even in the poor light, she could make out his khaki uniform and boots. He began to move swiftly across the room.

'Wilfrid!' Mrs Holland yelled, her voice trembling.

A little girl ran across the room and sat on Mr Peel's knee. She was wearing a long, Edwardian dress and carried an old spinning top.

'Come on, Reuben,' she trilled. 'Come and play!'

Mr Peel gawped at her and thrust her from his knee, a look of horrified revulsion on his face. 'No! No, not you!'

Jill looked about desperately. From every corner, dark figures were emerging, like bas-reliefs coming to life. Light trailed from their eyes and hands.

'Stella?' said Mr Peel in a disbelieving whisper as the little girl looked into his eyes. Jill knew about Stella. A little girl of eight or nine. Mr Peel's sister. She'd died after eating poisonous berries sometime during the First World War. Died.

The uniformed man blazed through the room towards Mrs Holland. Someone started screaming hysterically.

'Esmé,' said Wilfrid, his voice rustling like tissue paper. 'My darling.'

The old woman's jaw fell open. The figure stopped by her chair and opened its arms to embrace her.

Jill looked crazily about her. The old people were stumbling about in blind panic as shapes split off from the shadows and moved towards them. There was a thin woman in a black dress bearing down on Mr Messingham and a tiny baby crawling towards Mr Bollard. The old man's hoarse scream filled the air.

Mrs Holland rose from her chair, her bent back straightening determinedly as she stepped into her husband's arms. He smiled, and her face suffused with joy. Fountains of radiant light shot between their hands, cocooning them in a web of energy.

Then Mrs Holland cried out, her voice choking as ectoplasmic fluid erupted from her throat. Before her, Wilfrid's face began to fall away, flesh dripping from the awful darkness beneath. His bony arms seared into her sides and she vanished into a ball of light.

The monks who had remained were running for the doors. Mr Peel's sister was creeping remorselessly towards him, smiling a chilling smile. The room began to blaze with white light.

Jill panicked suddenly, her whole body trembling. She ran to the door and threw herself out into the cloisters, slamming the door behind her.

Ace, who was standing some way off, was by her side in a moment.

'What is it?'

Jill gestured towards the door. Ace peered through the dusty window and gasped. All she could see were people bathed in light, roaring like columns of fire. She turned around, brimming with questions. Jill was gone.

Ace turned back to the window, her eyes widening in shock. Then she saw something which froze her blood. The main doors had opened and Robin had stepped into the room. He was knocked off his feet in an instant as a wave of light tore through the place, crashing shut the doors, which buckled and expanded. Ace ran inside.

'Robin!'

The boy was standing stock still, staring at the terrible beauty of the apparitions before him.

Ace dived for his legs and brought him down. He seemed to snap out of his trance and hugged her to him.

'Come on! Come on!' Ace cried, dragging him to his feet. She looked around the room. Ethereal energy lapped at the walls, rising towards the ceiling like liquid fire.

Robin spotted the stairway to the tower and pointed. 'There!'

They ducked and weaved through the columns of light. Like running through a forest fire, thought Ace, grabbing Robin's hand as he stumbled.

She pushed him into the well of the staircase and his knees connected with the steps. He howled in pain but didn't stop, dragging himself upwards. Ace cast an anxious look behind. The room was humming with light, spindly fronds crackling their way towards them.

Ace pushed at Robin's backside and he clambered up the steps, using his hands for purchase on the cold stone. They seemed to go around and around endlessly.

After several exhausting minutes, they emerged on to a narrow landing which led to a long, long corridor. From behind one of the doors came the sound of prayer.

'Shh!' hissed Ace. They listened intently. The voice was cracked, defeated, mumbling the prayers in a hopeless dirge.

'It's the Abbot,' said Ace. Robin looked back the way they had come. The dark walls were already brightening.

'It's coming after us!' he cried. Ace grabbed his collar and they clattered up the next flight of steps.

'I know we shouldn't keep going up,' she gasped, her lungs bursting. 'In movies, if people go up buildings you know they're going to fall off sooner or later!'

'No choice,' called Robin over his shoulder, feeling dizzy as he ran round and round the never-ending spiral.

Behind them, the tide of light reached the landing, throbbing with power. It paused as though listening, fronds of buzzing energy retracting a little. The Abbot stopped praying.

Medway wondered whether he had a lunatic in the car. He'd listened with patience to Trevithick's story and accepted the reality of the missing persons and the landlady's death. Now the old man had insisted they drive to the radio telescope to find someone called 'the Doctor'.

'It's not that I don't believe you, sir,' he said, turning the car on to the moor road once again. 'It's just a little hard to take in.'

'I know, I know,' said Trevithick, biting his finger nails. 'But there's more.'

'More?' Medway raised his eyebrows. The old man looked out of the car window into the night. The headlights lit up dark bushes and indiscernible structures. 'I told you I was attacked and that the ... thing which attacked me was frightened off by Mr Yeadon's car.'

Medway nodded slowly. Trevithick took a deep breath. 'Mr Medway. It was a monster. Seven feet tall. Like a great insect.'

Medway opened his mouth but Trevithick pressed on. 'You came here to see me about *Nightshade*. Well, I can tell you for certain that the creature, that real creature, was the same thing which I used to fight on television!'

Medway didn't say anything. Trevithick rubbed his eyes. 'Not a man in a rubber suit. Not this time. A real thing. Trying to kill me. That's what I saw under the lamp last night and that's what smashed my window. They've come back to get me!'

'Right,' said Medway.

'Oh, I know you don't believe me. But it's true! I swear it! Look!'

He showed Medway the tear in his jacket and waistcoat where the creature's mandible had struck him.

Medway was grateful for the distraction of arrival. The security gate was wide open, just as the Doctor had left it, and the telescope dish plunged into darkness.

'We're here,' said Medway quietly.

Hawthorne sat on his bed, hugging his knees to his chin.

Bastards.

Who did they think they were?

Well, he'd soon sort them out. One phone call to Cambridge and he'd have the pair of them off the project.

He sighed. That was if the bloody phones ever started working again.

Anyway, his superiors were bound to recognize the truth of his statements. It was all well and good paying lip service to these fashionable ideas on racial harmony but it obviously didn't work in practice. He could show them that. Vijay Degun had admitted to taking illegal substances, had risked the entire project!

Hawthorne was disappointed in Cooper. He'd expected more. Didn't she realize where it would all lead? Powell was right. 'Rivers of blood,' he'd promised. Rivers of blood.

What was he doing skulking in his room? Who were they to tell him how to behave? They weren't his teachers. They weren't his mother.

Hawthorne wished she were here now so he could bury his head into the secure, perfumed folds of her dress. Perhaps she would read him a bedtime story. He stiffened. No. Not that. Not...now.

He could hear the frantic activity in the control room but didn't move from his bed. If they were so clever, they could manage without him. Couldn't they?

Medway and Trevithick opened the control room doors on to a scene of pandemonium. Cooper, Vijay and Holly were running about the place, trying desperately to fathom the explosion of data. The Doctor stood alone in the centre of everything, his eyes dark and fathomless.

'It's so strong!' cried Cooper.

'Doctor!' Trevithick called above the din.

'We've got to use the safety cutouts!' Vijay shouted. 'It's too big this time!'

Cooper nodded. 'See what you can do.'

Holly threw herself into a chair and began to hammer figures into a console. She frowned. 'It's no good. I can't stop it!'

'Doctor!' Trevithick advanced across the room and shook the Doctor's arm. 'I have things to tell you.'

Medway jumped as a hideous wail began to assail his ears.

'Klaxon?' said Cooper.

'Fence breached again.' Holly looked up from her work.

The Doctor glanced at Trevithick. 'Not now, not now.' He ran to the window and peered out into the darkness. Light was pouring from the silhouetted monastery.

Cooper pulled on a parka. 'I'm going to check the fence. Won't be five minutes.'

'No!' cried Holly. 'It's not safe.'

'Be careful,' said Vijay.

Cooper threw a glance at the bewildered Trevithick and Medway, and then disappeared through the doors.

'There's something happening at the monastery!' cried the Doctor, covering his ears as the klaxon honked deafeningly.

Then the lights went out.

Hawthorne lay back on his bed, chuckling to himself. He could

144

hear the klaxon wailing now. They *had* got themselves into a pickle.

Well, crisis or no crisis, he wasn't going to offer any advice. First thing in the morning he would take the Land Rover, drive to York and get the first train out of this rancid county. Then he would deliver his official letter of complaint and...

He turned over and pushed his hands under the pillow then jumped up in shock. There was a pool of sticky black liquid spreading across the sheet.

Surprised, he lifted his coated fingers to his face and sniffed. What was it? Pitch? Bitumen? No, it was... it was...

Tar

Hawthorne's spine froze. For several long minutes he was quite unable to move. The harsh, unshaded light above his head flickered, brightened and died.

He listened to the sound of his own stertorous breathing and then swung his legs over the side of the bed.

He would get up. Run to the door. Down the corridor. To the control room. Everything would be all right. Everything...

Strangely, he wasn't at all surprised when the tacky black paw grasped his ankle.

Winstanley didn't move. There had been a voice in his head. No words. Just a voice. A presence. Answering his prayers. He glanced around his cell quickly. A corona of light sparkled round the door.

With his heart in his mouth, he put a pudgy hand on the door and slowly opened it. He yelped in shock at the wall of energy which filled the corridor like sheet-lightning.

It was beautiful. Beautiful...

Backing into the room, he stumbled against a chair and fell to his knees.

Yes, that was only right. On your knees, he thought. He had doubted. His faith had been weak but now, oh now, his prayers had been answered. Winstanley prostrated himself before the light. Slowly, scarcely daring to breathe, he opened his eyes.

The energy before him had begun to assume a shape, pixels of delicate light swirling and swirling until a man stood before him, robed arms outstretched. The face was pale, bearded, ascetic. Light shivered over the shoulder-length hair.

'Oh my Christ!' sobbed Winstanley, reaching out trembling hands. 'Oh, Christ! Christ!'

He stumbled forwards on his knees. The man's face was kindly, the brown eyes warm and forgiving. He extended a hand: a long, finely boned hand in which a ragged hole had been torn. Blood oozed from the wound.

Winstanley took the man's hand and pressed it to his face.

'Blessed blood,' he wept. 'Sweet Jesus, forgive me.'

His eyes flicked upwards, catching a tiny change in the man's face. The brows drew together, eyes narrowing. The kindly smile creased into a mocking grin.

Winstanley felt the stigmatic hand close around his face, the bones of his jaw crumbling like powder. Then there was nothing but a searing pain: pain like a billion needles ripping through his mind as the apparition surged down his throat.

Winstanley's smile, so long forced and unreal, widened impossibly as energy roared into him. Then his broad head imploded with a vile clatter.

'You are forgiven,' chuckled the apparition as it closed around the Abbot's lifeless body.

8

Trevithick slid to the floor, his eyes darting to and fro as he willed them to become accustomed to the darkness. He could make out only indistinct shapes illuminated by the glow of the monastery. Something bobbed into view by him and he gasped, startled.

'Are you all right, sir?' It was Medway.

Trevithick nodded and then realized he'd have to vocalize his assent. 'Yes. Yes, thank you.'

Around them, the machinery was once again winding down. Vijay stumbled across the room and found Holly. He pressed his cheek to hers and called, 'Doctor?'

The Doctor moved to stand by the window, his figure silhouetted against the glow of the monastery like that of a child watching a bonfire.

'Please excuse me,' he said quietly. 'I must return to the monastery. Ace may need me.'

He dashed across the room without knocking over a single stick of furniture.

'I'll be back,' he called over his shoulder. 'Try and stay together. Things are getting serious.'

The double doors clattered and he was gone.

Holly jumped as Medway flicked the flint of his lighter, his face looming into view close by. 'I suggest we find some illumination,' he said, standing up.

'There are some candles in my room,' said Vijay.

'No,' said Holly quickly. 'I don't want you to go back there.'

'It's all right. I'll be careful.' He laid a hand on her arm. 'Listen out for Cooper. I don't like the thought of her on her own out there.'

Medway swore as the flame scorched his thumb. 'I'll come with you.'

'What about Hawthorne?' cried Holly. 'I'd forgotten all about him.'

'He can do what he likes just as long as he stays out of my way.' Vijay's voice was strained and angry.

Medway flicked the lighter again and they set off into the interior.

Trevithick stumbled towards Holly. 'Hello, my dear. I'm Edmund.'

'Holly. Hi.' She looked about in the darkness, evidently unnerved.

'Reminds me of the War,' said Trevithick, struggling to make conversation. Holly smiled and nodded.

'Perhaps,' began Trevithick, 'perhaps you'd like to fill me in on what's been going on here?'

Holly shrugged. 'I don't know. Strange things. It's like a dream . . .' There was a shriek from somewhere in the corridor. Holly stiffened. 'Vijay?' she shouted.

Trevithick backed against the console as running footsteps echoed around the room.

'Wait!' It was Vijay's voice. Holly sighed with relief. Two candle flames bobbed across the room like will o' the wisp. Dark figures flashed by. Trevithick frowned in confusion.

Vijay tripped over Holly. 'Wait!' he called. She grasped his hand. 'What is it?'

The double doors opened again and Medway ran through into the night.

'We found Hawthorne. In his room,' whispered Vijay.

'Dead?' said Trevithick.

'Yes. All rotten. Decayed.'

Trevithick sighed. 'Just like Mrs Yeadon.'

Vijay looked at the old man's candle-lit features. 'Mrs Yeadon too? God help us . . .'

They could hear Medway's car stuttering into life and reversing out of the compound.

'Well, that's my interview gone for a burton,' said Trevithick.

Medway spun the wheel, prickles of sweat shimmering over his back and shoulders. He was breathing hard, panic coursing through him.

They had pushed open the door of Hawthorne's room on their way back from getting the candles. He was lying on the bed with his back to them and the Asian bloke had shaken his shoulder to wake him. But Hawthorne wasn't asleep. He was withered and dry like an unwrapped mummy. And the strench...

Medway shivered, did a three-point turn and careered on to the moor road. He was getting out.

The tower was dark and silent. For some time, Ace had been aware of a deep, resonant throbbing sound from the monastery below but now that, and the accompanying light, seemed to have subsided.

They had staggered up the final flight of spiral stairs and emerged through a trap door into a long, empty room, its corners sheathed in dusty shadow. A solitary window was blank and open on to the night outside.

In a voice cracked by emotion Robin had told Ace about his stepmother. She'd pulled him close to her, letting hot, salty tears flood over her shoulder. Unable to think of the adequate words, she had simply kissed him, feeling him relax into her arms. Desire swept over her and she ran her hand through his hair, pressing her lips to his quaking face. He tasted like sugar.

Robin pulled away, adding little kisses to her cheeks and neck, breathing haltingly as his sobs died away.

'Thanks,' he said.

Ace smiled and stroked his forehead. 'No problem.'

She held him for several blissful minutes.

'Dorothy?'

She tensed, then laughed. 'The Doctor told you?'

Robin nodded, shifting to lay his head in her lap. He gazed up at her face, side-lit by the frosty blue night outside.

'Hello.'

She looked down at him and brushed the fringe from his eyes. 'Hello.'

There was a gentle bleep from Ace's watch. She touched the mechanism with her finger and silenced it.

'What's that?' said Robin, his brow creasing.

Ace shrugged. 'Some alarm call I forgot about.'

'You have an alarm on your watch?'

'Yeah.'

'Where did you get it?'

'Camden Market.'

Robin frowned again. 'What was it you said earlier on? When the Stones were on?'

Ace felt a little uneasy. 'Nothing. I didn't mean . . .'

'You said "You should see him now". What did you mean?' He smiled, no malice intended.

'I'm not from round here,' was all she managed to say.

'I gathered that much. Who is the Doctor anyway? Your dad?'

She laughed, a funny, snuffly laugh. 'Oh, that's a good one. He's worse than a dad sometimes. But mostly he's just my friend.'

Robin rested his head on one hand and looked thoughtfully into the corner. 'Ace, whatever's going on here, you seem . . . you seem to know more about it.' He shook his head hastily. 'No, I don't mean that. You just seem to take it all in your stride. Like you've seen it before.'

Ace sighed, wondering whether to make a clean breast of things there and then. She thought of something the Doctor had said and whispered, with as much gravitas as she could muster, 'I've seen some things in my time.'

'That's what the Doctor said.'

They both laughed.

The Doctor was halfway to the monastery when the illumination faded, the light bleeding from the monastery windows falling back like a retreating tide. There was a disquieting silence and then the low moan of the wind returned.

The looming monastery tower was now indistinguishable in the dark night.

The Doctor stopped and stared at the building, his breath shimmering in clouds. Gradually, he became aware of the sound of running feet slip-slapping across the moor. He peered into the night and made out Jill Mason, haring across the blasted landscape with mud belching underfoot. She ran straight into him and the Doctor held her arms firmly.

'Doctor!' she cried. 'Oh God, Doctor. They're all dead!'

The Doctor's face froze. 'Who? Who's dead?'

Jill bit her lip, her voice broken into hiccough-like sobs. 'My old folks. My responsibility...' she wailed.

'And Ace?'

'What?'

'My friend, Ace...'

'Oh, I don't — I don't know. She was OK. I don't know! The place is full of ghosts!'

The Doctor thought for a moment and then took Jill's hand kindly. 'Go back to the village and find that policeman friend of yours. Get as many people as you can and stay together. Somewhere safe. Everyone is at risk! Do you understand?'

Jill looked dazedly at him.

'Do you understand?' The Doctor shook her violently.

She nodded repeatedly and put an unsteady hand to her forehead.

'Very well,' said the Doctor determinedly. 'I'd better get up there.'

He strode off into the night.

'Good luck,' Jill called, her voice scarcely a whisper.

The Doctor didn't look back.

Vijay was sitting, eyes closed, in a ring of candles. He reminded himself of the icons and embroidered pictures his mother used to dot around the house back in Pakistan: angular, mystical faces full of wisdom and heavenly virtue. But there was no such atmosphere of stillness now.

Trevithick sat in a swivel chair, twiddling his thumbs anxiously. Holly stood by herself at the window, chewing her fingernails down to the quick. Vijay realized she would need some time to get over the shock of seeing James, or whatever it was that had appeared in her room. She was shuddering involuntarily, her eyes twitching as though pained.

Vijay rose from his position on the floor and stepped over the sputtering candles. He put out his arm to hold Holly, withdrew it uncertainly and then tried again. She shrugged him off at once.

'No.'

He sighed. 'Come on, Hol. You've got me.'

She looked at him unsteadily, her eyes flicking about. Vijay touched her cheek. 'I don't want you to suffer this on your own. There's no need.'

Holly frowned. 'I'm sorry. I just can't.'

Vijay let his hands fall to his sides, helpless. He wandered out of the control room to the coffee machine which was still, miraculously, functioning. Then he fumbled through the darkness to Trevithick, holding two plastic cups in his hands.

The old man yawned and stretched, peering about as Vijay approached.

'Ah, tea. Smashing.'

'Coffee, I'm afraid. All we've got.'

Trevithick took the cup gratefully. 'Never mind. I love coffee, I love tea, I love the java jive and it loves me, eh?'

Vijay smiled indulgently. 'You're Edmund Trevithick, aren't you? I heard you were in the village. Always meant to come down and see you. Big hero of mine, you were.'

Trevithick shrugged. 'Yes, it's been lovely having all this attention again, I can tell you.'

Vijay took a swig of his coffee. 'I remember all the kids at school used to want to be the monsters. But I wanted to be Professor Nightshade. I suppose it got me started on physics in a way. All that rocket stuff.'

Trevithick chuckled. 'Well, I'm very honoured.'

He gulped down his coffee in one go. It was black and bitter. 'Funny that life seems to be stranger than fiction now,' he continued. 'I gather you've had some experiences up here?'

Vijay nodded, stooping to relume a candle which had blown out. He briefly outlined Ace's discovery of the dead security guard and Holly's experience in his room. 'And you too?'

'Oh yes. Things I would never've believed possible. Those monsters you mentioned, for instance.'

'Monsters? What? From *Nightshade* you mean?'

Trevithick nodded heavily. 'I saw one. It attacked me. Really. A bloody monster.'

Vijay's mouth set in a grim line. 'I saw . . . a ghost, I suppose. That's all I can call it. It was as real as you are. It even threw me against the wall. And there was this stuff, like ectoplasm, condensing all over me.'

152

Trevithick put down his cup suddenly. 'Your young lady's late fiancé, you say?'

'Yes.'

'That's interesting.'

Vijay put his head on one hand. 'What is?'

'Miss Kidd saw her dead friend. I saw the creature from my old series. Mrs Yeadon believed that the ghost of her late brother appeared to her.'

Vijay's lip turned down in a grimace of puzzlement. Trevithick's eyes lit up. 'Well, don't you see? They're all elements from our past. Our memories. Things we probably haven't thought about in years, come alive!'

Vijay folded his arms. 'But what's behind it?'

He frowned and then glanced over at the dead consoles. 'We're being bombarded by data from space, maybe...'

'Invaders from Mars, eh? Well, that's your province, not mine. At least, in the real world.'

Trevithick hooked his thumbs into the pockets of his waistcoat. 'I need a drink. A proper one, I mean.'

Vijay looked across at Holly. 'I wish the Doctor would come back. He seems to know more than he's saying.'

'He knows more than we do, that's for sure,' muttered Trevithick.

Vijay sighed. 'I just wish my mind wasn't so closed. I mean, we're here to monitor radio signals from space. Why should I be surprised if something ... something intelligent has turned up?'

There was a gentle whirring sound as one of the consoles flashed back to life. Holly was by it in an instant, her fingers tapping away at the keyboard. Vijay dashed across the room, knocking down a couple of candles.

'What is it?'

Holly scanned the screen. 'Power's coming back. Slowly. There's the same data from the Bellatrix nova. And something else. A sort of ... pulse. Steady pulse in the background. Like interference. But with a pattern.'

'Getting stronger,' stated Vijay, flatly.

Medway changed gear and slammed his foot on the accelerator.

The car had spent several agonizing minutes stuck in the marshy ground by the station's security fence before he'd persuaded it on to the road.

Ahead, the monastery seemed to burn like a Roman candle, but, when he looked again, the old building was invisible against the night sky.

He was getting out. Away from this strange place with its missing persons and stinking corpses. Back to London and safety, somewhere he knew well, where there were people to love him. No, even better, he would go home. Home for Christmas, just as he had been promising himself all these years.

Home.

He would make the tea tomorrow morning. Hold his parents tight and tell them how much he loved them.

Home.

Medway's stomach lurched as if he'd been punched, a wave of dizziness flooding through him. There was a dull, thumping ache at the back of his neck. Sickly pain shot across his temples and over his eyes. He took one hand off the wheel and rubbed his forehead which was prickled with icy sweat. His stomach heaved involuntarily and vomit trickled down his chin.

The car jerked as he took his foot off the accelerator. He couldn't stop now. He had to get out. Had to.

Then there was a wild, appalling sickness spinning through him and he cried out, almost losing control of the car as his hands twitched and shook. The road ahead was a dark black ribbon, shifting and blurring as he fought to keep a grip on his senses.

Suddenly there was someone in his headlights, looming into view like a spotlit statue, her hands flying to her mouth as she screamed and threw herself off the road.

Medway spun the wheel to avoid her but the road ahead had vanished in a mist of pain and nausea. There was just the moor now, somersaulting into his mind's eye as the car rolled and rolled.

Medway's last thoughts were of the old tinselly Christmas tree, now dazzlingly bright and beautiful. Then he screamed and rammed his head under the dashboard as the car erupted in flame.

154

Jill Mason ducked down as the explosion lit up the night, chunks of red-hot metal whooshing across the moor. She stood up, her legs almost buckling with exhaustion and fear, as the skeleton of Medway's car burned before her.

'Bloody hell!' Robin pulled Ace to the tower window and both their faces flashed orange as the car exploded out on the moor.

'We'd better try and find the Doctor,' said Ace, turning back. 'We're no use to anyone stuck up here.'

'No!' barked Robin. Ace looked at him.

'No,' he said more softly, 'I don't want you to. We still don't know what's down there, do we? Let's stay where we're safe, at least till it's light.'

Ace checked her watch. It was close to five in the morning. 'Yeah. I suppose you're right.' She looked at him steadily. 'I'm really sorry about your mum.'

Robin nodded. 'I was too old to think of her as my mother. Never really got to know her, I suppose. But we were good friends. I can't believe she's gone, I just can't.'

'Maybe that's good,' said Ace quietly.

'What d'you mean?'

'Maybe it's good that you can't take it in. You've got to keep your wits about you. I think the best thing you can do for her is to stay alive.' Ace took his hand and pulled him to her. They kissed again.

'Tell me about the Doctor,' said Robin at last, stroking her hair from her eyes with his delicate fingers.

Ace shrugged. 'We travel together. He's a sort of . . . guru for me, I suppose.'

Robin laughed. 'You're not into all that hippy shit, are you?'

'No!' Ace grinned. 'The Doctor's . . .' She thought of a word she'd found in a little yellow-backed novel in one of the TARDIS's less dusty rooms. 'The Doctor's . . . my mentor. He teaches me things, shows me places. Helps me to grow up.'

'You don't seem like you need much help.'

'Oh, I did. Still do, I suppose. Sometimes I feel like he manipulates me. But it usually turns out for the best. Usually.'

'Cruel to be kind, eh?'

Ace nodded. 'Something like that.'

She stared into the darkness and smiled. 'He's shown me so many things, so much beauty . . .' Ace looked at Robin, suddenly embarrassed. 'Stuff like that.'

Robin could sense she was troubled. 'But?'

'I'd do anything for him,' said Ace. 'But now . . . now he's talking about jacking it all in.'

Robin squeezed her hand. 'All good things come to an end.'

Ace ruffled his hair. 'You're full of those clichés, aren't you?'

They laughed again, eyes shining.

Perhaps she would tell him everything soon. Tell him of the wonders and the horrors she'd seen. And who she and the Doctor really were. Perhaps . . .

The floorboards creaked loudly and Ace jumped in shock. She peered into the dusty corners.

'There's somebody there!'

'Can't be.' Robin began to advance towards the trap door.

'There is!' Ace grabbed his arm. 'Listen!'

A heavy silence followed and then they heard the same creaking of boards followed by a deep moan.

'What the hell is it?' Robin whispered from between clenched teeth.

Ace shook her head. Something small and dark scuttled into view, starlight from the window picking out its bent contours.

Billy Coote walked slowly towards them, his arms stiff and his hair swept back from his head like a halo.

Ace gasped. 'Look at his eyes!'

The old man's black orbs jerked and twitched in their sockets. A voice, deep and rumbling, rose from the depths of his chest.

'I can see it! I can see it!'

Then, more powerfully, the timbre becoming almost musical: 'I can *see* it!'

Trevithick, Vijay and Holly shot to their feet. For an instant, the sky was like an upturned crucible, fire leaving a starburst after image on their eyes.

Holly gasped and jumped back from the window, shielding her eyes.

'Mr Medway, I presume,' said Trevithick hollowly, clasping his hands behind his back.

Vijay pulled a parka off the back of his chair. 'I'm going to find Cooper.'

He expected Holly to react, to ask him to stay with her as she had done before, but she just slid to the floor, gently rocking herself. Vijay didn't really want to go outside at all.

Trevithick came to his rescue. 'Are you sure about this, young fella? We don't want to risk any more of us, do we? It's rather like those Hammer horrors I used to do where people get bumped off one by one. You always end up saying "Why do they go off on their own? It's so obvious!" Maybe we should stick together.'

Vijay gave a relieved sigh. 'Well, if you think...'

Shattering cracks echoed through the room as the main window imploded. Vijay and Trevithick threw themselves to the floor as shards of glass streaked through the air. The floor was suddenly thick with glittering particles. Vijay crunched towards Holly and pulled at her shoulders. 'Hol! Come on, back this way. Come on!' He jerked her round but she continued to stare at the gaping window which opened like a burst eye on to the terrifying sight beyond.

Standing in a staggered line, their black carapaces glinting in the moonlight, were half a dozen of Trevithick's monsters.

Holly felt her skin crawl as one cocked its huge head and glared at her with compound eyes, liquorice-black mucus spilling from its mouth.

One, a good foot taller than the rest, jerked its muscle-bunched legs forward, crushing glass beneath its feet. It reared up on its legs, mandibles clicking, and the others followed suit as though obeying a silent command.

Gradually, very gradually, the soft rustling sound whispered into the air, rising in volume like the sound of an expectant crowd.

'You see!' cried Trevithick. 'It's them! Remember!'

Vijay's gaze was forced away from them for a moment as more consoles blinked back to life. He grabbed Holly's hand but she resisted, pressing her feet against the floor tiles. Vijay gritted his teeth and picked her up bodily.

'Mr Trevithick. Into the interior. Quick!'

The row of insectoid creatures sprang through the window,

157

gutteral screeches escaping their jaws.

Trevithick yelped in fright and pelted across the room towards the interior door. The creatures' huge, glistening bodies flashed green, then white in the glare of the consoles as they careered across the room.

Vijay hauled Holly through the door and pulled Trevithick by the hand till he too was through.

'Chairs! Anything! Quickly!' Vijay shrieked as he slammed the door on the creatures. A mandible caught in the jamb and there was a terrifying howl as it shattered into a bloody stump.

Lungs bursting, Holly and Trevithick reached the TV room in thirty seconds flat, and dragged three chairs and a table back down the corridor. Vijay slammed the table under the door knob as the woodwork began to splinter. A mass of spindly mandibles erupted through the frame. Trevithick hurled the wooden chairs at them.

'It's no good,' cried Holly.

'Listen,' said Vijay, grasping Trevithick by the shoulders. 'This is a big place. Lose yourself. We'll have to split up. If you can get outside, you might stand a chance.'

'But surely . . .'

'There's no other way.'

The door shattered and three massive insectoid heads punched through. Without another word, Holly, Vijay and Trevithick turned and ran into the darkness of the corridor. The old man skidded as he reached a corner and held on to the wall for support, spluttering for breath. His chest felt tight and painful. He was too old for this. Far too old.

Holly and Vijay had gone in the general direction of their rooms. Trevithick glanced after them and headed right, catching sight of a lift at the end of a long corridor.

There was a tremendous clatter and disgusting twitter as the creatures burst through the door and flooded in. Trevithick threw himself down the corridor, banging into a fire extinguisher which thudded on to the floor. He stopped sharply and pounded his fists against his temples.

Think. Think.

A triumphant roar boomed down the corridor. Trevithick fell to his knees, hands clapping on the floor tiles, and scrambled about for the fire extinguisher. It would do as a weapon of sorts.

He cast a glance at the lift doors. If the power was off he was as good as dead. But some of the consoles had come back to life. There was just a chance ...

Trevithick strained his old eyes, cursing himself for leaving his spectacles, and just made out a tiny winking red light by the lift buttons. He sighed with relief and paddled his arms across the floor.

Got it.

He grasped the fire extinguisher and hugged it to his chest, then sprinted as best he could towards the lift and pressed the summons button. There was a distant clunk.

Couldn't be far up, he thought. Perhaps most of the complex was underground? Or perhaps — he felt his heart sinking — the lift ran all the way to the telescope dish?

He turned and felt sick as the creatures scrabbled around the corner like monstrous crane flies, their clawed limbs skittering against the walls and floor. Trevithick hammered on the lift doors.

'Come on! Come on!'

The taller creature crouched low and began to bound down the corridor towards him. Once it had just been a man in a rubber suit. Now it was real, a flesh-and-blood killer.

There was a gentle ping and the lift doors sprang open. Trevithick fell inside and stabbed desperately at the buttons. The doors began to slide closed with agonizing slowness. The creature slammed into them, its massive head beating at the metal and its mandibles thrashing in fury.

Trevithick crashed the extinguisher to the floor of the lift and aimed the nozzle at the beast. A torrent of spray erupted into its maw and it howled in protest, head cracking against the doors as it fought to clear its vision.

Trevithick pushed his finger on to the button again and the doors began closing once more. Still the creature fought on, hooking its claws around the creaking metal doors. Trevithick bit his lip and caught hold of its eye with shaking hands. It was cold to the touch. With a great cry of effort, he brought down the extinguisher on to the compound lens and beat at it repeatedly as the creature wailed and chittered in pain. Again and again he struck till the eye fractured and exploded, splattering his coat in colourless fluid.

With one final heave, he pushed the great head back into the corridor and the doors clanged shut. A beautiful humming silence met his ears and he slid to the floor. The lift went up.

Something bulky was pressing into his side and he grabbed at his jacket to remove the obstruction. With a sigh of disbelief, he pulled out his service revolver. Curse his useless memory! All this time attacking the thing with a fire extinguisher when he could've...

There was a dull thud below. The lift shook slightly but continued its flight upwards. Trevithick looked at the floor indicator. He had been on Level 8, it appeared, so there were seven floors below ground. The indicator went up to 27. Right the way up to the dish. He swallowed nervously, never having been good with heights. In his agitation he had pressed randomly. Level 15 was his destination, but that was bound to be beyond the creatures' reach, wasn't it?

At Level 15, the lift shook again. Trevithick frowned, got to his feet and waited for the doors to open. Nothing happened. He placed the flat of his hands against the cool metal and tried to push the doors apart.

With a terrifying screech, the lift floor buckled as the creature attempted to punch its way through. Trevithick gave a little whimper and thrust his fingernails between the doors. He had been so desperate to get in, now...

Please, please, please...

The creature must have forced its way through the exterior set of doors and clung to the bottom of the lift as it ascended. Trevithick felt his pulse hammering in his temple. He looked down at the floor which had cracked right across. A harpoonlike claw was thrashing through the hole, attempting to gain purchase on the floor.

It's going to get through. It's going to get through.

Trevithick gave up on the door and looked around the lift. There was a knee-high tubular astray in one corner. In the ceiling was the familiar escape door he'd seen in countless films. He'd even crawled through one in some cheap American picture his wife had persuaded him to do in order to pay for a new fridge.

But this was now, this was real. Could he even squeeze through the hole? And what would he do when he got there?

Trevithick jumped as the creature ripped through the floor. The bristly head lolled back mockingly. Trevithick gave it two bullets in its uninjured eye.

The creature bellowed in pain and fell back some way through the hole in the floor. Fist-sized lenses spattered against the walls.

Trevithick pulled at the ashtray which fell and spilled its contents. He picked it up and jammed it against the wall, pocketing his revolver and casting an anxious glance at the hole in the floor. The creature's claws were scrabbling about again, making a fresh attempt to pull it into the lift.

Trevithick tore at the expensive lining of his jacket until it ripped across, then stuffed the fire extinguisher inside. It was bulky and heavy but, once he was out of bullets, it was the only weapon he had.

Without another moment's hesitation, he climbed on to the wobbling ashtray and reached towards the ceiling hatch. He pushed with his fingertips but the hatch resisted. Why was nothing going right for him?

With a roar, the creature hauled itself over the lip of the hole and clawed at the carpet, dragging its disgusting body inside. This was all the incentive Trevithick required. He punched the hatch out and gazed through at chilly darkness.

The creature had one leg through now, sliding through the hole like a monstrous dragonfly sloughing off its old skin.

Trevithick managed to get his arms through the hatch up to the elbows and howled with effort as he tried to pull himself through. The ashtray below him shook unsteadily as the beast fell inside the lift. Trevithick was through up to his waist, his old arms seared by pain. Cold sweat flooded down his face.

The creature stood upright, uncurling its enormous body and chittering in triumph. Trevithick thanked God he was wearing his steel-toed boots, and kicked it savagely in both wounded eyes. It lashed out instantly, ripping through his trousers to his bare flesh underneath. Trevithick cried out in pain and kicked again, struggling to retain his fragile grip on the top of the lift.

The creature's maw dripped with fluid as it thrust its head towards Trevithick's legs. With a titanic effort he pulled himself right through the hatch, curled around, pulled out his revolver and pumped two more bullets into the creature.

Again it fell, spraying the lift walls with black blood. Trevithick looked about him desperately. The lift shaft was totally dark. His only choice was to attempt a climb up to the next level and somehow prise open the doors which led to safety. But, in his heart, he knew this was impossible. He hadn't the strength left and his plans failed to include one thing. The creature.

It was roaring and slamming at the ceiling hatch now, determined to break through and find him. Trevithick shivered, half through fear and half through cold. He glanced at his old revolver. Two bullets left.

Then a wild idea lit up his brain. He scrabbled about inside his jacket and pulled out the fire extinguisher. The creature was half blind now anyway. All he needed to do was complete the process and then ... It was too perfect! The extinguisher didn't spray foam; it was for electrical fires, obviously the main worry in a place like the tracking station. So it contained carbon dioxide. Compressed carbon dioxide!

Trevithick checked his gun again unnecessarily. Two bullets. He would need only one. He tore off his jacket and crouched by the hatch, holding his breath. The creature's head was through now, peering about in the gloom to locate him. Trevithick slid across the lift so he was behind it, holding his jacket in one hand and the extinguisher in the other. He said a silent prayer and then launched himself at the creature.

He delivered a kick to its eye and instantly sprayed its entire head with carbon dioxide, then cocooned the head with his jacket and flung himself and the creature back into the lift.

Trevithick's whole body screamed in pain but he wouldn't give up now. Whilst the creature thrashed about the confined space, utterly disorientated, he fired one more bullet into its head. It reeled and fell to the floor. Summoning all his strength, Trevithick fell to his knees and barged the creature through the hole it had ripped in the floor. Its claws clattered desperately for purchase. Trevithick looked at its knobbly back and at one hooked spine in particular. That would do very well, he thought.

Dodging to evade its razor-sharp claws, Trevithick hooked

the extinguisher on to the creature's back and then jumped on to the huge black head like a child on a trampoline, beating and beating till his boots sank into the brittle tissue. The creature screeched, twisting around in an effort to save itself. Trevithick gave one last kick and the thing slid through the hole into the shaft.

Immediately, it lashed one claw on to the cable and tried to haul itself back inside. Trevithick was prepared, however, and stabbed his finger decisively on to the Level 18 button. The lift began to ascend immediately, stranding the creature on the cable, its claws scraping and slipping on the metal.

Trevithick lay down by the hole and took out his revolver with careful deliberation. He gazed through the hole in the floor and watched the creature diminish in size.

At Level 18, the lift stopped and, to Trevithick's relief, the doors sprang open. Instantly, he slid the tubular ashtray on to the threshold to prevent the doors closing, then looked back down the hole.

The creature was struggling up the cable, the shiny extinguisher glinting on one of its hooked spines. He cocked his revolver and took aim.

The creature's head rolled back as it saw his face. It roared in fury and redoubled its efforts, wrapping its vicious claws around the cable.

Trevithick had been a crack shot during the War, had even won medals for it. But this shot had to count. Had to. He aimed for the extinguisher and pulled the trigger.

The bullet hit the compressed carbon dioxide and Trevithick was out of the lift in seconds, wrenching the ashtray away so the doors would shut.

The creature was instantly consumed by fire, guttural screams forcing their way through its dreadful gullet. It let go of the cable as flames tore through every fibre of its body, falling backwards and down, down into the shaft like a shooting star.

Trevithick watched the lift doors close and listened to the satisfying roar as the extinguisher exploded. He dragged himself to the wall and closed his eyes.

Did it. Did it.

He allowed himself a little smile.

It was almost dawn as the Doctor pulled open the doors of the monastery. The hinges had buckled and the wood itself seemed to have expanded against the stone frame.

The room beyond was unnaturally quiet, lit only by a couple of stubby candles. The smell hit the Doctor almost immediately and he thrust his coat sleeve across his face.

Over by the long-extinct fire, several indistinct shapes were huddled. The Doctor picked his way through the smashed furniture, steeling himself for what he knew he would find.

Three monks lay curled like embryos. The Doctor recognized them only by their scorched habits. All other features were ravaged and wasted, skeletal hands projecting from folds of grey material.

The Doctor looked across towards an old armchair in which a just-recognizable Mr Peel was sitting, his blotched, purple head thrust back against the antimacassar. The Doctor stepped over to the corpse and, almost without thinking, touched the bony head. It fell forward with a splintering crack, hit the floor and vanished like a mushroom spore in an explosion of dust.

The Doctor's gaze ranged around the room at the scores of lifeless figures, petrified in attitudes of horror like the residents of Pompeii.

'As if the life had been drawn out of them,' he muttered.

Without the fire, a creeping dampness had gripped the room. The Doctor wandered towards the cloister door, shivering in spite of himself.

'Ace?' he called, half-heartedly. Could she have escaped this carnage? Was she one of the unrecognizable corpses strewn about the room? 'Ace?'

The monastery had lost all the cheeriness of his earlier visits. Now it was a cold and lonely place. No wonder the Abbot had seemed so maudlin.

The Doctor looked down at the dusty flagstones, half-reminded of something. There was another smell in the air: a musty, neglected smell so common in old religious buildings.

There was a sudden, distinct plop as a rain drop fell to the floor. The Doctor gazed up at the darkened roof. Another drop fell and splashed coldly on his forehead.

Leaking roof.

All at once, he knew what it reminded him of. A forbidden place. A chamber with a secret door, the key to which he had once stolen. Such a long time ago...

There was a light scampering of feet in the darkness and the Doctor whirled round.

In the dim candle-glow, he could make out a small, dark-haired girl, though her face was lost in shadow.

His stomach turned as he recognized the neat grey pinafore with its red and gold embroidered badge.

'Grandfather?' said the girl, giggling. 'Where have you *been*?'

The Doctor's mouth went dry as dust. His shoulders fell and an exhausted gasp slipped from his lips.

'Susan!'

9

Christmas Day dawned with some uncertainty, the sun a pale circle of light against the white sky, like a neat hole punched in the clouds.

Freezing fog began to roll over the moor, drifting around the base of the monastery like smoke from an Arctic fire.

In the attic chamber, Ace and Robin were running out of options. Billy Coote stood above the trap door, gurgling softly. His skin was giving off a faint luminescence and his twitching, glazed black eyes were focused directly at them.

'We can't get past him,' cried Ace, looking around the room desperately. Her rucksack, with its precious load of climbing ropes, was propped against a wall, far too close to the advancing stranger for her to retrieve.

Robin popped his head through the stone arch of the window. Dawn light bled feebly inside.

He looked down at the moor. Too far to climb unaided. But the slate-covered roof of the tower was only a few feet above them.

'We can get to the roof with a bit of effort,' he said.

Ace nodded quickly. 'That's an idea. But we could wait till he moves away from the trap door and then try and get down the stairs.'

'Down the stairs to whatever was in the Hall? That's why we came up here, remember?'

Ace grinned. 'Oh yeah.' She shot another glance at her rucksack. 'If we can get...'

Billy Coote took a step towards them. His mouth clicked open, saliva dribbling over his lips. An anguished, chilling moan echoed throughout the room.

'Roof it is,' said Ace, quickly.

They clambered through the window and crouched on the

stone sill. Ace looked up. It was a climb of about five or six feet, over a section of ancient lead guttering and then on to the roof. She scanned the masonry with expert eyes. There were a couple of good handholds.

Billy Coote arched his back and emitted another deep moan.

'Come on, then,' cried Ace, reaching for the lintel.

The Doctor leant against a wall, his whole frame bent with emotion.

'Susan,' he said dully.

Yet it couldn't be. Couldn't be...

A tide of regret and grief overwhelmed him and he almost cried out.

'I've missed you so much, my dear,' he croaked, breath broken by sobs.

There was already a curious luminescence in Susan's dark hair. She turned her elfin face towards him and her eyes were full of forgiveness.

'You were always such an old worrier, Grandfather.'

The Doctor's mind raced, recalling all the precious times he'd spent with her. Then a dark strand of memory rose up in his consciousness and he saw again Dalek-ravaged London, Ian and Barbara, and Susan with the man she had grown to love.

'You had to leave me with David, Grandfather. It was what I wanted, after all,' she said, as though reading his thoughts.

He'd abandoned her on an alien world in an alien time, losing his last link with all that he could call home. Since then, there had been but one brief meeting, during the Borusa incident. No time to talk. No time to make up for all those lost years.

'One day, I shall come back,' he had said. But that day had never arrived. He had been too caught up in his own selfish concerns, his ceaseless journeying through the Vortex. What was he running away from anymore? Only himself.

Susan gave a little laugh, the light, lovely laugh he had always cherished. She had called him 'Grandfather', and in that simple phrase was bound up so much feeling, so much tenderness. Had he ever let anyone else get so close?

What was before him now was not Susan. He knew that. But seeing her there, just as he remembered her, was almost too much to bear. He could feel himself moving towards her.

'Susan,' he whispered.

She smiled, and in that moment, the Doctor caught a tiny flicker in her expression. The eyes seemed suddenly colder, harsher.

'No,' he said flatly.

Susan reared up, her body elongating like an uncoiled snake. For an instant, her smiling face remained. Then it fell away, leaving only a terrible darkness around which her hair whispered.

She held out her hands in an embrace and began to giggle, an awful, sick sound that made the Doctor's hair stand on end.

Susan's body was expanding now into trails of light, her mocking laughter echoing around the deserted hall.

The Doctor cried out in anguish and grief, looking around frantically for an exit. He spotted the well of the spiral stairs and bolted across the room, running for his life.

The fog from the moor poured down the empty streets of Crook Marsham, blanketing the peal of the distant bells of York Minster, six miles away. It was a rousing, jubilant sound, greeting the festive morning effusively.

Yet in the village no one stirred.

An icy wind whipped through the main street, setting the butcher's sign swinging.

Somewhere, there was a soft, soft rustling sound.

One man stirred, however, and the weak sunshine made Lawrence Yeadon squint as he turned up the collar of his overcoat and made his way towards The Shepherd's Cross.

He glanced around at the eerie emptiness, straining to hear any sign of life. With a heavy sigh, he pushed open the door of the pub and stepped inside.

The taproom was silent and deserted, discarded glasses and plates littering the tables. Lawrence walked listlessly around the room, his face drawn and haggard. He glanced at the tinsel which hung across the bar and shuddered as a sob caught in his throat.

Betty.

She was gone. The woman who had brought meaning to his

life. Gone.

It had been hell after the death of his first wife. He had struggled to bring up Robin as best he could. No one, Lawrence included, ever really expected him to get over it. But Betty's love had helped him, healed the wounds, restored the joy to his existence.

He could see her now, just as she had been that summer's afternoon in York, the sun beating down on her hair, her laugh echoing through the hot, still streets.

Now she was gone. Claimed by some force he couldn't even begin to comprehend.

Lawrence slid into a chair. He had to pull himself together.

George Lowcock had called at Mrs Bass's place late the previous night, talking about Jill Mason having some terrible fright over at the monastery and how important it was to get everyone together for their own safety.

Lawrence had suggested the church and said he'd meet them all there at eight on Christmas morning. He checked his watch. Nearly time.

First, though, he had needed to see the pub again, needed to put himself in touch with Betty by seeing the things she'd seen.

He got to his feet and forced himself up the stairs. The police had taken away what was left of her and the bedroom door had been nailed shut.

Lawrence paused by the door and pressed his cheek against the panels, sobbing.

He checked his watch again through tear-misted eyes.

Get a grip.

He would talk to George. Everything would be fine. Everything could be explained. Then he had to find Robin. Say sorry. Make sure he was safe.

Lawrence turned from the door. There was a sudden, sharp noise like scratching. He froze.

It came again. An insistent scraping like a dog demanding to be let outside.

Lawrence looked down at the door. It was shaking slightly.

'Lol?'

His name. Stated in a dry, dead whisper.

'*Lol?*'

He bent down and stared at the door. Something was pawing at the broken lower panels, pleading to be released.

Quaking with fear, Lawrence put an eye to the splintered wood and peered through into the room.

He caught his breath. Then a laugh resounded through his mind. A hearty musical laugh he'd first heard on a faraway summer's day . . .

Vijay opened exhausted eyes, lifted his head experimentally and found his neck to be stiff and painful. Holly lay asleep next to him, a few filthy blankets thrown over her.

They had hidden themselves in the security guard's hut after a petrified dash through the station. Luckily for them, but unluckily for Trevithick, the creatures seemed intent on pursuing the old man, racing after him into the interior of the building.

Holly had been keen to make for the village but Vijay thought this might expose them to still more danger. Better to hide till they could get their bearings.

Sometime during the night, there had been a tremendous, muffled explosion from somewhere inside the station and Vijay had uttered a silent prayer for Trevithick. If the old man had gone down, he would certainly have been fighting to the end.

Holly had slept better than Vijay and this troubled him. It was as if she had found an easy escape route from her troubles, blocking out the horrors by refusing to accept them.

Vijay stood up stiffly, carefully resting Holly's head on his discarded blanket, and tiptoed through the piles of rusted junk towards the door.

Daggers of icy wind slipped under the door. He opened it and grimaced as the harsh white daylight dazzled his eyes. He could scarcely see the moor which stretched out before him. Dense fog and heavy clouds had blended together, forming a freezing envelope around the station.

Then he noticed the fence and dashed outside, slamming the door without thinking.

The perimeter fence, whose impregnability had so impressed Dr Hawthorne, lay broken and smashed. It was how Vijay imagined a prison camp to look after a mass breakout. The steel mesh was beaten down and each post was missing or broken off like a cemetery pillar.

Vijay spun around, the telescope dish looming overhead, and took in the devastation. Something extraordinary had happened during the night.

Holly appeared, rubbing her face. She seemed a little brighter, kissing her lover full on the lips and hugging him close. She saw the fence over his shoulder and gasped.

'Think it was those things?'

Vijay shrugged. 'Can't have just been them, the whole fence is down.' He peered across at one of the posts. 'Hang on.'

Holly pulled her blanket tightly around her as Vijay wandered over to the fence. She watched him feel about in the heather for a moment then look around himself again. 'Holly!' he called.

She wandered towards him, stepping over the remains of the fence.

'The ground's uneven,' said Vijay, wonderingly.

'Subsidence?'

'Must be. The fence hasn't been knocked down, the ground itself has been disrupted.' He squatted on his haunches and indicated the heather. 'And look at this.'

Holly bent down. 'It's scorched.'

Vijay nodded and swung his arm around in an arc. 'All the way round, I reckon.'

Holly frowned. 'Like a giant fairy ring.'

An icy gust ruffled her hair. 'What about Mr Trevithick . . . and Cooper?'

Vijay sighed. 'Maybe they got away.'

Holly hung her head despondently.

Vijay stood up. 'We'll drive into the village. They must have some idea what's going on by now. Maybe we can do something.'

'I think we should find the Doctor.'

'Yeah. So do I. But let's get away from here first, eh?' Vijay hooked his arm around her and held her chin in his other hand. 'I love you, you know.'

She smiled sweetly, squeezed his hand and set off for the Land Rover.

Vijay pulled open the door and leant across to open the

passenger side. He stiffened as a low groan murmured through the air. Holly looked at him through the windscreen and shrugged. Vijay got out of the Land Rover.

The groan came again, stronger this time. Vijay pushed Holly away from the truck and pricked up his ears. It was coming from underneath the vehicle. Gingerly, he squatted down and blinked into the shadows.

'Christ! Holly! Give me a hand!'

He thrust his arm under the chassis and pulled at the prostrate figure lying there. The grizzled hair was matted with blood and the fierce blue eyes flickered weakly.

'Dr Cooper!' cried Holly delightedly, shunting her colleague into a sitting position against the wheel.

Cooper lifted an eyelid. 'Holly?' She inclined her head. 'Vijay?' A sigh bubbled from her lips. 'Thank God.'

'We thought you were dead,' said Vijay.

Cooper coughed. 'Should be, by rights. Those beasties...' She shook her head disbelievingly. 'One caught me across the forehead but I managed to get under here. Must've passed out.'

Holly hugged the older woman. Cooper patted her back affectionately.

Vijay stood up suddenly, his keen gaze fixing on something. He wandered away towards the fence.

'Hawthorne?' croaked Cooper weakly. Holly shook her head. 'The old man too, probably. The Doctor went off to the monastery.'

Cooper nodded, her eyes closing.

'Holly?' Vijay's voice cut through the moan of the wind.

'Will you be OK a moment?' asked Holly urgently. Cooper nodded, fingering the wound on her forehead with some distaste.

'Holly!'

Vijay was walking up and down in agitation just beyond the edge of the fallen fence. Holly ran over to him, the question on her lips answered by the sight of the great, tumulus-like mound of earth heaped before her.

The subsidence had opened a gash in the moor some thirty feet across. The soil yawned above a crooked cave mouth, with broken stones and clods of earth littering the entrance. The ring of scorched heather extended right around it.

'What did the Doctor say this place was built on?' said Vijay, knowing the answer. Holly nodded excitedly.

Vijay turned back to the pitch-black chasm. 'I think we've just found his palaeolithic quarry.'

The stones of Crook Marsham's little church had echoed to the sound of Christmas Day worship for almost nine hundred years. Rows of creaking pews gave on to an aisle so worn down that it formed a channel rather than a straight path, making the whole interior resemble a heavily rigged ship, the towering pulpit looking like some ecclesiastical fo'c's'le.

Attendance had dwindled to such an extent that the church had been closed for all but the most special occasions. Those villagers still devoted enough took the bus over to York. George Lowcock, however, kept the keys in the bottom drawer of his desk and that Christmas morning, he opened the ancient doors to convene his meeting.

Now the dingy interior was crammed with villagers. Lowcock had done his rounds late on Christmas Eve, telling everyone to be in the church for eight the next morning as there was a bit of a flap on. He was shocked to discover how few people answered his knock. It was almost as though they had all gone away.

Mr Bayles, Crook Marsham's butcher for thirty years, seemed to have upped and left, fresh turkeys abandoned on his counter. Old Mr Pemberton at the post office, who had never been more than thirty miles from the village in his life, had similarly vanished.

It was only when Lowcock called on Win Prudhoe that his suspicions became a sick certainty. These people hadn't left Crook Marsham. They had been taken, consumed, just like the others they had found.

He'd knocked lightly on the door and pushed it slowly open until it banged against the umbrella stand. There was a burnt smell in the air and clouds of what appeared to be steam hanging low under the rafters.

Gingerly, with heart pounding, Lowcock walked through the sitting room, looking about at dusty furniture and old photographs. There was one of Jack Prudhoe and old Andrew

Medcalfe, shoulder to shoulder on the day they had both gone off to war.

'Hello? Mrs Prudhoe?'

He knew, with a dread that made his head reel, that she was no longer alive. Easing open the kitchen door, he noticed at once that the kettle had boiled itself dry on the stove, little tongues of gas flame licking at its blackened underside. Then he glanced down at the bundle of rags in the corner and failed to stifle a scream.

'Mrs Prudhoe, then?' Jill asked him as he ushered the last of a depopulated village into the church.

Lowcock nodded heavily. 'Same as the others. Withered. Decomposed.' He slammed shut the church doors. 'You sit yourself down, love. You've done enough.'

'I'm all right,' said Jill determinedly, resenting his patronizing tone in spite of her experiences.

The confused residents of Crook Marsham, some fifty or sixty people, were conversing in low, frightened voices. Lowcock strode up the aisle and mounted the pulpit to make the most difficult speech of his life.

The Doctor was running blind, the curved walls of the tower blurring past him. He forced himself to concentrate on the steps under his shoes, stone by stone, as he rose ever higher. The Abbot's landing appeared and then was gone.

Stone by stone. Stone by stone.

Up and up he ran, his legs wracked with pain and his mind reeling, a succession of confusing images glittering before his eyes.

Susan.

Susan but ... not Susan. Why did it have to be her? As if the thing were focusing in on his darkest thoughts, exacerbating the very feelings which had brought him to such a crisis.

It knew. It knew.

With a cry, the Doctor banged into the trap door which led into the attic chamber. He sat down wearily, wheezing for breath, and buried his head in his hands. The steps up which he had run remained dark and silent. There was no sign that the apparition had followed him.

174

The Doctor's head brushed against the trap door and he stood up, pushing against the wood with the flat of his hands until it gave, crashing against the stone floor of the attic chamber.

He poked his head through and peered into the gloom. A moaning wind, accompanied by a beam of weak, diffused sunlight, was blowing through the glassless window. All else was shadow.

The Doctor hauled himself through and, with a grunt, slammed shut the trap door.

He walked to the window and gazed out on to the moor a hundred feet below. The light made him wince and he turned back to the room. Tears sprang to his eyes. Just the light, he told himself, just the light.

Sliding down the wall, the tails of his duffel coat folding under him, the Doctor breathed in deeply.

He'd been through so much. Ridden so many of the waves of Time.

Yet, for all those years, he'd put his own feelings to one side, tucked them away as if they were of no importance. Now the full weight of his troubles was becoming clear.

Instead of trying to confront his insecurities, like any rational being, he had buried them deep in his psyche.

He was the Doctor, after all, and expected to be immune to such things. Above such trivial matters as emotion and longing and . . . love.

It was only a matter of time before all those repressed feelings flooded his system like poison from an untreated wound.

Something glinted in the hard winter sunlight and the Doctor reached out a trembling hand to pick it up. It was a flat, coiled metal object, cool to the touch. With a start, the Doctor recognized it as the earring Ace had picked up on their visit to Segonax. The one she had taken to wearing in her left ear.

'Ace?'

She was here then, or had been. The Doctor stood up, sensing movement in the dusty shadows.

Twin oak beams dominated the far corner and, between them, a shambling figure was stirring.

The Doctor recognized Billy Coote from their encounter in the Great Hall. But there was something different about him now.

As the Doctor moved closer, Billy emerged into the light, stumbling forwards on his knees as though in great pain. His face was deathly pale and clammy with little beads of sweat.

The Doctor shuddered as tiny particles of skin fell away from Billy's face like old plaster, allowing radiant points of light to shine through the pock-marks.

The Doctor put out his hand with some trepidation.

Billy Coote's eyes snapped open and the Doctor gasped. There was no colour in those orbs now, not even the opaque black which had so scared Ace and Robin. Billy's eyes were utterly transparent, like two spheres of aspic jelly, a strange, dull light exposing every capillary and nerve.

Ace jammed her feet into the guttering and clung on to Robin. He responded by nudging closer, placing his warm hand over hers.

They had been lying against the slates in this way for some time. It was freezing cold and Ace would rather have attempted escape, but without her rucksack it seemed impossible. Still, she could wait. And as soon as that bloke in the attic got out of the way...

Ace remembered suddenly that her rucksack might contain something even more useful, that was, if she'd bothered to pack it. She looked up at the featureless sky.

Any attempt to negotiate the frost-covered roof would be suicidal, so they had remained perched on the sheer slates, clinging together for dear life and bodily warmth. Under different circumstances it would have been a delight, thought Ace, tightly gripping this lovely bloke, feeling the pressure of his warm body against hers. But circumstances weren't different. They were the same as they always were when travelling with the Doctor. Bloody dangerous.

Ace checked her watch. It was well after eight in the morning.

'Ace?'

She jerked alert as the Doctor's voice sounded from the room below.

'Robin!' she hissed. 'It's him. The Doctor! He's in there!'

The boy craned his neck to look at her. 'What can we do?

176

Get him up here?'

Ace shook her head. 'No point. Maybe things've quietened down in there. If the Doctor got in, we should be able to get out.'

Carefully, she slid down the roof and leant over the gutter, straining to hear more. She closed her eyes, feeling sick, as the ground jumped into view a hundred feet below. What was the Doctor doing in there?

Billy Coote was slumped against the wall like an abandoned scarecrow, his arms limp at his sides. The Doctor was crouched on his haunches, gazing in awe at the old man's luminous eyes and the weird light streaming from every crevice of his leathery skin.

'Who are you?' said the Doctor gently.

Billy stirred slightly, his hair rustling agitatedly as energy began to build around him. Filigrees of electric-blue light shivered over his flesh.

'Who *are* you?' said the Doctor again.

Billy's eyes rolled in their sockets, the dull light suddenly blazing intensely from them. He opened his wizened mouth and a chunk of light, solid as a film beam in a dark cinema, poured out.

The Doctor moved back a little.

Some sort of mental link, he thought.

Possession?

Billy Coote's wizened chest began to heave. From deep, deep within his ribs came a rustling sound. He began to mouth noiselessly, his lips splitting and cracking as light flooded through.

Something inside the old man gave out a dreadful croaking moan and the Doctor shuddered. Then it spoke.

Nightshade was running.

There wasn't much time, he knew, and the rocket had to be launched soon or else − or else . . .

Around him, the air steamed and hissed, smoke belching from the massive steel furnaces which crowded the complex.

Three domes, their fabric buckled and blackened, loomed into view and he chose the first, scurrying up the twisting ladder

177

on to the gantry section. He looked down at the flat concrete far below and felt queasy. Heights had never been his strong point.

But what was that below? A body? Lying lifeless on the baked ground, its features coated in black slime. Of course. Barclay! How could he have forgotten? Barclay was dead. Barclay had sacrificed his life so that they might escape. But where had he, Nightshade, been? Why hadn't he even tried to save the young man?

There had been something else. Something very pressing. 'Nightshade . . .'

That voice again. Chuckling. Chuckling.

And suddenly the complex vanished, replaced by the deeply inset window of an eighteenth-century farmhouse. Nightshade looked down. There was a television in the corner of the room and his own face was on the screen, grimacing in horror as a vicious insectoid claw burst through the window.

Nightshade turned around and retched as an appalling smell assaulted his nostrils. This was all wrong. This belonged to someone else's life.

He fell back against the armchair as the window shattered, a great, glistening black claw ramming its way inside.

'Trevithick,' rustled the voice.

Trevithick
Trevithick

Trevithick blinked twice and opened his eyes. He was lying with his back against the wall of the same corridor into which he had tumbled the previous night.

He craned his neck and looked over towards the tiny portal through which daylight was streaming. The dish of the telescope dominated the view.

Of course, he was on Level 18. That's where he'd reached after destroying the creature. Then he must've dropped off to sleep.

He cursed his old body again. This wasn't the time for frailty. He had to make sure the others were all right. He had defeated that monster, but there had been at least five others. Getting back to the control room was now a priority.

Trevithick looked about for a doorway, expecting an entrance to a flight of stairs, but the corridor walls were blank. He turned and regarded the closed lift doors with dread. That was obviously his only way down.

He struggled to his feet and, with some trepidation, pressed the summons button. The doors sprang open immediately.

There was a strong smell of burning inside the lift and Trevithick held his breath as he crossed the threshold, carefully avoiding the gaping hole which the creature had ripped through the floor.

His jacket lay in tatters in the corner next to the tubular ashtray and there were black bloodstains all over the walls. It had been real, then. He breathed out noisily.

Trevithick pressed the Level 8 button and the doors slid shut with a soft click.

He had little idea what he would do when he got to the control room; after all, daylight was only safe in fairy stories. What if there were more of them waiting for him? It would certainly be the end. He hadn't the strength left to. . .

Trevithick frowned as the floor indicator reached Level 8 and then continued downwards. A cold chill ran through him. Not again. Not more.

He'd always had a horror of being inside a plummeting lift. Was this it? Wasn't there a position he had to assume, bend his knees or something? Or was that just an old wives' tale?

The lift, however, continued to descend in its own stately way.

Trevithick jabbed at the Level 8 button again but there was no response. He glanced down at the floor and felt compelled to peer through the hole out into the dark shaft.

Grunting with effort, he crouched down on his hands and knees and put his face as close as he dared to the hole.

Expecting only darkness, Trevithick was taken aback by the sight which met his eyes.

The lift was descending into a network of glowing light, wisps of fiery energy cocooning the entire shaft like a spectral spider's web.

There was a deep, throbbing pulse emanating from the light as it progressed upwards.

Upwards.

Trevithick got to his feet and pressed the first button that met his trembling fingers. Nothing happened.

He swore savagely and kept his finger on the button until the nail whitened.

It seemed as though the lift were being dragged inexorably down into the pulsing entity below. Insubstantial tendrils were already groping their way through the hole in the floor.

Trevithick panicked and stabbed at the 'doors open' control, his whole frame shaking in fear. The floor indicator showed Level 5.

To his inexpressible relief, the doors sprang open and he threw himself out of the lift into another darkened corridor.

Trevithick groped his way through the blackness and his hand clapped on to a cold, steel banister. Thank God, at least there were stairs at this level.

He forced his weary legs on to the damp concrete. It was now vital that he found his friends. There was something alive down here. Alive and growing.

Holly and Vijay helped Cooper through the double doors and then into the control room.

'Now what?' said Holly. 'The village?'

Vijay shook his head. 'No, this changes things. If Dr Cooper survived, then maybe old Trevithick did too. I think we owe it to him to at least look.'

The room was buzzing with energy once more, the noise from various machines almost deafening.

'Any change?' said Vijay as Cooper hobbled back to her consoles.

She sifted through a sheaf of paper and frowned. 'There's a real pattern now. Still makes no sense, but it's a pattern. Regular. Like a pulse.'

'A pulse,' said Holly calmly.

Vijay ran his fingers through his hair. 'I still don't see how a nova could produce this kind of data...'

Holly slapped herself across the forehead. 'It's so bloody obvious!'

Cooper smiled. 'What is?'

'The Doctor was right all the time, only he didn't know what about. We've been acting on the assumption that all this data is coming from space. Because that's where it's *supposed* to come from!'

'From the nova?' said Cooper quizzically.

'No! We couldn't see the wood for the trees. The nova is incidental. The energy isn't coming from space at all. It's *underneath* us.'

Cooper whistled. 'That would explain why it's flooded the systems. Too local to make any sense.'

Vijay looked at her excitedly. 'But what is it? The Doctor's ghost thing?'

Holly shook her head. 'I don't know.'

Cooper sat down and pouted her lower lip. 'Well, call me alarmist if you like, but it strikes me we're not in the best of positions here.'

Vijay looked down gravely. 'We're sitting on a powder keg.'

The Doctor rocked on his haunches.

'How long?' he whispered.

Billy Coote inclined his head, his whole frame now flickering with light.

'How long have you been here?' urged the Doctor.

There was a strange, whispering groan, merging with the familiar rustling sound. Then the voice, halting, dry and dead as stone: 'All time. Since before the world.'

The Doctor frowned. 'Before the world?'

Billy raised a spindly arm along which flurries of blue light were dancing. 'All time.'

The Doctor changed tack. 'What are you?'

The thing within Billy Coote seemed to shudder and for an instant there was a vile movement beneath his transparent skin, like a specimen in a jar suddenly jerking to life.

'Know not,' it mumbled. 'Know not. Just am.' Billy's head slumped on to his chest, columns of light bursting from every pore. 'So tired. So tired.'

The Doctor rubbed his chin thoughtfully and moved back still further. Energy seemed to be seeping from Billy's body, pooling under his legs and beneath his back.

'Do you know . . .' the Doctor began. 'Do you know where

you've come from?'

The voice gave a guttural choke, as though willing itself back into life. 'Only ever here. Alone. Cannot rest. Cannot rest.'

The light in Billy's eyes seemed to blaze again for an instant. 'Need!' it rustled. *'Need!'*

Ace was hanging from Robin's legs as he hooked his fingers into the guttering. It was horribly unsafe and he gritted his teeth, mixing blind optimism with prayers to his neglected deity.

'OK?' he gasped.

'Yeah. Hold on.' Ace scrambled down his legs and pushed her boot into the same wall crevice she had found the previous night. If she could just keep a grip on the stone and swing herself back through the window...

'You get back on the roof!' she shouted to Robin. 'I'll get the rope strung up and then you can come down. OK?'

He hissed his assent, struggling to breathe as Ace clambered down him.

She reached his ankles and her feet found the top of the stone window. Carefully, she pushed her fingers into the crumbling masonry and scrambled through into the attic chamber.

'Doctor!'

He held up his hand to silence her. Ace gawped at the thing in the corner.

Billy Coote's whole body was alive with crackling light, billowing around him in nebulous clouds.

'He's possessed,' whispered the Doctor. 'Possessed by whatever it is.'

'All time,' it burbled, ectoplasmic fluid gushing from the light-blanched mouth. 'Need! Need!'

The Doctor leant forward as close as he dared. 'What do you need?'

Billy Coote's body flickered for a moment and then, like a distant image in a heat haze, vanished into the shimmering wall of light.

Ace spotted her rucksack, now a good few feet from what was left of Billy Coote. She scrambled across the room and picked it up, immediately retreating to the window.

'We've got to get out, Doctor!'

The Doctor glanced at the trap door, which was now totally enveloped by the clouds of whispering energy.

'*Need!*' bellowed the disembodied voice.

Ace found a coil of rope in her rucksack and hastily tied one end around the nearest beam. It was further from the window than she would have liked but it would have to do. She ran back to the window and fed the rope down the wall. It was a good twenty feet short.

'Robin!' cried Ace, pushing her head through the stone arch. 'Come on!'

'What do you need?' shouted the Doctor to the air around him.

A tendril of energy appeared and stroked his face almost tenderly.

'Need you,' gushed the voice. 'Need your life. Warm life!'

'Doctor!' screeched Ace. She tipped up her rucksack. No more rope. Just a small collapsible ladder and...and...

Two globes of nitro-nine-A.

She'd been right then. Thank God she had foresight.

It was the same formula she'd brewed up in Nazi Germany during their fight with the Timewyrm. Bit of an unstable formula but effective. And that was what they needed now.

Robin pulled himself through the window but Ace immediately shook her head.

'No time! Get down the rope!'

'It's too short!' he cried.

'Just have to try it, mate,' she said, smiling.

Robin launched himself back through the window and began to descend the rope.

Ace cupped the explosives in her hand and turned around. The Doctor was against the wall, the huge miasma of energy floating about him. It was roaring with power now, beautiful colours like frozen flames rippling within its nebulous structure.

'*Need you!*' came the chuckling voice.

'Doctor! Get away from it!' cried Ace in a hoarse whisper. She rolled the globes of nitro-nine-A across the floor.

'No, Ace!' yelled the Doctor.

The cloud's tendrils retreated a little, slipping around the explosives inquisitively.

Ace grabbed the hood of the Doctor's coat and dragged him

towards the window. She found the rope and pulled herself through, abseiling down the face of the tower. Freezing wind bit at her face and hands. She looked up. The Doctor was just emerging through the window. Looking down, she saw Robin gazing up at them. He was all right.

Ace pushed her feet off the stones and slid down the rope, trying to ignore the vicious burning sensation it induced.

The end of the rope came in sight and she jammed her fingers into the brickwork. Twenty feet to go. Twenty feet. And that nitro was so unstable...

She looked up anxiously. The Doctor was still too high up.

'Come on, Doctor!'

Her voice was blown back at her by the wind.

'Ace!' Robin cried, holding out his arms to grab her. 'Jump! You're close enough!'

She saw that there was only ten or twelve feet to go. Time to put some of that training into action. She thought of Sergeant Drew Smith and the parachute team he had brought to Perivale Youth Centre one wet bank holiday. He'd been one of her earliest crushes. This one's for you, Drew, she thought.

Ace threw herself to the ground, rolled expertly and found herself gripped by Robin's hands. He kissed her gratefully. Then they both looked up at the tower.

The Doctor was reaching the end of the rope. He swung in the wind, trying to get a grip on the loose masonry of the tower wall.

In the attic chamber, the cloud of energy shimmered over the globes of explosive. There was potential energy in there, it knew. Delicious energy. And any moment now...

The tower roof erupted in flame as the entire attic disintegrated. Chunks of stone and roof-slate blasted into the air. The whole structure tottered on its foundations.

The Doctor felt the heat first and a blinding light as he lost his grip on the rope. Then there was terrible empty air around him and his senses cried out in shock, his stomach lurching. He hit the ground with tremendous force.

Ace and Robin were by him in an instant.

'Doctor!' Ace wailed, running her fingers over his blackened face.

The ruined tower crackled with flame behind them and lumps of stone continued to fall. Robin coughed as a blanket of smoke drifted down to ground level.

The Doctor lay sprawled on the grass, deathly still.

10

Trevithick pulled at the banister and leant heavily over it, wheezing and spluttering. He stared into the gloom and made out a large red sign on the far wall. Level 8. He was almost there now. Just through the door and back down the corridor towards the control room.

There was a sharp pain in his leg and he reached down, wincing as his fingers contacted a vicious cut. The tweed material of his trousers hung in shreds.

Trevithick took a deep breath and hauled himself to the top of the steps. He allowed himself a little smirk of satisfaction. He'd fought off that creature. Come through it alive. Him! A seventy-year-old man. That was something to tell his granddaughter, should he ever chance to see her again.

He pulled open the doors and stumbled as black dots crowded his vision. Shaking his head, he advanced down the corridor, leaning against the wall for support. For an instant, everything went black.

No. He'd never fainted in his life. This was no time to start.

Oh but he had, hadn't he? After the window had been smashed.

Don't think about that. Don't. . .

He had to tell them what he had seen in the lower floors. It was too important to ignore.

The corridor walls seemed to close in on him.

Dicky ticker, he thought to himself. No surprise at his age, and after the strain he'd put himself under. . .

With a low moan, Trevithick slid to the floor, unconscious.

'Doctor!'

Ace pulled at the hood of the Doctor's duffel coat in an attempt to rouse him. Robin put his ear to the Doctor's chest and blinked anxiously. He frowned and moved his ear to the other side.

'He's got...'

'I know,' said Ace quietly. 'Two hearts.'

She knelt down and held the Doctor's hand in hers. His face was pale and waxen, little curls of sweat-soaked hair plastered to his forehead.

'You might as well know,' she said, hopelessly. 'He's an alien and I'm from the future. We travel through Time.'

Robin looked up from his scrutiny of the Doctor. He shrugged and smiled slightly. 'Well, you did say you weren't from round here.'

Ace put her hand on the Doctor's brow. 'Why won't he wake up?'

Robin sighed. 'I don't know. His heartbeat is very shallow. Maybe that's normal for him...'

Suddenly, the Doctor sat bolt upright and yelled in pain.

Ace sat back on her haunches in surprise, staring at the Doctor's wide open mouth. He roared and screamed and howled in agony until Ace thought she'd be deafened.

'What is it? What *is* it?' she cried desperately.

The Doctor fell back, tears springing to his eyes, and bit into his lower lip.

'It's his shoulder,' yelled Robin. 'Look!'

Ace looked and felt suddenly sick. There was an ugly lump projecting from beneath the sleeve of the Doctor's coat.

'Dislocated,' gasped the Doctor, weeping in agony. 'Have to put it back.' He was panting in distress.

'What?' said Ace. 'I can't...'

'Do it!' ordered the Doctor. 'Please ... please. Can't stand it...'

He arched his back and screamed. Robin put his hands on the Doctor's right shoulder, eliciting an immediate howl from the prostrate Time Lord.

'I'll hold it,' panted Robin. 'You push it back in.'

Ace looked down worriedly.

'Please!' hissed the Doctor between his teeth. 'Quickly!'

'Sorry about this, Doctor,' said Ace grimly.

Robin pushed his knee under the Doctor's back and Ace rested her hands on the dislocated shoulder, gritting her teeth as though she were feeling the pain herself. She grasped the bones firmly and, holding her breath, slammed them back into place.

The Doctor emitted a stream of oaths not heard since the very darkest days of Gallifreyan history and then fell back, sobbing, on to the moor.

'Thank you. Thank you both,' he muttered, eyelids flickering.

'Did I do good?' asked Ace eagerly. 'Blowing up the tower?'

The Doctor opened one eye painfully. 'Nothing could've been worse. It feeds off energy. You gave it a nice hors d'oeuvre for the main dish.'

Ace looked crestfallen.

The Doctor looked up and smiled. 'But you did get us out of there,' he croaked. Ace grinned back.

'What d'you mean, "main dish"?' said Robin worriedly.

The Doctor struggled into a sitting position. 'That thing in the tower . . . that Sentience . . . is of incalculable age. I believe the Earth formed around it. It runs through space like a vein of mineral in the rocks. It's growing and it's hungry.'

Robin looked ashen faced.

The Doctor seemed to recover with remarkable speed and was on his feet within minutes. 'You see,' he said, pointing to the ruined tower, 'you've only made it stronger.'

Ace and Robin looked up. The air around the blackened stonework was alive with roaring energy, a cloud of whispering light growing by the second.

Ace looked across the moor and then at the Doctor. His expression was dark and forbidding.

'What now, Doctor?' said Ace quietly.

The Doctor glanced up at the tower and then over the moor to the fog-shrouded telescope.

'Come on,' he said. 'It's time to lay some ghosts.'

Jill Mason sat hugging her knees to her chin in one of the cold church pews. It felt like an age since they'd closed the church doors and almost as long since George Lowcock had made his 'difficult' announcement. He had stuck to his idea of a poisonous gas leak and the reaction hadn't been as incredulous as expected, several villagers having already made their own grim discoveries.

There had been several ideas to perk everyone up, some of the residents organizing things with all the gusto of a boy-scout jamboree, although Jill had violently vetoed someone's notion of a singsong.

Now they were huddled together in the pews, wrapped in the blankets they'd been requested to bring. A few children were dashing unconcernedly up and down the aisle.

Only Mr Medcalfe, one of Crook Marsham's oldest residents, stood alone, gazing out of the back window into the misty churchyard.

George Lowcock sat down next to Jill and undid his tie. 'I feel so ... useless,' he exclaimed.

'I know,' said Jill calmly, 'but until we have a clue what's happening we'd better stay put. I know what it can do.'

'It?'

Jill shrugged. 'You know, I never believed in anything out of the ordinary, supernatural ... even as a child. But I've seen things today...'

Lowcock sank his head on to his chest. 'Well, whatever it is, I want it out of my village. I want things back the way they were.'

Jill put a hand on his. 'I don't think they can be, George. Things change. They have to.'

Andrew Medcalfe watched his breath steam up the window. He felt safe here in the old church, lost amongst the cold shadows.

As a boy, he had often hidden from his parents in this bit of the building, enjoying the feel of the cool stone against his hands and face as he gazed out of the stained glass. He'd seen a good few headstones spring up since then and knew that his own, the one he was never destined to see, was not too far off. He was getting on.

This gas scare he could have done without, especially since his declining years had been so free of incident: calm, unspectacular and peaceful. Medcalfe turned the word over in his mind. Peace. Full. It had such a beautiful sound.

Some people said he was a dull old dog but he never complained, never answered back. Because they didn't understand. Could never hope to understand.

Oh, he had been a hot-blooded youth like the rest of them, a bit of a rebel even. He was going to get away from this miserable village and see the world. China, India, Africa or even America, which sounded so exciting in the Conan Doyle books.

There'd even been one or two brushes with the law back at the turn of the century. Nothing too serious of course, but it had taken more than a magistrate's fine to sort out Mr Woodall's daughter when he'd got her in the family way.

But after the Somme, he had never yearned for excitement again.

Of all the men in Crook Marsham who had joined up (and almost all had gone voluntarily, poor devils), only he and Jack Prudhoe had returned alive.

They'd never really been friends before but after the Great War they had an unspoken bond, something no one else could penetrate. Even though neither said a word about their experiences, both recognized the haunted look buried deep at the back of the other's eyes.

Medcalfe coughed loudly and spat up a ball of phlegm into his grubby handkerchief. He'd caught a whiff of gas in the trenches and was still suffering for it.

Now old Jack was gone too: a victim, so George Lowcock said, of this mysterious accident. Ironic that it should be gas too.

Medcalfe rubbed his hand against a crimson-hued pane of glass and peeked out into the frost-rimed churchyard. There it was. The one monument he could hardly bear to look at.

AICKMAN, ROBERT, PTE
ATKINSON, WILLIAM, PTE
COCKAYNE, CYRIL, PTE
CLEMINSON, JOHN, PTE
MAYNARD, EDWARD, PTE
SHACKLETON, GEORGE, SRG

His gaze moved swiftly to the base of the broken pillar where a fairly fresh wreath of poppies fluttered in the wind.

WE WILL REMEMBER THEM

The sky above the ruined monastery tower rippled like water, great bolts of burning light shooting through the clouds. There

190

was a distant rumble of thunder followed only seconds later by a vicious fork of lightning.

The Sentience licked about the tower and slowly, almost unconsciously, began to swirl into a vortex. This time the thunder seemed closer, booming from horizon to horizon, the accompanying lightning flared across the sky. The atmosphere crackled as though alive.

A massive shock ripped through the tower and the ancient masonry shattered into limestone dust. Trails of light sparkled in the vortex, spiralling from a rich purple to a dense, terrifying blackness. Wind roared across the moor, tearing up clumps of heather and rock. The old bus shelter and the road sign gave little resistance, exploding in a cloud of rotten wood. Only the TARDIS stood firm, like a watchful policeman, calmly biding its time.

The Sentience spread its nebulous fronds, gushing down from the heavens like an avenging angel. The sky boiled with fire.

It felt the blackness at its heart, the great, awful hollowness. There had to be more. There was still need.

Need

Flicking a shimmering tendril, it covered the whole distance to the village in a fraction of a second. For a few moments, it gurgled and twisted around every house, loosening bricks and shattering roofs.

Need

Then there was a tiny trace in its mind. Insistent. Powerful. Bountiful.

Need

A torrent of emotion raced through every brilliant particle of its essence and sadness overwhelmed it. Such regret. Such regret.

Regret was good. Regret was strong.

Need

Need

Suddenly, there were images too. Faces and names and voices, all perfectly clear and unsullied.

Without the slightest hesitation, the Sentience moved in for the kill.

* * *

191

Vijay found Trevithick slumped in the corridor just outside the control room. He appeared to be asleep through sheer exhaustion, his empty revolver gripped tightly in one hand.

Vijay was so delighted to find the old man alive that he kissed him, an action which roused Trevithick faster than any smelling salts.

Hooking one of Trevithick's arms around him, Vijay carried the battle-weary actor into the control room where he was enthusiastically received by Cooper and Holly. It was better than a hundred ovations, he thought, chuckling to himself.

Trevithick recounted his adventures with some pride and then told them of his discovery in the base of the lift shaft.

Cooper threw him a glance. 'Describe it.'

Trevithick sat back in his chair. 'I can't. It's all lit up like a TV studio. Too bright to make anything out. But it's pulsing, as if it were alive. I managed to get back up the stairs to this level but I think I must've passed out. Getting to be a bit of a habit, I'm afraid.'

'Well,' said Vijay, 'we're delighted...'

The double doors burst open at the suggestion of Robin's foot and he, the Doctor and Ace ran into the room, bringing a mass of wind-blown foliage with them.

'Doctor! Thank God!' exclaimed Trevithick.

Cooper ran a hand through her blood-stiffened hair and grinned broadly. 'Good to have you back.'

'What's the situation?' said the Doctor quietly.

Cooper gestured around desperately. The room was clattering with data again.

'It's coming from under the ground, not space,' said Holly, triumphantly.

The Doctor blinked. 'Yes. Yes, that would make sense.'

Trevithick stepped forward. 'Doctor, I've seen it. Down there. You wouldn't believe it. All the lower levels, full of light and...and...' He stammered and shook his head.

'I've spoken to it,' said the Doctor gravely.

'You've what?' cried Vijay.

'I don't know what it is. I don't even know if it's alive in any sense we understand. It's like a virus. Or a vampire. Feeding off energy.'

Ace shot a look at the shattered window. 'What happened here?'

Vijay smiled. 'You wouldn't like to know.'

Robin was also by the window, gazing at the boiling sky. 'Doctor, I think you should see this.'

The Doctor appraised the violent heavens with one look and then turned back. 'We're running out of time. It's spreading all over the moor.'

'But what *is* it?' insisted Cooper.

'I've told you, I don't know!' bellowed the Doctor, angrily. 'I can't have an answer for everything.'

Oh, that's a good one, thought Ace.

The Doctor sat down. 'It's incredibly ancient. Older than the Earth itself. It runs *through* the planet.'

'Like the letters in Blackpool rock?' said Trevithick brightly.

The Doctor glared at him. 'If you like.'

Cooper looked at the Doctor earnestly. 'But all these incidents, ghosts . . .'

The Doctor's voice was husky and exhausted. 'My guess is that, powerful as it is, it can't feed directly. It needs something to latch on to, to give it time to feed.'

'Memory?' said Vijay.

The Doctor nodded. 'For the most part. Strong associations. Regrets. Desires. They're formidable emotions. Think how one little thing can stir up a flood of nostalgia in all of us.' He glanced down. 'All of us.'

'Like that French chap and his teacake!' announced Trevithick triumphantly.

'So the power of our emotion, our memory, summoned these ghosts into being?' whispered Holly.

'Exactly.' The Doctor rose from his chair. 'And the stronger your belief in it, the more powerful it becomes until you haven't the will to deny it. And then it consumes you.'

Robin thought of Betty. What had she seen? What was the dreadful death he had condemned her to?

'What can we do?' he said at last.

'We have to fight it at source,' declared the Doctor firmly. He turned to Trevithick. 'Edmund, you said something about the lower levels . . .'

193

'There's no need, Doctor,' cried Vijay. 'I think we've found a more direct route downwards.'

The Doctor frowned.

Andrew Medcalfe jerked back from the window in surprise. There was someone standing by the war memorial, their face in deep shadow.

He almost turned to call Lowcock. Everyone was supposed to be inside the church. For their own good. He almost turned.

But then the figure raised its face and gazed directly into Medcalfe's bleary old eyes.

Need

The young man was wearing a knee-length trenchcoat and high boots. His hair and skin were fair, almost radiant, flushed with youthful vigour. He smiled warmly.

'John?' whispered Medcalfe.

John Cleminson

Need

Need

Need

The Sentience hissed with delight. Perfect.

'John?' croaked Medcalfe in disbelief.

His mind raced, unbidden, through the other names on the memorial. So many friends.

Medcalfe backed away. There were others now, appearing out of the mist in a staggered line. Some he recognized. Billy Atkinson with his shiny black moustache. Cyril Cockayne, his arm in a sling just as it had been the day the shell wiped him off the face of the Earth.

Others were anonymous behind gas masks, strutting remorselessly across the graveyard like hideous blind pigs.

Medcalfe felt someone by him and turned in fear. It was George Lowcock.

The policeman stood and stared at the spectres through the frost-covered window. He didn't recognize a single one, but he believed in them.

He believes

Need

Need

194

The Sentience relished Lowcock's contact and grew stronger still.

Suddenly, there were faces crowding the window, pressing their features against the cold panes and grinning. Grinning.

One of the gas-masked figures pushed itself to the fore and Medcalfe saw his own face reflected in the blank glass sockets. He screamed.

'Not this time!' insisted the Doctor.

'But why?' cried Ace plaintively.

The Doctor looked about evasively. Cooper was staying behind to monitor things on the surface. Holly, Vijay and Trevithick, who wouldn't hear of being left out of the adventure, had elected to accompany him below ground. But Ace was not to come.

'You're . . .' The Doctor looked up but managed to avoid Ace's eyes. 'You're too important.'

Ace frowned but then decided this was a rare compliment, something not to be sniffed at. She smiled warmly.

'OK. No tantrums. You win, Doctor.'

He touched her arm and smiled thinly.

'Is it really that bad?' said Ace.

The Doctor didn't reply. Ace sighed. There were deep shadows under his eyes. He looked fit to drop.

Robin put his arm around Ace and the Doctor clapped a hand on the boy's shoulder. 'Look after her,' he whispered.

Ace watched the party leave through the double doors, shrinking back as another blast of wind from the moor flooded into the station.

It was as if he didn't expect to come back.

The moor was like a battleground, a fierce gale whipping and lashing through the heather. The Doctor pulled up the hood of his coat and wrapped his scarf over his mouth as he, Trevithick, Vijay and Holly struggled towards the cave entrance.

'There, Doctor!' called Vijay, his face hidden by the bulk of his parka.

The Doctor ran towards the cave mouth which the subsidence had uncovered, plunged his hand into his pocket and produced his torch.

'Are you going to try and reason with it?' shouted Trevithick above the noise of the wind.

The Doctor scowled and didn't reply. Instead, he swept the torch-beam around the cave, the beam creating a broad yellow cone of light in the fog.

'Man made,' he said softly. 'Well done, Vijay.'

'But if this is the quarry, Doctor, what's made it show up? Why has the ground . . .'

The Doctor looked Vijay in the eye, crinkling his face against the onslaught of the elements. 'This thing has come fully to life, probably for the first time, and it's growing. Expanding under the ground. That's what Edmund must have seen in the lower levels of the station: a tremendous build up of energy. It's shaking off its earthly shackles and this is the result.' He gestured around at the scorched, disrupted ground.

Trevithick stepped forward. 'Well, let's see where it goes, shall we?'

The cave floor began to dip almost immediately, leading into a steep tunnel. The rock walls glistened with moisture.

Holly wrinkled her nose. 'Can you smell that?'

The Doctor sniffed. There was a faint but noticeable odour of decay.

'It's the same,' said Trevithick in a sepulchral whisper.

Holly moved off into the darkness. 'It's stronger further down.'

The Doctor pointed his torch before them and led the way.

Trevithick looked back as they descended deeper into the tunnel, the rain-lashed entrance now a diminishing half circle of grey light.

Ace stapled the last sheet of polythene across the shattered window and watched the rain drum against it. Even through the distortion of the plastic she could see the fantastic display lighting up the sky. If she hadn't known how sinister were its implications, she would have marvelled at its beauty. It was as if the oceans had been drawn up into the clouds, torrents of light creating a magnificent effulgence against the pale December sun.

Cooper had given up even attempting to make sense of the data overwhelming her computers. She sat rubbing her temples as sheaves of paper pooled around her shoes.

She glanced up as lightning spat across the sky, illuminating the whole room. Robin caught her eye and smiled.

'Had enough?' he said.

'Now I know it's not from space,' she gestured at the steady pulse of data, 'it's not such a burning issue. I was giving myself a heart attack trying to make sense of it. Turns out to be just nonsense. This "thing" below us flooding the systems.'

Robin sensed her helplessness and felt sorry for her. It couldn't be easy having so many of one's certainties turned on their heads like that. He looked at the chattering consoles with interest and decided to engage Cooper in conversation, preferably on a topic she was expert at. Almost guaranteed to perk her up.

'And what's that?'

He pointed to the small bank of monitors to Cooper's left. She smirked. 'That, son, is the only thing we can get a fix on at the moment. Our own private nova.'

Robin chewed his thumb, struggling to recall his half-heard science lessons. 'And that's an exploding star, right?'

Cooper nodded. 'Mmm.'

Robin held up his hand and looked into space thoughtfully. 'So what's the difference between that and a — what d'you call it — *super* nova?'

Ace saw her chance. This was going to sound impressive. 'A supernova is...' she hesitated, remembering one of the Doctor's short but instructive lectures, 'a supernova is an old star. Its centre gets hotter and hotter till it tries to burn heavier elements...'

'Helium, carbon, nitrogen, oxygen, silicon...' added Cooper helpfully.

Ace cast her eyes upwards, praying she wouldn't forget. 'And finally iron,' she said triumphantly.

'So?' Robin shrugged.

'When the centre of a star is made of iron,' said Cooper with mock gravity, 'it has an energy crisis, because the thermonuclear fusion of iron *absorbs* energy instead of releasing it.'

Ace knew that bit and was a little annoyed she hadn't been allowed to say so. 'Anyway,' she put in, before Cooper could steal any more of her thunder, 'the star collapses like a house of cards and *boom*!'

Cooper smiled. 'You're remarkably well informed.'

Ace grinned. 'The Doctor taught me everything I know.'

'Anyway, they're very rare,' Cooper continued. 'One of the reasons we're here is to look for their remains. We call them pulsars. A friend of Holly's discovered the first one in February.'

Ace sat down next to Robin, deciding to continue privately with her impressive monologue. 'The iron core collapses and becomes so dense that the, that the . . .'

'Atomic nuclei,' called Cooper, without looking up. Ace smiled ruefully at Robin. 'Those, anyway, are crushed together. It spins on its axis and produces pulses which they can detect with the telescope.'

Robin grinned at her. 'Right.'

'Anything else you'd like to know?' said Ace chirpily.

'Yes. How long you'll be staying around.'

Ace's face fell. She'd been expecting this moment. 'Well . . .'

Robin looked at her. 'You said the Doctor wants to stop travelling. Settle down. Is he likely to do that here?'

Ace shook her head. 'He's got universes to choose from.'

'Any time, any place, any where. He's not called Doctor Martini, is he?'

Ace smiled sadly. 'Anyway, I doubt he'll choose Yorkshire in the late sixties.'

Robin shifted uncomfortably. She knew so much that he wanted to know.

'Tell me about the future, Ace. Will things be OK?'

Ace frowned. 'I can't tell you that. It's not fair. You'd be expecting things, or dreading them.'

Robin took her hand. 'Well, there is one way of making sure I just take things as they come.'

Ace looked at his serious expression, his thick black hair, brilliant eyes and oh-so-delicious lips.

'Stay with me,' he said at last.

* * *

Holly, Vijay and Trevithick had hung back a little whilst the Doctor went ahead with his torch. After a time, he returned, a look of puzzlement on his face.

'Come on. It's all right.'

They followed him down the narrow tunnel until they emerged in a large cavern, its black rock walls glistening with moisture. Rain from the drenched moor above trickled down through the roof.

Trevithick chose a boulder and sat down, tired by his exertions. The Doctor shone the torch around the cavern, picking out chunks of stone upon which the mark of human interference was obvious.

'The quarry,' said the Doctor. 'Smothered by soil over thousands of years.'

Holly picked up a small figure, crudely carved out of limestone. There were others dotted about the ground, some almost perfect, others with only rudimentary work on them.

'It's like Easter Island,' she breathed.

'What do you think we'll find here, Doctor?' said Vijay.

The Doctor was examining the walls. 'I don't know. I suppose I half expected it to be here waiting for us.'

'But the sky,' said Trevithick. 'All that activity. Surely it's on the surface now.'

'No,' said the Doctor. 'I'm convinced it's just sending out feelers. The main body is still here. This *has* to be it.'

There was a dull crackle from his pocket and he swiftly removed the walkie-talkie.

'Dr Cooper?'

'No. It's me.' Ace's voice was indistinct through the hiss of static. 'Dr Cooper's monitoring a slow build-up. The pulse is getting stronger. I think it's on its way. Over.'

'Right. Thank you. Over and . . .'

'Doctor?'

'Yes?'

There was a long pause. 'Nothing. Take care. Over and out.'

Vijay's eyes widened in fear. 'Let's get out of here.'

'No,' muttered the Doctor. 'We came here to confront it and that's what we must do.'

Trevithick looked about uneasily in the darkness. 'I say, gone awfully quiet, hasn't it?'

They all exchanged glances. A thick hush had descended on the cavern. Even the steady drip of water from the surface appeared to have ceased.

Holly shivered. 'It's so cold,' she said wonderingly.

The Doctor was conscious of it too. 'Temperature drop. Like a cold spot in a haunted house.'

'Over there!' Vijay pointed to the far wall of the cavern in which a dark fissure was visible. As they watched, the wall began to glow, almost as though a gateway were opening to the outside. There was a deep, thunderous rumble and tiny spheres of light began to split off and dance about in the cold air, colliding off the walls to coalesce above their heads. The Doctor gazed up in awe. The light continued to sparkle, shifting colours from gold to a brilliant cobalt blue.

'It's so beautiful,' whispered Holly.

'The song of the Siren,' said the Doctor cryptically.

The cavern was suddenly alive with blinding light. Trevithick shielded his eyes against the painful glare, his brows knitting together. The Doctor peeked through his fingers. 'So strong,' he breathed.

Waves of heat shimmered towards them.

'Clear your minds!' called the Doctor. 'It's the only way to remain safe.'

Holly had seen this display before, the hypnotic light drenching her brain. The thought came before she could even acknowledge it and then refused to go away, like the refrain of some annoyingly catchy tune. She shook her head and looked away from the burning gold light.

Vijay caught hold of her arms and shook her. 'Holly? What is it?'

She snapped shut her eyes and fought to wipe the image from her brain.

'Can't! Can't do it!' she whimpered, grasping her temples, her face screwed up in agony.

'Look!' It was Trevithick's voice, hushed in awe.

The Doctor and Vijay turned. Holly ran to the wall and buried her head in her hands.

Out of the flood of light, a man was emerging, tall and

smiling, his arms open in welcome. His skin shone beautifully, patches of golden light woven together to form the image.

The Sentience could taste the strength of Holly's memory. Part of it had sensed her presence, shooting out tendrils from its massive core to find and isolate her.

There was resistance too, but that would pass. Somewhere, in the darkest corners of her mind, Holly wanted to believe.

She turned from the wall.

'James!' she screamed, gagging with emotion.

'It isn't real, Holly!' bellowed the Doctor above the rising noise. 'The more you believe...'

'I need him. I still need him,' she sobbed.

Need

Need

The Sentience throbbed with delight.

'Let it go,' cried the Doctor. 'You can't bring him back.'

'Hol,' pleaded Vijay. 'Let it go.' He gazed into her frightened eyes. 'Need *me*.'

The Sentience rippled and grew more substantial, ethereal light glancing off every feature. It opened its mouth, rushing through Holly's memory and piecing together fragments of Time, moments of experience. Constructing a voice.

'Holly,' it stammered.

Holly froze. The voice was strange, indistinct, as though heard underwater. But it was James.

'Holly.' The voice was already stronger, almost commanding. The Sentience beckoned.

Trevithick moved forward. The Doctor held him back. 'We can all see it, Edmund. It knows we believe too. We're all in danger.'

Vijay grabbed Holly by the shoulders. 'Holly! For Christ's sake! Think of us. Think of me. James is dead. D'you understand?'

Holly wriggled in his grip, shaking her head in confusion.

Holly...

Holly...

The voice was inside her head now, quiet and calm. Peace descended on her mind and suddenly everything became clear to her. It was so easy. So obvious.

Holly...

She turned to look at Vijay and nodded. 'It's OK. I'm all right.'

Vijay's grip on her arm loosened. In an instant, she was sprinting across the cavern.

'James!' she yelled, tears flooding her eyes.

'Holly, no!' Vijay pelted after her.

The Sentience grinned broadly. Holly jerked to a stop directly before it. She extended a shaking hand.

James's smile faded a little. 'It's been so long,' he whispered. His voice was as soothing as the babble of clear, mountain water.

'James.' Holly felt her grief easing away moment by moment, a healing joy washing through her mind. 'I *love* you!'

'Kiss me,' instructed James, his red lips alive with pixels of light.

Vijay caught hold of Holly's hair and swung her round.

'No!' he screeched. Holly looked at him with a strange hatred in her eyes and he felt his heart sink.

Then, gritting his teeth, Vijay brought round his fist and punched Holly into unconsciousness. She crumpled and fell to the rocky floor.

The Sentience billowed like a sail, regarding the three men below it with detached interest.

'Leave us,' hissed the Doctor. 'Why can't you leave us alone?'

'*Need!*' thundered the Sentience, pillars of fire shooting from its outstretched arms.

It grew suddenly larger, patterns of gold filigree sparkling across its eyes as it turned to observe Holly where she lay. There was a huge inrush of air, it closed its eyes and, in an instant, was gone.

Vijay looked about desperately. 'Doctor? What's happened to it?'

The Doctor shook his head wearily.

The Sentience squirmed and gushed with pleasure. Didn't he realize that sending the female into unconsciousness was the worst thing he could have done? The belief of the dreaming mind was so much stronger. So much sweeter...

202

It had almost consumed her before whilst she slept, like the woman in the village, but this time there would be no escape.

The Sentience entered Holly's willing mind and began to gorge itself on her life force.

'Vijay!' Trevithick pointed down at Holly's inert body and felt his blood run cold.

Vijay dashed across to Holly and lifted her in his arms. A tide of light was drifting over her skin in sweeping waves.

'No, no!' Vijay sobbed angrily, running his fingers through Holly's hair and across her face.

He could see through her skin now, as the Sentience burrowed through her flesh. Fragments of bone shattered and burned before his eyes.

Vijay dropped her and wept into his hands, scarcely daring to watch the appalling sight before him.

The Sentience ripped and pummelled through Holly, draining every morsel of her energy. A great wash of light exploded around her.

For a moment, she shone with magnesium brightness and then the glare faded. There was nothing left behind.

'No.' Vijay sank to his knees. Trevithick put his arm around the young man's shoulder and shot an anxious look at the Doctor who was struggling to his feet. 'Let's go, for heaven's sake.'

The Doctor was already making for the tunnel. 'It's so strong,' he said again. 'Not even a body left this time. I must ... I must think.'

A huge sigh, almost a sob, was wrenched from his chest.

Trevithick pulled Vijay to his feet. The young man was shaking his head silently, tears running down his cheeks.

He had been too weak, then, after all. Unable to fight against a dead man. Now she was gone.

The Doctor strode down the tunnel, scarcely bothering about the rocks into which his shins slammed. Trevithick hobbled behind, helping Vijay as best he could.

'What are we going to do?' cried Trevithick to the little figure ahead of him. The Doctor said nothing. In fact, Trevithick thought he might not have heard until the Doctor stopped abruptly just in sight of the tunnel entrance.

Trevithick wheezed and let Vijay slide to the ground. 'Doctor, I said . . .'

He stopped, conscious of the Doctor's back turned towards him. 'What is it?' he asked, turning to look out into the open air.

The light was still a dismal grey, wind and rain lashing down on to the moor, and lashing also on to three of Trevithick's monsters; their obscene heads twisting and clicking in pleasure . . .

Lowcock and Medcalfe had jammed over a dozen pews against the window. The figures outside continued to press against the glass and Medcalfe kept a weather eye on their activity.

Jill had managed to keep the villagers calm, using an authoritative voice of which she didn't know she was capable. She did know, however, that, sooner or later, faces would begin to appear at every window. And when they did . . . Well, they would cross that bridge when they came to it.

The beamed roof shook and plaster cascaded down on to the frightened survivors.

Outside, the Sentience lashed about the church gables like a kraken attached to a storm-tossed ship. Tendrils of golden light ranged through the graveyard, lapping at tombstones.

There was a deafening roar as the portion of its consciousness which had been below ground blasted back through the village like a typhoon, flattening houses in its path.

The Sentience felt almost whole again and flexed itself, the energy infusion from Holly gushing through it. Soon it would be strong enough to summon its entire self from below.

But still there was need. There was always need.

It scanned the minds of those gathered in the church below and felt good. There were rich pickings to be had.

The Sentience prodded and encouraged every fugitive memory.

Believe

The soldier in the church promised most. He was old and steeped in Time, like the other it had encountered in the monastery.

But was there yet more?

The Sentience scanned experimentally and picked up a trace from Trevithick's mind. He had defeated it once...

Instantly, the Sentience propelled a tendril to the tunnel entrance, assuming the familiar image of Trevithick's monsters.

The Doctor stepped back from the entrance. 'Impasse,' he said under his breath.

Vijay looked up from the ground. 'No. No more. Please.'

Trevithick regarded the creatures with tired old eyes. He had given them a good run for their money.

The Doctor grasped his arms. 'Don't remember them, Edmund! Don't you see that they can have no existence without you?'

Trevithick closed his eyes and concentrated, but the images became stronger not weaker. In his mind, he was shoulder to shoulder with young Jimmy Reynolds, fending off the razor-sharp claws as they ripped through the walls. And there was Margaret, his dear wife, standing just off the set as the cameras rushed in for the close-up. Little Paula had been so frightened of the creatures that he'd arranged for one to unmask itself in front of her.

'You see, my dear,' he had said, holding her in his arms, 'just a fella in a costume.'

But now she was gone. Margaret too. And he was just an old man with nothing but memories left to him...

'Edmund?' The Doctor touched his hand.

Trevithick opened his eyes and smiled. 'I'm an old fool, Doctor. Never been a real hero. Not the way people thought I was.'

The rain hissed down. Trevithick looked at the silent, waiting creatures.

'They're a part of me. I can't be rid of them, hard as I try. I'm the only one who can get you out of here.'

'There must be another way, Edmund,' cried the Doctor, his voice hoarse with despair.

'Not this time, Doctor. No cliffhanger with a miraculous escape. It's time for Nightshade to do his bit.'

The old man's wrinkled face creased into a sad smile, his eyes misting over. He held out his hand. 'Goodbye, old fellow.'

The Doctor took his hand and looked down at the ground. Vijay scrambled to his feet. 'Mr Trevithick! Wait!'

'Use the chance I'm giving you, my boys,' called the old man. 'And don't look back. Never look back.'

With that, he ran out into the fog.

For a moment, he faced the three creatures, the rain soaking his hair. He looked at them steadily, his eyes steely and thoughtful.

Then he launched himself at the central creature, grabbing its thick neck with both hands. The other two were upon him immediately, their vicious claws flailing at his skin.

Trevithick managed to rain several good blows on to the creature's eye before he felt a strange numbness rising through him. Light began to sparkle under his skin and he felt unconsciousness overwhelming him.

Believe

Believe

With one last effort, he flung his arms around the creature's head and fell with it on to the moor, kicking his boots into its brittle eyes.

The Doctor grabbed Vijay by the scruff of the neck and dragged him outside. Then they sprinted across the ground towards the telescope, trying to ignore Trevithick's agonized screams as he twisted and melded into the beasts.

They didn't look back, even when they reached the double doors.

The Doctor slammed and bolted both doors and, turning, put out his hand to enter the control room.

Vijay stopped him and shook him desperately. 'Why do people have to keep *dying*?'

The Doctor looked at him grimly, then pushed open the interior door.

11

The church shuddered again as the Sentience heaved itself together, sliding and thrashing about the eves with Trevithick's energy within it.

The dead figures pressed to the window had redoubled their efforts and Medcalfe picked up a heavy brass candle snuffer with which to defend himself.

A pane of ruby-coloured glass shattered and John Cleminson's pale hand pushed its way through.

Lowcock watched Cleminson's wrist scrape against the broken glass and wondered why it didn't bleed. Instantly, the cold flesh was bright with blood.

It was necessary to maintain the illusion. To keep them believing.

Need

Need

'Who are they?' cried Jill, throwing her arms around a couple of terrified children.

Medcalfe tried to reply but his throat was bone dry. Cleminson's fingers began to pull at the leadwork.

Lowcock looked about the church for weapons. There were none visible.

A gas-masked soldier thrust his face at the glass and the snoutlike filter crashed through.

There was a strangled cry from a woman crouched by the altar and Jill whirled around. Just as she'd feared, there were dark shapes hovering outside the other windows, their shadows lurching against the glass.

At once, another gas-masked soldier smashed through, his breathing hoarse and terrifying.

Lowcock glanced up at the vaulted ceiling and his heart leaped. He threw himself on to a pew and began wrestling with a mouldering banner which projected over the aisle. He succeeded in prising the lance out of its socket and tottered back to floor level, brandishing the faded colours of some forgotten Yorkshire regiment.

The soldier stood on the wide sill of the shattered window, gazing impassively around him. There were people screaming now and further ghostly figures attempting to force their way inside.

Lowcock sprinted down the aisle, holding the lance like a pole-vaulter, and clambered over a row of broken pews towards the window. He rammed the lance into the soldier's neck and the apparition fell with an agonized cry, blood fountaining from the wound.

Lowcock crouched down and ripped off the gas mask. His spine froze as he took in the soldier's perfectly blank face: a smooth, round head without a single feature.

'George! The door!' Jill called.

Lowcock spun round. The big oak doors were beginning to shake as something battered at them from the outside.

Lowcock bit his lip. 'Albert, Harry, Alan,' he cried rapidly. 'Get those lances down.' He gestured at the remaining banners projecting from the walls. 'And push the pews against the doors. Quickly!'

The villagers were mobilized now, ramming anything they could find against the windows and doors.

'It's no good,' whimpered Medcalfe. 'They'll be in any minute. Oh, God!'

Lowcock began to move towards the doors but stopped as his shoes clanged on a floor tile. He looked down. The tile had a brass ring set into it.

Lowcock rubbed his chin thoughtfully.

The Doctor and Vijay almost fell into the control room. Ace ran to them.

'Doctor? Are you all right? What happened?'

Cooper looked across from the buzzing consoles anxiously. 'Vijay? Where's . . .?'

Vijay looked at her steadily. Cooper felt her throat constrict. 'Oh no.'

'And the old bloke too?' said Robin incredulously.

Vijay nodded. 'It's because of him that we got back.'

Ace looked at the Doctor. 'What were you trying to do?'

He shook his head hopelessly. 'I thought I could reason with it. I'd already spoken to it once. I thought I might find out how to stop it.'

'And did you?' asked Ace.

The Doctor didn't look up. 'I've failed. It's simply grown more powerful.'

Cooper crossed the room and sat down next to him. 'Don't blame yourself, Doctor. You've done your best. No one could ask for more.'

'No one did ask,' he said bitterly. 'I came here to get away from this kind of . . .' His voice trailed off hopelessly. 'There's no rest for me. I got involved. Yet again.'

Cooper rubbed her eyes. 'What I don't understand is why it — whatever it is — has suddenly become active. I mean, if what you said is right, it's been here millions of years.'

The Doctor shrugged. 'I don't think it was strong enough. Those incidents in the past. The Civil War ghosts. Things before that, even. It must've detected them and made what it could of the situation without being fully aware. Like a hibernating animal turning over in its sleep. For some reason, it's never realized its full potential. Perhaps because this has always been such an underpopulated place.'

'No food,' said Ace gravely.

The Doctor nodded, gazing around the room with red-rimmed eyes. 'Or at least, not sufficient to give it a critical mass. . .'

Cooper whistled slowly. 'Until they built this place on top of it!'

'Very probably, yes. All that activity, followed by huge amounts of electricity, must've acted as a lure. It started sending out feelers, gauging the potential energy in the village population. So many people with fond memories. . .'

Ace shuddered. 'It's horrible.'

'Just trying to survive,' said Vijay quietly. 'Like all the rest of us.'

Ace felt Robin's hand slip into hers and was glad of it. 'What can we do then?'

The Doctor rested his head on his hand and sighed. 'I don't know any more. I can't think. I just can't...'

His voice broke into a sob and Ace ran to him, cradling his slight frame in her arms.

'It's OK, Doctor. Come on. You'll be fine. You always are.'

He looked at her but once again his eyes were focused somewhere far distant.

'I saw Susan,' he whispered. 'It knew. It knew everything I'd been feeling. Every pain. Every regret.'

Ace stroked his hair. 'Come on, Doctor. You've got to help us. You've got to give us some ideas.'

'I don't know what to do, Ace! Not this time...'

Ace looked down sadly at her friend. She'd never known him to be indecisive. Even when he was wrong, he would at least put his all into it. Now he sat like a broken man, his spirit crushed by the grief and emotion of a lifetime.

Robin tugged at her sleeve and led her to one side. 'He's lost it, Ace. Can't you see? We can't wait for him to get us out of this. It's up to us. If we can get out of the village...'

'We can do *what*?' spat Ace, angrily. 'Call the police? The army? Look, Robin, we haven't a clue how to even begin to fight this thing. Besides...'

'Besides?'

'I have to believe in the Doctor. Otherwise there's no point in going on.'

Robin lowered his eyes, defeated.

Ace looked around the control room.

Vijay was sitting in a chair, hugging himself, Cooper with a consoling hand on his shoulder. The Doctor sat close by, head bent, eyes closed.

There'll be no better time, thought Ace. And this was the only way to prove to herself it was true.

She picked a chair some distance away from the others and closed her eyes.

Robin noticed it first, a chill spreading through the air and a pungent smell which reminded him of Dr Shearsmith's empty front room. He looked around rapidly, almost as if he could detect movement in the atmosphere itself.

'Ace!' he called.

The Doctor looked up from his brooding and noticed his companion. She was gripping the arms of her chair, her brow furrowed in concentration.

'Ace? What're you doing?' the Doctor cried, getting to his feet.

'You taught me so much, Doctor,' she shouted, eyes clamped shut. 'Taught me to face my fears, not run away from them. Remember Gabriel Chase?'

'No, Ace! You don't know what you're doing. It'll destroy you!'

The Doctor hared across the room and stood by her, hands shaking.

'I have to know if you've succeeded, Doctor. That we've both come through it together. It's the only way to make you see. You're the only hope we've got of destroying this bloody thing!'

'No! Ace!'

The Doctor reached out a hand to touch her but immediately swung round as light began to dance through the air.

Ace smiled to herself. She had to be strong. Concentrate. Remember. She let distant images swim before her mind's eye.

Yes, that would do...

She was small. Perhaps five or six. The sun was hot and very high in the cloudless sky. There was sea and the reassuring tumble of the frothy waves. White horses, her mum always called them. *Mum...*

'Dory?'

Her mother was calling for her now. Across that stretch of yellow sand on a faraway summer's day. And calling across the years...

Ace could feel gritty sand between her toes, taste warm lemonade and tomato and egg sandwiches. Feel her cheeks burn as she was forced to change into her little swimming costume without the camouflage of the beach towel. Feel the crack of her mum's hand across her backside when she'd pee'd in the car on the way home...

'Mum?'

'Dory?'

The voice came to her like a rolling wave, breaking on the bank of her subconscious.

211

A burning, delicious yearning swept through the Sentience and it rippled with pleasure. There was a radiant contact somewhere out on the moor.

It paused in its attack on the church and sent a portion of itself shooting towards the telescope.

Lowcock stood on the threshold of the open vault. The church had become unnaturally quiet, the ghostly soldiers falling back from their assault and stumbling about as though struck blind.

Lowcock lost no time. 'Everyone! Down into the crypt. Quickly!'

He gestured feverishly with his hands and ushered the villagers through the floor and into the vault. If they were lucky, whatever was directing the attack wouldn't know what had happened to them.

Lowcock shoved a young boy down the crypt steps and looked around anxiously. There was no one left to come. No one except...

Andrew Medcalfe was backing away from the window, a fair-haired man in a trenchcoat advancing down the aisle towards him.

'Andrew!' bellowed Lowcock. 'Get down here!'

Medcalfe stumbled and almost fell over his own feet. He looked over his shoulder, panic-stricken, as Lowcock scrambled out of the crypt.

'Get away from me, John!' shrieked the old soldier. 'You're dead. You can't be here!'

'But I *am* here,' purred the fair-haired apparition. 'Just an old friend coming back to see you. It's been so long...'

Lowcock swivelled his eyes and fastened his gaze on the church's eagle lectern. With a cry, he stormed up the aisle and lifted it into the air.

Cleminson's ghost marched relentlessly towards Medcalfe and the old man fell to the floor, his knees cracking off the floor tiles.

'Please, John. Leave me alone.'

'You were lucky that day, Andrew,' hissed the apparition, its voice disintegrating into a low rustle. 'Some of us weren't so fortunate. I've come back for the future they stole from me.'

He extended a khaki-clad arm and grasped Medcalfe's chin

in his pale hand. 'Now, old man,' Cleminson breathed.

Lowcock sprang up behind the figure and swung the massive lectern with every shred of his strength. The great brass eagle slammed into Cleminson's head and took it off in one movement. There was an appalling crack of splintering bone and the head thudded into the pews.

Cleminson's body stood for some seconds like a side-show dummy and then toppled to the floor.

Medcalfe stared at it in horror.

'George...' he began.

Lowcock grabbed his arm. 'No time. Come on.'

He thrust him down the stairs into the crypt and followed immediately after, slamming shut the floor plate with a resounding boom.

Ace had formed a picture of her mother now, a composite of every Christmas morning, summer holiday, every blazing row. How many times had that face burned itself into her sleeping mind. She had hated it. *Hated* it.

The Doctor was standing with his back to the wall, staring up at the auroral display which crackled through the air.

Cooper moved behind the consoles in disbelief. 'Look! Can you see...?'

She jammed her fingers into her mouth as a figure shimmered into view, hovering a few feet from where Ace was sitting.

It was a pretty, middle-aged woman, her face wreathed in smiles.

'Hello, Dory, love. Where on earth have you been? I was worried sick.'

Ace opened her eyes and jumped, shocked at the perfection of the apparition.

The Sentience had found the image of Audrey easy to assume. There was much bile in the girl's memory, much resentment. It shivered inside the golden particles of the woman's body, light bleeding from every pore.

'I'm fine,' said Ace, carefully.

'Ace,' said the Doctor, concernedly.

'It's OK, Doctor.' She stood up. 'I'm fine,' she repeated, turning to address the apparition. 'It's you that's in trouble.'

Audrey smiled. 'Come on, Dory. Don't play games. We're going to the school today to see the Head about that nasty boy Chad Boyle.'

Ace half smiled. It had done its homework. 'You're not my mother,' she said quietly. 'Whatever you are, you're not her. You're not real and I'm not afraid of you. I deny your reality. You have no claim on *me*!'

The Sentience within Audrey grew taller, glaring down at Ace, its face darkening in fury.

'You cannot. . .'

The voice began to tremble a little, breaking up into a soft rustling sound.

'You cannot. . .'

Need

Need

The Sentience felt the great hollowness returning. There was nothing for it here.

'Get out! Get out of here!' shouted Ace.

Audrey's image began to disintegrate; glittering particles swirled into a vortex around it.

Ace picked up a sheaf of papers and hurled them at the apparition.

'Get *out*!'

The papers fluttered to the floor. When they settled, the Sentience had gone.

'Ace!' Robin ran to her and flung his arms around her. She grinned broadly and kissed him.

'Don't worry. I knew what I was doing,' she lied.

Ace turned to the Doctor who was staring at her in disbelief. 'I can face my past, Doctor. Now, what about you?'

The Doctor continued to stare and then ran across the room to Cooper, his hands flapping in agitation. 'Show me your nova! Show me!'

Cooper tapped some figures into the console. The Doctor's eyes flicked down the screen. He drummed his fingers against the console and ran a hand through his hair.

Ace felt a bit deflated. A bit of recognition wouldn't do any harm, she thought.

The Doctor turned full around and his face was suffused with joy.

Lowcock held his breath. The crypt was completely dark but he felt a little cheered by the close proximity of his fellow villagers. Several had pressed themselves between ancient tombs, as if trying to vanish into the walls themselves.

Above them, the stone floor echoed with the sound of footsteps.

Lowcock crossed his fingers.

Please, please, please . . .

Jill Mason grasped his hand. He could hear her frightened breathing fluttering in his ear.

The footsteps came closer.

The Sentience was on the point of withdrawing from the moor and it boiled and swirled in the atmosphere, struggling to understand its failure. No life form had ever had the will to resist it before. The lure of the past was always so great. .

Need

Need

There was still energy to be had, however.

It would simply concentrate its efforts on the church. Drain those creatures dry.

Then came another contact. Begging it to stay, demanding it to stay. A strong contact, no . . . an unprecedented contact. It was the creature from the monastery again! And this time, he wasn't shielding himself.

There was so much energy there, such a wealth of experience – almost as if he had lived several lives.

The Sentience pulsed an urgent signal and finally pulled free of its earthly prison. Light blasted from beneath the moor, sending tons of soil shooting into the heavens.

The bulk of the Sentience joined with the portion wrapped around the church eves and scorched across the moor, coagulating into a vast, glorious cloud around the dish of the telescope.

'At your mark, Doctor,' said Cooper coolly.

The Doctor nodded and shut his eyes. Ace had shown him the way. If he could only manage it half as well as she...

Memories flooded his mind.

That first visit to Revolutionary France. Times before that. He and Susan travelling alone in the TARDIS, or the Ship as he had liked to call it then.

Fleeing through that terrifying forest to the plain where the TARDIS stood. The months in China with that Venetian traveller. Slowly dying from the deadly radiation of the planet Skaro. And it was Susan who had gone off into the jungle to save them. Brave Susan...

He forced himself to concentrate on her image. That dark, pretty face. That uniform she had first worn at the school and so hated that she'd buried it deep in the TARDIS.

'Oh, Grandfather. I can't be seen wearing *that*.'

Not 'with it', she had told him. Not the sort of thing for a fan of John Smith and the Common Men.

Susan...

And then that terrible day. Defeat of the Daleks and the liberation of Earth but... but he had been forced to make her stay behind. It had been what she needed, what she wanted in her heart. To stay with David Campbell and make a life for herself. A life away from him...

She had stood outside the TARDIS, tears pouring down her face, the key to the Ship clutched in her hand.

'*One day, I shall come back. Yes, I shall come back...*'

He was here now. Waiting.

'*Until then, there must be no regrets, no tears, no anxieties...*'

Come back to me. Come back to me...

'*Just go forward in all your beliefs, and prove to me that I am not mistaken in mine...*'

Come back...

'*Goodbye, Susan. Goodbye, my dear...*'

Susan...

'Grandfather?'

The Doctor's eyes snapped open. Susan was standing before him, a beautiful apparition, like a shaft of sunlight pouring through storm clouds. Her dark hair wafted around her face

216

and her hands were held open in welcome.

Like an angel, thought Ace.

Light poured from Susan's eyes and mouth like sand from a punctured bag.

'Susan?'

The Doctor's voice was calm and assured.

'I'm here, Grandfather.'

Her voice was strangely beautiful, haunting...

Ace shivered.

'Tell me who you are,' urged the Doctor.

'I am Susan...' the apparition murmured.

The Doctor chewed a fingernail thoughtfully. 'Yes, you're Susan. But tell me why you're here. Tell me what you seek.'

Susan fluttered her eyelids and the light streaming from them stuttered. 'I have always been here. There has always been me. But....'

'But?' The Doctor held out his hands.

Susan's face seemed to fall, as though overwhelmed with sadness. 'There must be more than this. There must have been a better time. Not this *need*.'

'A better time. A simpler time,' said the Doctor. 'That's what we all yearn for. The pain of wanting to belong somewhere. To go home.'

'Home,' repeated Susan.

The Doctor stepped back a little. Susan raised her head. 'But there is always need. I cannot rest.'

'You have to feed?'

'At first, I had only to consume a very little and was content. But I have grown now, and the need has grown with me.' Susan's eyes began to shine with a fearful incandescence. 'I can smell them,' she hissed, her voice harsher now. 'Their regret. Their yearning for times past. It is so strong, so sweet. They fashion me into what they desire, or what they fear and then... then I harvest.'

'Harvest?' Cooper spat the work disgustedly.

The Doctor silenced her with a gesture. Susan inclined her head.

'There was much energy to be had. I grew stronger as the years passed. I learned how to shepherd my prey together and

217

prevent them from leaving me . . .'

'What does it mean?' said Ace.

'The sickness anyone feels if they try to leave,' said the Doctor without taking his eyes off the apparition. 'It creates a barrier, preventing them getting out.'

'But not getting in,' said Vijay quietly. 'Like Mr Medway?'

The Doctor nodded. 'Bees to a honeypot.'

Susan smiled slightly. 'I found one who could see as I did. An old man. Through his mind I saw the potential of this world.'

Billy Coote, thought Robin. So his second sight had been real after all.

'And now?' said the Doctor. 'Now that you have grown?'

Susan rolled back her head and laughed, delighting in her own power. 'I shall go on from here till the need is gone. I shall *consume*!'

The Doctor whipped around. 'Now, Dr Cooper! Now!'

Cooper slammed her fingers across various keyboards and each monitor screen flared with identical data.

There was a distant clunk from the dish above. Vijay and Robin looked up.

'Doctor?' said Ace in puzzlement.

Cooper ran a hand over the console. 'That's it, Doctor. All systems overridden and concentrating on Bellatrix.'

The room began to throb with power. The Doctor turned back to Susan. 'Can't you feel it? Can't you feel the energy?'

Susan twisted about, her figure stretching and distorting as she attempted to locate the energy source. Radio waves honed in on the dish of the telescope.

'What is it?' hissed Susan, her hair streaming behind her as though stirred by unseen currents. Light was forcing its way through every part of Susan's face, as though the Sentience were shaking off the image.

'A star,' said the Doctor calmly. 'An exploding star. Pushing outwards in a pure, brilliant surge of light and energy. Can't you feel it? Can't you *taste* it?'

The Sentience thrashed against the walls, Susan's image flaring and billowing as light fountained from it.

The Doctor ran closer, pressing home his advantage. 'Can't you *feel* it? The energy of a whole star. It's all yours. Take it. *Take it!'*

Susan's face seemed to break into a smile before evaporating into a surge of blinding light. Golden fire roared through her until there was only a blazing column of light dominating the room like some biblical miracle.

'I can feel it!' screamed the Sentience, its terrifying voice resonating around the room. The walls began to shudder and crack.

'I can taste it!'

Ace, Robin and Vijay threw themselves to the floor as chairs and papers crashed around the room The Doctor and Cooper gripped the benches for dear life as a freezing wind blasted through the room.

'Is it not... beautiful?'

The Doctor turned away as the column of fire expanded across the room, dazzles of brilliant white light searing his eyes. A screeching cacophony pounded at his ears and he thrust his head under the bench, sweat washing down his forehead.

'Beautiful! Beautiful!'

The Doctor lay down flat and covered his ears with his hands. There was a tremendous wave of energy and he felt his whole body being flattened. His eyes lolled back in their sockets and blood roared in his ears. He rolled himself into a ball and came to rest against the console. Then he opened his eyes.

The makeshift polythene window had burst asunder and a fine rain was blowing through.

Cooper poked her head over the top of the bench and looked around.

Papers fluttered over the consoles.

'It's gone,' said the Doctor, sighing with relief. 'Gone to find its star.'

The Sentience consumed the ancient radiation as it rushed into the telescope's feed. Even at this distance, there was much to enjoy. So much energy pouring out of the dying stellar body. But it was still so far away. So far away.

To consume properly, the Sentience would have to get closer.

It was strong enough now, strong enough to leave behind the planet in which it had always existed.

219

The energy was weak, *but once it had been fresh*. The Sentience would have to go back. Back to when the star exploded. And then it would *feast*.

Back. Back. Back.

Cooper hugged Vijay to her. 'I'm so sorry, my dear friend.' She kissed him and then held him at arm's length. 'There's just the two of us now, I'm afraid. Think we can manage?'

Vijay smiled thinly. He thought of Holly and immediately pushed the thought to the back of his mind.

No.

That was wrong. That's how Holly . . . that's *why* Holly died. By not accepting James's death and letting his memory fester inside her. Holly was dead.

He would grieve, very publicly and for as long as it took. But he would remember her with joy.

'I think we'll manage,' he said at last, kissing Cooper fondly on the forehead.

Robin grasped Ace's hand tightly. 'Well?'

Ace gazed into his lovely green eyes and bit her lip. 'I'm going to tell him. Tell him now.'

The Doctor was rummaging through his pockets. He pulled out the small, vellum-bound book which the Abbot had lent him and looked up, as though struck by a thought.

'Doctor,' said Ace quietly. She placed a hand on his sleeve. 'Mm?'

'Doctor, I've . . . I've decided to stay . . .'

The Doctor blinked as though waking up. 'Stay? Here? But you can't. You . . .' He stopped and sucked his lower lip. 'Of course you can.'

Ace looked at her shoes. The Doctor turned and regarded Robin. 'I take it you've got something to do with this, young man?'

Robin smiled his cheeky smile. 'Guess so.'

Ace looked deeply into the Doctor's eyes. 'What about you?'

He smiled encouragingly. 'I'll be all right.'

'I will miss you, Doctor.' Ace felt the familiar numb pains spreading to her palms and throat.

'And I shall miss you too, dear Ace.'

She flung herself into his arms and he held her tightly.

Ace pulled away, tears stinging her eyes.

The Doctor looked at the book in his hand. 'Would you do one last thing for me?'

'Of course,' she said, sniffing back tears.

'I want to test out a theory. Will you come with me, in the TARDIS? One last time?'

Ace was taken aback. She looked over at Robin and then back at the Doctor. She owed it to him. 'Er ... yeah. Yeah! Why not?'

The Doctor smiled and hurried over to Vijay and Cooper.

Ace embraced Robin and kissed him fondly. 'Won't be long. Promise.'

He kissed her full on the lips, lingering for a long minute.

'Vijay,' said the Doctor. 'This nova of yours. What's the distance from Earth?'

Vijay shrugged. 'About a hundred and ten parsecs.'

The Doctor did a lightning calculation. 'Of course!'

He dashed across the room and lifted his hat. 'I hate goodbyes. I'll have Ace back here before you can say John Robinson.'

He pushed open the double doors and was gone.

Ace turned to them all and shrugged. 'I'll be back soon. Promise. Bye!'

Robin looked longingly after her. The doors clattered and then immediately swung open again. Ace popped her head round the jamb. 'Merry Christmas!' she cried and vanished.

The Doctor was scrabbling at his watch chain for the TARDIS key. He looked up at the sky which had cleared completely, leaving a dark, star-filled expanse. In Orion, one particular star was blazing wonderfully.

Ace ran up behind the Doctor. 'What's the theory then, Doctor?'

He spoke as he walked. 'The nova is one hundred and ten parsecs away, or thereabouts.' He pointed into the night sky. 'See it?'

Ace craned her neck. 'Oh yeah.'

'Well, what's that distance in light years?'

Ace grimaced. 'Erm...'

221

'There's 3.259 light years to a parsec, or 19,160,000,000,000 miles, so . . .'

'About three hundred and thirty light years?'

The Doctor smiled triumphantly. '*About,* yes, *about.* But I'm willing to bet on another figure.'

Ace was intrigued. 'What?'

The Doctor pulled up sharp. 'Three hundred and twenty-four,' he grinned.

George Lowcock counted to ten and pushed at the floor plate. He looked around the darkened church. Starlight glinted off the fallen lectern. The place was utterly silent.

Lowcock threw back the floor plate and clomped his way up the steps from the crypt.

He wandered down the aisle, conscious of the shadows looming in every corner, and grasped a tall candle. Fumbling in his pockets he produced a lighter and lit the candle, holding it high above his head.

'Nothing,' he whispered, then raised his voice so that the villagers in the crypt could hear him. 'Nothing! They're gone!'

Slowly, like shell-shock victims staggering from a bunker, the residents of Crook Marsham filed from the vault, blinking bemusedly.

Jill ran straight over to Lowcock. 'Are you sure?'

Lowcock held up his hand. 'Listen.'

Jill pricked up her ears, expecting the tinkle of breaking glass. But a gentle sound was struggling to make itself heard at the edge of her awareness. A low, repeated hoot.

'It's an owl,' she whispered.

Lowcock smiled.

The Doctor patted the TARDIS affectionately and pushed the key into the lock.

'Have you back in two shakes,' he said to Ace, pushing open the door. Then he looked at her. 'Thank you for coming with me.'

She smiled. 'Least I could do.'

They went inside.

The tertiary console room was just as they had left it. The

Doctor stepped over to the console and let his fingers flutter over the controls.

Ace picked up Susan's uniform and folded it neatly over the mirror, smiling wanly to herself. The TARDIS had been her home for so long. The only real home she'd ever known, and now . . .

'Aha!' cried the Doctor. 'I knew it. It's travelling backwards in Time. Fingers crossed, we should be able to get there first.'

'Get where, Doctor?'

The Doctor turned and his eyes were twinkling with mischief. 'Why, Crook Marsham, of course.'

Ace frowned.

The night was warm and balmy. Campfires glowed distantly.

'Captain!'

Phillip Jackson turned to the soldier behind him. The fellow was pointing towards the castle.

'What is it?'

'There's someone there, sir. I swear it. Down there, by the gates.'

The Doctor stepped from the TARDIS and looked around. The night was pleasant, the air sweet. This was more like it.

Ace emerged behind him. 'Where are we?'

'I told you. Crook Marsham.'

Ace looked at the imposing castle next to which the TARDIS had materialized. 'When?'

'Sixteen forty-four,' said the Doctor.

Ace laughed in surprise.

The Doctor gazed up at the battlements. 'The light from the exploding star has taken three hundred and twenty-four years to get to Earth. Which means?'

'Which means that it actually went nova in 1644!' cried Ace delightedly. 'You are devious, Doctor.'

The Doctor shrugged and smiled. 'I aim to please.'

He strolled over to the cold stone walls. 'My guess is that the Sentience will follow the fossil radiation back to when it was new, by going back through Time. To this evening.'

'But how can you be so exact?'

'Another guess. This is Marsham Castle, in which our friendly local Cavaliers are currently being frightened out of their wits. Ah, there they go!'

The castle gates burst open and the Royalists ran out, screaming in terror.

The Doctor pointed up at the battlements, where a ball of fiery light was forming. Ralph Grey looked over, his face a mask of horror, and then threw himself into space. Ace grimaced.

'It must've returned to its normal state now,' said the Doctor. 'And remained undisturbed as its future self arrives.'

He looked about. There was silence. The Doctor checked his pocket watch.

Phillip Jackson rode up to the gateway, dismounted, stepped over Grey's body and disappeared inside the castle.

The air was suddenly alive with power. Ace felt the hairs on her arms and neck stand up.

'Here it comes,' whispered the Doctor.

The castle began to seethe with light, the old stones themselves rippling and blurring.

'The castle was destroyed by a mysterious fire!' shouted the Doctor above the rising din.

'This is it?'

The Doctor nodded, beginning to run back to the TARDIS.

A few moments later, Jackson dashed from the gates, mounted his horse and galloped away.

Ace could feel the heat blasting against her as the castle became virtually transparent. Halos of blistering fire roared through the masonry.

'This is it!' cried the Doctor. 'The Sentience leaving Earth to find its star. Come on!'

He pushed open the doors of the TARDIS and ushered Ace inside. Seconds later, the old ship protested out of solid existence.

The castle reached optimum brightness and then erupted into an immense fireball with a sound like planets colliding.

The Doctor fussed over the console, mumbling to himself. He glanced at the scanner and then whooped with delight. 'There!'

They were in space now, and the roundel screen was

dominated by an incredible outpouring of light and energy.

The Bellatrix double comprised a white dwarf star and its companion. In the course of time, the companion star had grown enormously, but its evolution had been halted by the proximity of the white dwarf.

Material began to bleed from the companion on to the dwarf until it reached its maximum permissible mass. At this point, the Chandreskhar limit, the dwarf underwent a massive thermo-nuclear explosion.

The Sentience, however, knew nothing of this. All it could feel, all it could taste, was the bounty of the exploding star. It slipped free of Earth's atmosphere and sped across the galaxy at incredible speed, throbbing with power.

In an instant, it was there, writhing and wallowing in the astonishing blast of energy.

'*Need!*' it sang to itself.

'It'll stay there until the star has exhausted itself,' said the Doctor. 'Let's nip forward a bit . . .' His fingers danced over a row of buttons.

Ace checked her watch. They'd been gone a good while now but this *was* a time machine, after all. The Doctor could drop her off only a minute after they'd left. She thought of Robin and smiled.

The Doctor glanced at the scanner and frowned. 'It's gone.'

'What about the star?'

'Finished. Dead.' He stabbed at a display before him. 'Wait, I've got a trace. We can follow it.'

Ace joined him at the console. The Doctor frowned and then smiled. 'Clever. Very clever.'

The Sentience had sensed the star diminishing. How long it had hovered there, drinking in the beautiful energy, it couldn't tell. But what was time to it? Now it was free to roam through space, consuming anything it came across. The eater of stars!

It sent out a portion of itself and suddenly shuddered with delight. There was another star, somewhat more distant, but so powerful!

Seconds later, the Sentience was storming out of the galaxy.

Ace regarded the Doctor steadily. 'Where's it going?'

'Out of the galaxy,' said the Doctor wonderingly. 'Out towards Andromeda.' He looked up and smiled. 'M31. The Great Spiral.'

'And what's it looking for? Another nova?'

The Doctor leant on the console and looked at her. 'No, better than that. A supernova.' He checked his instruments. 'Yes, there it is. It's found one. A big one too.'

The Sentience groaned with delight as the energy from the blazing red star flooded into it. If it could go on discovering these sources, these dying stars then, perhaps, the need would be fulfilled. Perhaps it might rest, at last...

The Doctor chewed his fingernails anxiously. 'We'll go forward in Time again and see what it's up to.'

He cast a glance at the scanner and his eyes began to widen.

'What is it, Doctor?' said Ace worriedly.

'If we're lucky...' he said under his breath.

Ace shrugged. 'What? The star burns out?'

'No, no. Remember what I told you.'

'It turns into a pulsar, right?'

'Yes,' said the Doctor quietly. 'Unless the core of the star is too massive for the neutrons to support it against gravity. In which case the core continues to collapse.'

Ace shrugged. 'Well?'

'Continues to collapse until the gravity at its centre is strong enough to form...?' The Doctor raised his eyebrows expectantly.

Ace frowned, then smiled, then grinned as she realized what the Doctor was implying.

The Sentience was aware of the star's death. Immediately, it began to monitor the space around it for more energy. It was colossal now, stretching shimmering tendrils into the vacuum.

It would leave and find more stars.

Nothing happened.

226

Once again, it attempted to leave and found that it could not. It desired to be elsewhere and this had always been easy to accomplish. Why not now? Besides, since it had grown greater the need was greater.

Already, the yawning emptiness seemed to burn within it.

The Sentience flexed a tendril but was dragged back remorselessly towards the dead star.

This was impossible. It had to move. Get away. The star had nothing left to give. There was no more energy. There was nothing but oblivion.

For the first time in its ancient life, the Sentience felt something akin to panic. It tried to wrench itself free, lashing its tendrils in fury, but the gravity of the star wouldn't permit it. Not even the Sentience could escape from a Black Hole.

For a long moment, an eternity of experience flashed through its consciousness. Sir Brian de Fillis and his wife, Harry Cooke and his daughters. Dyson and Scott from the archaeological expedition. Dr Shearsmith, Jack Prudhoe, Win Prudhoe, Betty and Lawrence Yeadon, Abbot Winstanley...

Need. Cannot die. Still need. Must go on. Must...

Holly Kidd. Edmund Trevithick...

Must go on...Must...Must...

The Sentience shimmered briefly like a firefly.

Then a curious peace came over it as it vanished forever. Perhaps it had finally come home.

The Doctor flicked a switch and the scanner roundel darkened to the same hue as the others.

'It's over,' he sighed. 'Consumed by the black hole.'

Ace breathed out delightedly. 'Well...'

'Yes. Time you were getting back.'

The Doctor looked at her steadily. He didn't want to let her go but under normal circumstances he would have done.

Under normal circumstances.

But there was more at stake now...

'Crook Marsham 1968, here we come,' he said brightly.

Ace had nothing much to pack and returned to the tertiary console room with her rucksack and bomber jacket. Her tape

227

deck would have to stay as it was anachronistic and liable to cause a few raised eyebrows. Come to think of it, by the time Ian Brown and the Stone Roses came round, she'd probably be too old to like them any more. Funny thought. But she had Robin now...

She walked into the room uncertainly. The Doctor was at the console and the TARDIS was just materializing.

'Doctor?'

He turned.

Ace bit her lip. 'Everything we talked about before. You *will* be OK now?'

The Doctor smiled. 'You know, the Elizabethans thought nostalgia was a diagnosable disease. Perhaps they were right.' He sighed. 'Thanks to you, Ace, I know that what's done ... is done. No sense living in the past. The only way for me is forward. Always forward.'

Ace moved to hug the Doctor one more time but he shook his head. 'Just go. I'll slip away quietly. No fuss.'

Ace nodded silently, feeling the tears well up in her eyes. Then she ran through the double doors without looking back.

Expecting the familiar moorland, she was somewhat surprised to find herself on a broad stretch of beach.

The sand glistened like pomegranate seeds and the sky above her was a lovely, dusky purple. A breeze was blowing through a dense forest to her right. Three moons hung low over the horizon.

'Doctor,' she said in a low whisper. 'You've got it wrong.'

She ducked back into the TARDIS. The tertiary console room was empty and silent, save for the familiar hum of machinery. Ace noticed several switches clicking into life.

Ace stepped over the threshold. The doors swung shut of their own accord and the TARDIS dematerialized automatically.

She grasped the brass door knob and threw open the interior door, racing into the corridor beyond.

'Doctor! Take me back! I have to go back! I have to!'

There was no reply. Ace ran down the corridor, fresh tears springing to her eyes. 'Doctor! You promised! Take me back!

The light in the grey corridor was dim and cheerless. Ace

228

wheeled around, already hopelessly lost. She slid down the roundelled wall and buried her head in her hands.

'Take me back.'

Epilogue

Robin waited for a very long time. In fact, for over five months, never a day passed without him making the trip to the telescope. Just in case. But she never came back.

Perhaps it was for the best. If, as she'd said, she *was* from the future, then living through her time again might have proven very difficult. But Robin missed her so much.

He became very close to Dr Cooper and Vijay Degun and it was good to have friends who understood what he was going through now that Lawrence was gone too. It had been a terrible time for them all.

Robin read the official account in the paper some time later. Poison gas, they said, from under the ground. Couldn't have been anticipated. Nobody's fault. He was surprised to see how many of those who'd had the worst scares were the first to deny anything out of the ordinary. Probably just their way of dealing with it.

Robin didn't stay long in Crook Marsham, however. He moved to York and then to London. Occasionally, he got a postcard from Jill Mason. She seemed never to settle down. Always at some political flashpoint or another.

Vijay and Dr Cooper he saw more frequently now they were back in Cambridge. They had all put the village behind them. Too many memories. Far too many...

The tracking station was closed down almost at once, dark noises being made about risking government property and lives (in that order) in such an unstable geological area.

The great telescope dish stood through another three winters until it was dismantled. Eventually, even the concrete shell of the station buildings, stained and broken by the elements, disappeared.

And there was only the rain.
And the moor.
Always, the moor.

THE DOCTOR'S ADVENTURES CONTINUE IN DOCTOR WHO MAGAZINE

Every issue of *Doctor Who Magazine* is packed with new stories, archives, news and features about the world's longest running SF television programme. Special reports cover subjects such as new books — including the New Adventures — visual effects, design, writers and new merchandise.

For full details of the latest subscription details and other Marvel *Doctor Who* products, write to: *Doctor Who Magazine* Subscriptions, PO Box 500, Leicester, Great Britian LE99 0AA.